BRIAN FLYNN

THE CASE OF THE PAINTED LADIES

With an introduction by
Steve Barge

DEAN STREET PRESS

Published by Dean Street Press 2021

Copyright © 1940 Brian Flynn

Introduction © 2021 Steve Barge

All Rights Reserved

The right of Brian Flynn to be identified as the Author of the Work has been asserted by his estate in accordance with the Copyright, Designs and Patents Act 1988.

First published in 1940 by John Long

Cover by DSP

ISBN 978 1 914150 67 8

www.deanstreetpress.co.uk

BRIAN FLYNN
THE CASE OF THE PAINTED LADIES

BRIAN FLYNN was born in 1885 in Leyton, Essex. He won a scholarship to the City Of London School, and from there went into the civil service. In World War I he served as Special Constable on the Home Front, also teaching "Accountancy, Languages, Maths and Elocution to men, women, boys and girls" in the evenings, and acting in his spare time.

It was a seaside family holiday that inspired Brian Flynn to turn his hand to writing in the mid-twenties. Finding most mystery novels of the time "mediocre in the extreme", he decided to compose his own. Edith, the author's wife, encouraged its completion, and after a protracted period finding a publisher, it was eventually released in 1927 by John Hamilton in the UK and Macrae Smith in the U.S. as *The Billiard-Room Mystery*.

The author died in 1958. In all, he wrote and published 57 mysteries, the vast majority featuring the super-sleuth Antony Bathurst.

INTRODUCTION

"I believe that the primary function of the mystery story is to entertain; to stimulate the imagination and even, at times, to supply humour. But it pleases the connoisseur most when it presents – and reveals – genuine mystery. To reach its full height, it has to offer an intellectual problem for the reader to consider, measure and solve."

Brian Flynn, *Crime Book* magazine, 1948

BRIAN Flynn began his writing career with *The Billiard Room Mystery* in 1927, primarily at the prompting of his wife Edith who had grown tired of hearing him say how he could write a better mystery novel than the ones he had been reading. Four more books followed under his original publisher, John Hamilton, before he moved to John Long, who would go on to publish the remaining forty-eight of his Anthony Bathurst mysteries, along with his three Sebastian Stole titles, released under the pseudonym Charles Wogan. Some of the early books were released in the US, and there were also a small number of translations of his mysteries into Swedish and German. In the article from which the above quote is taken from, Brian also claims that there were also French and Danish translations but to date, I have not found a single piece of evidence for their existence. The only translations that I have been able to find evidence of are *War Es Der Zahnarzt?* and *Bathurst Greift Ein* in German – *The Mystery of the Peacock's Eye*, retitled to the less dramatic "Was It The Dentist?", and *The Horn* becoming "Bathurst Takes Action" – and, in Swedish, *De 22 Svarta*, a more direct translation of *The Case of the Black Twenty-Two*. There may well be more work to be done finding these, but tracking down all of his books written in the original English has been challenging enough!

Reprints of Brian's books were rare. Four titles were released as paperbacks as part of John Long's Four Square Thriller range in the late 1930s, four more re-appeared during the war from Cherry Tree Books and Mellifont Press, albeit abridged by at least a third, and two others that I am aware of, *Such Bright Disguises* (1941) and *Reverse the Charges* (1943), received a paperback release as part of John Long's Pocket Edition range in the early 1950s – these were also possibly abridged, but only by about 10%. They were the exceptions, rather than the rule, however, and it was not until 2019, when Dean Street Press released his first ten titles, that his work was generally available again.

The question still persists as to why his work disappeared from the awareness of all but the most ardent collectors. As you may expect, when a title was only released once, back in the early 1930s, finding copies of the original text is not a straightforward matter – not even Brian's estate has a copy of every title. We are particularly grateful to one particular collector for providing *The Edge of Terror*, Brian's first serial killer tale, and another for *The Ebony Stag* and *The Grim Maiden*. With these, the reader can breathe a sigh of relief as a copy of every one of Brian's books has now been located – it only took about five years . . .

One of Brian's strengths was the variety of stories that he was willing to tell. Despite, under his own name at least, never straying from involving Anthony Bathurst in his novels – technically he doesn't appear in the non-series *Tragedy at Trinket*, although he gets a name-check from the sleuth of that tale who happens to be his nephew – it is fair to say that it was rare that two consecutive books ever followed the same structure. Some stories are narrated by a Watson-esque character, although never the same person twice, and others are written by Bathurst's "chronicler". The books sometimes focus on just Bathurst and his investigation but sometimes we get to see the events occurring to the whole cast of characters. On occasion, Bathurst himself will "write" the final chapter, just to make sure his chronicler has got the details correct. The murderer may be an opportunist or they may have a convoluted (and, on occasion, a somewhat over-the-top) plan. They may be working for personal gain or as part of a criminal enterprise or society. Compare for example, *The League of Matthias* and *The Horn* – consecutive releases but were it not for Bathurst's involvement, and a similar sense of humour underlying Brian's writing, you could easily believe that they were from the pen of different writers.

Brian seems to have been determined to keep stretching himself with his writing as he continued Bathurst's adventures, and the ten books starting with *Cold Evil* show him still trying new things. Two of the books are inverted mysteries – where we know who the killer is, and we follow their attempts to commit the crime and/or escape justice and also, in some cases, the detective's attempt to bring them to justice. That description doesn't do justice to either *Black Edged* or *Such Bright Disguises*, as there is more revealed in the finale than the reader might expect . . . There is one particular innovation in *The Grim Maiden*, namely the introduction of a female officer at Scotland Yard.

Helen Repton, an officer from "the woman's side of the Yard" is recruited in that book, as Bathurst's plan require an undercover officer in a cinema. This is her first appearance, despite the text implying that Bathurst has met her before, but it is notable as the narrative spends a little time apart from Bathurst. It follows Helen Repton's investigations based on superb initiative, which generates some leads in the case. At this point in crime fiction, there have been few, if any, serious depictions of a female police detective – the primary example would be Mrs Pym from the pen of Nigel Morland, but she (not just the only female detective at the Yard, but the Assistant Deputy Commissioner no less) would seem to be something of a caricature. Helen would go on to become a semi-regular character in the series, and there are certainly hints of a romantic connection between her and Bathurst.

It is often interesting to see how crime writers tackled the Second World War in their writing. Some brought the ongoing conflict into their writing – John Rhode (and his pseudonym Miles Burton) wrote several titles set in England during the conflict, as did others such as E.C.R. Lorac, Christopher Bush, Gladys Mitchell and many others. Other writers chose not to include the War in their tales – Agatha Christie had ten books published in the war years, yet only *N or M?* uses it as a subject.

Brian only uses the war as a backdrop in one title, *Glittering Prizes*, the story of a possible plan to undermine the Empire. It illustrates the problem of writing when the outcome of the conflict was unknown – it was written presumably in 1941 – where there seems little sign of life in England of the war going on, one character states that he has fought in the conflict, but messages are sent from Nazi conspirators, ending *"Heil Hitler!"*. Brian had good reason for not wanting to write about the conflict in detail, though, as he had immediate family involved in the fighting and it is quite understandable to see writing as a distraction from that.

While Brian had until recently been all but forgotten, there are some mentions for Brian's work in some studies of the genre – Sutherland Scott in *Blood in their Ink* praises *The Mystery of the Peacock's Eye* as containing "one of the ablest pieces of misdirection" before promptly spoiling that misdirection a few pages later, and John Dickson Carr similarly spoils the ending of *The Billiard Room Mystery* in his famous essay "The Grandest Game In The World". One should also include in this list Barzun and Taylor's entry in their *Catalog of Crime* where they attempted to cover Brian by looking at a single title – the somewhat odd *Conspiracy at Angel* (1947) – and summarising it as "Straight tripe and savorless. It is doubtful, on the evidence, if any of his others would be different." Judging an author based on a single title seems desperately unfair – how many people have given up on Agatha Christie after only reading *Postern Of Fate*, for example – but at least that misjudgement is being rectified now.

Contemporary reviews of Brian's work were much more favourable, although as John Long were publishing his work for a library market, not all of his titles garnered attention. At this point in his writing career – 1938 to 1944 – a number of his books won reviews in the national press, most of which were positive. Maurice Richardson in the *Observer* commented that "Brian Flynn balances his ingredients with considerable skill" when reviewing *The Ebony Stag* and praised *Such Bright Disguises* as a "suburban horror melodrama" with an "ingenious final solution". "Suspense is well maintained until the end" in *The Case of the Faithful Heart*, and the protagonist's narration in *Black Edged* in "impressively nightmarish".

It is quite possible that Brian's harshest critic, though, was himself. In the *Crime Book* magazine, he wrote about how, when reading the current output of detective fiction "I delight in the dazzling erudition that has come to grace and decorate the craft of the *'roman policier'*." He then goes on to say "At the same time, however, I feel my own comparative unworthiness for the fire and burden of the competition." Such a feeling may well be the reason why he never made significant inroads into the social side of crime-writing, such as the Detection Club or the Crime Writers Association. Thankfully, he uses this sense of unworthiness as inspiration, concluding "The stars, though, have always been the most desired of all goals, so I allow exultation and determination to take the place of that but temporary dismay."

In Anthony Bathurst, Flynn created a sleuth that shared a number of traits with Holmes but was hardly a carbon-copy. Bathurst is a polymath and gentleman sleuth, a man of contradictions whose background is never made clear to the reader. He clearly has money, as he has his own rooms in London with a pair of servants on call and went to public school (Uppingham) and university (Oxford). He is a follower of all things that fall under the banner of sport, in particular horse racing and cricket, the latter being a sport that he could, allegedly, have represented England at. He is also a bit of a show-off, littering his speech (at times) with classical quotes, the obscurer the better, provided by the copies of the *Oxford Diction-ary of Quotations* and *Brewer's Dictionary of Phrase & Fable* that Flynn kept by his writing desk, although Bathurst generally restrains himself to only doing this with people who would appreciate it or to annoy the local constabulary. He is fond of amateur dramatics (as was Flynn, a well-regarded amateur thespian who appeared in at least one self-penned play, *Blue Murder*), having been a member of OUDS, the Oxford University Dramatic Society. General information about his background is light on the ground. His parents were Irish, but he doesn't have an accent – see *The Spiked Lion* (1933) – and his eyes are grey. Despite the fact that he is an incredibly charming and handsome individual, we learn in *The Orange Axe* that he doesn't pursue romantic relationships due to a bad experience in his first romance. We find out more about that relationship and the woman involved in *The Edge of Terror*, and soon thereafter he falls head over heels in love in *Fear and Trembling*, although we never hear of that young lady again. After that, there are eventual hints of an attraction between Helen Repton, but nothing more. That doesn't stop women falling head over heels for Bathurst – as he departs her company in *The Padded Door*, one character muses "What other man could she ever love . . . after this secret idolatry?"

As we reach the halfway point in Anthony's career, his companions have somewhat stablised, with Chief Inspector Andrew MacMorran now his near-constant junior partner in investigation. The friendship with MacMorran is a highlight (despite MacMorran always calling him "Mr. Bathurst") with the sparring between them always a delight to read. MacMorran's junior officers, notably Superintendent Hemingway and Sergeant Chatterton, are frequently recurring characters. The notion of the local constabulary calling in help from Scotland Yard enables cases to be set around the country while still maintaining the same central cast (along with a local bobby or two).

Cold Evil (1938), the twenty-first Bathurst mystery, finally pins down Bathurst's age, and we find that in *The Billiard Room Mystery* (1927), his first outing, he was a fresh-faced Bright Young Thing of twenty-two. How he can survive with his own rooms, at least two servants, and no noticeable source of income remains a mystery. One can also ask at what point in his life he travelled the world, as he has, at least, been to Bangkok at some point. It is, perhaps, best not to analyse Bathurst's past too carefully . . .

"Judging from the correspondence my books have excited it seems I have managed to achieve some measure of success, for my faithful readers comprise a circle in which high dignitaries of the Church rub shoulders with their brothers and sisters of the common touch."

For someone who wrote to entertain, such correspondence would have delighted Brian, and I wish he were around to see how many people have enjoyed the reprints of his work so far. *The Mystery of the Peacock's Eye* (1928) won Cross Examining Crime's Reprint Of The Year award for 2019, with *Tread Softly* garnering second place the following year. His family are delighted with the reactions that people have passed on, and I hope that this set of books will delight just as much.

Steve Barge

Chapter I
THE THREE INCIDENTS

Aubrey Coventry frowned heavily and turned somewhat impatiently at the noise of the ringing telephone. "See who that is, Rayner, will you? Unless it's something terribly important, say that I'm out. I'm not in the mood for sour somethings with anybody."

"Very good, Mr. Coventry." The secretary answered the ring. Almost against his will, and despite his protestation of a moment ago, Coventry found himself listening intently to the conversation as he heard it from his end.

"Mr. Coventry's secretary speaking," said Rayner. "Well . . . I'm not altogether sure with regard to that . . . I can find out for you, of course . . . if it's important. What is the name, please? Montgomery? Mr. Silas Montgomery?"

Coventry saw Rayner furrow his brows. A completely puzzled look took possession of the secretary's face. He nodded his head two or three times in answer evidently to what was being said to him by the caller. "If you'll hang on for a moment or two, sir . . . I'll see what I can do for you. Thank you."

Rayner placed his hand over the telephone's mouthpiece and, still wearing his puzzled look, turned towards his employer.

"A Mr. Silas Montgomery, sir . . . from New York . . . wishes to speak to you on what he describes as a most important matter. If you are in, he says, he would like to speak to you 'at all costs.' They were his very words, Mr. Coventry. . . . A rather extraordinary procedure, don't you think?"

Aubrey Coventry frowned for the second time. As he had previously indicated to Rayner, he was not in the mood that morning for interruptions of any kind. He repeated the name that his secretary had mentioned to him.

"Silas Montgomery did you say . . . of New York . . . just a minute, Rayner . . . let me think . . . it must be *the* Silas Montgomery, I should imagine . . . one of the biggest operators on Wall Street for many years. Head of the Transatlantic Oil Trust. I suppose I had better speak to him—though for the life of me I can't think what he can have to say to me."

Rayner handed the telephone receiver to his chief without speaking. Still frowning, Coventry took it.

"This is Aubrey Coventry speaking. What is it, please?" There came a long silence as Coventry listened. "But this is most extraordinary," Rayner heard him say, "and . . . er . . . altogether without precedent. I don't know what I can really say to you. Besides being . . . er . . . extremely inconvenient." The harsh and strident voice of the American came to him again after an appreciable wait. "Well . . . you can please yourself, of course, Mr. Coventry, but if you refuse to see me it will be the worst day's work you've ever done in your life. Big money's big money . . . and whether it's you or I that's primarily concerned . . . you can't alter that fact."

Coventry hesitated and glanced towards Rayner. He knew the reputation of Silas Montgomery on Wall Street when big deals and daring ventures were being put through, and was loth to throw away anything in the nature of a golden opportunity. Such an action was in direct contrast to his principles. He attempted, therefore, to compromise. "But I'm not refusing to see you," he urged. "I'm simply telling you that two a.m.'s the most inconvenient time to expect anybody to see a complete stranger on business! Why, damn it all, man, it's a most unusual request! Surely you yourself can see that?"

Coventry had to wait again for the reply. But it came.

"Stranger—say, I like that! I should have thought that the name of Silas Montgomery would have been good enough for anybody! Should have thought it would have crashed into Buckingham Palace itself, if needs be! Very well—have it your way, Mr. Coventry. I dare say I can find somebody else in your big city who'll be ready and willing to listen to Silas Montgomery when he's ready to spill his mouthful and put a few court cards on the table."

Coventry's frown deepened. He was beginning to feel just a little uneasy. This man had touched him on the raw. After all, Silas Montgomery was a man of powerful interests and subtle influences. It would be an appalling mistake to offend him. Perhaps he had been a trifle too . . . He collected his thoughts and came to a quick decision. "Look here, Mr. Montgomery," he said hastily, "I've changed my mind. Your arguments have convinced me. I'll expect you at two o'clock to-morrow morning. Here, as you request, in my study. I'm sorry if I appeared a little discourteous to you just now . . . but you'll admit that the arrangement isn't one that you'd make every day of the week."

"Silas Montgomery isn't in London every day of the week either, Mr. Coventry . . . so we can cry quits on that. Very well, then. Two o'clock to-morrow morning at your place. I'll be there on the dot. Good-bye till then."

Aubrey Coventry was left holding the receiver. He smiled cynically at Rayner. "Well, you heard most of that, Rayner. Mr. Montgomery calls here at two Ack Emma to-morrow. Though what he wants of me at that absurd time the good Lord alone knows."

Rayner looked appropriately dubious. He sounded a warning note. "Do you consider it altogether wise of you, sir, to take this man for granted, as you appear to be doing? He may, for all we know, be an impostor. Why not make a few discreet inquiries before you definitely decide on this course of action?"

Coventry bore all his remonstrances good-humouredly. "Silas Montgomery should be good enough in himself, Rayner. The man's name alone spells money—money in capital letters at that. Besides, I can take care of myself in most circumstances. I suppose that even you, Rayner, would admit the truth of that?" Coventry's mood of irritation seemed to have passed and been replaced by one of good-humoured geniality.

But the secretary shook his head. "Even if I do admit that, Mr. Coventry, it doesn't alter my opinion about this appointment. Why should a man in your position take unnecessary risks?"

"I'm not going *out*, Rayner. Don't forget that. I shall be here in my own place when he comes. Surely that condition alone makes all the difference? It isn't as though I'm being inveigled to a low den somewhere to be knocked on the head and robbed. If that were going to happen, I might agree with you as to the risk. No. Don't you worry about me, Rayner. I shall be all right."

Rayner shrugged his shoulders with a hopeless gesture, and surrendered his position. "Very well, Mr. Coventry, if you say so. I must, of course, abide by your decision. All the same, I shall feel very thankful when I hear that the affair is over and that no evil consequences have resulted from it."

Aubrey Coventry laughed again at his secretary's persistence and turned away. "You're the faithful retainer, Rayner, I must say. All right."

This was the first of the three remarkable incidents that were due to occur to him on that particular day.

The second of these extraordinary incidents of which mention has been made happened in a tent at a garden-party held in the Vicarage grounds of the village of Leyland in the county of Essex. The Vicar of Leyland at that time was the Rev. Noel Duff—known to his intimates, naturally, as 'Christmas Pudding.' Mrs. Coventry had been Susanna Duff in her maiden state, and was to-day fulfilling a long outstanding promise to her brother to open a Bazaar in the grounds of his Vicarage on behalf of the Church Building Fund. Aubrey Coventry had come to Leyland on that particular afternoon in support of his wife (verbally) and in support of the Building Fund (financially). The opening speeches had all been made, and, in addition, certain other people had contributed a few remarks. Gradually the more impatient people who were present drifted away with pilots, and without pilots, to patronize the various stalls and sideshows that had been erected by individual enthusiasm for the good of the cause, Seeing that his wife was very well looked after by her brother and a number of ecclesiastical luminaries, who had ranged themselves in her attendance, Aubrey Coventry wandered off on his own bent and eventually found himself beside a tent which exhibited the notice 'Madame Zylphara, Palmist and Clairvoyante.' 'The wonderful woman who reads the Future for you.' Aubrey Coventry smiled cynically to himself as he read the announcement. As he did so, he suddenly thought of the strange telephone message he had received that morning from Silas Montgomery, and the appointment he had arranged for two o'clock on the following morning. He thought of these matters, too, in terms of Madame Zylphara. The wonderful woman in the tent but a few yards away from him, who claimed to be able to read the future. Yielding to an insistent whim which was strangely unlike the normal

Coventry, and which he would have been entirely unable to explain had he been asked to, he strode across the grass strip and nailed open the canvas of the tent in front of him. A brown-eyed girl with a yellow bandeau round her hair was sitting at the entrance. She was evidently of the lineage of St. Matthew judging by the question she put to him. Coventry laughed at the challenge and plunged his hand into his pocket.

"Oh—in that case, I'll lash out and have the full five bob's worth," he answered.

The girl laughed at his reply, took the two half-crowns he handed to her, and jingled them into a bowl which stood on the table at which she sat. "If you will kindly pass behind the screen, sir, you will find that Madame Zylphara is disengaged and ready to see you at once."

"Thank you," said Aubrey Coventry curtly. She handed him a pink ticket and he did as he had been instructed. Beyond me screen he saw the usual appointments of the commonplace palmist. Madame Zylphara sat at a square table upon which stood the inevitable globe of crystal. She was short and stout. Her hair was black. Her eyes were blacker.

"Good afternoon," she said. The foreign accent was unmistakable.

"Good afternoon," responded Aubrey Coventry.

The woman had dignity, he concluded, despite the garish conditions in which she was framed. He handed over the pink ticket which the girl at the tent entrance had given to him. Madame Zylphara accepted it and nodded. It occurred to Coventry as he stood there that vouchers worth five shillings to her, came but very occasionally.

"Sit down," she said.

He took the chair indicated.

"You desire the full reading . . . so . . . so?"

"If you will be so kind." The woman interested and, in a way, fascinated him.

"Give me your hand . . . no, the other one, if you please." She looked at the palm of his hand. "And your birth date . . . if you will please tell me."

"May the twenty-ninth."

"Ah," she muttered . . . "So . . . so . . . a son of Gemini, of course." She rattled off a few of the stock phrases of her trade. Coventry bore patiently with her for some little time. He remembered that he had heard most of them before at odd times and in odd places. Then he put forward a gentle remonstrance.

"This is all very interesting . . . and I must candidly admit almost all true . . . but I am really much more concerned with the future than with what has gone. Your claim is that you can foretell the future."

"I make no claim that I cannot substantiate," she answered almost haughtily . . . "because you find me at a Church Bazaar at an obscure village in the country, that makes no difference to my powers, even though it may to your judgment. Don't judge me by my circumstances. If you do, you will be making a very great mistake. I am Bianca Zylphara. Let me look at your hand . . . so . . ." She bent his palm back and peered into it. Her black brows puckered into a frown. Coventry smiled at her encouragingly.

"Well?" he asked, "and what have the Gods of Chance to tell you about that?"

She put his hand away from her with a sharp exclamation and turned towards the table.

"Look into the crystal with me . . . so . . . will you, please?"

Coventry, urbane as ever, obeyed the request. The woman was seated opposite to him, but he knew instinctively that her attitude was tense and rigid. There came a silence. At length Madame Zylphara broke it. Her voice was harsh and highly charged, as it were, with emotion. "That will do. It is not necessary for you to gaze into the crystal any more. I have seen enough."

Coventry relaxed. The woman relaxed with him. "Well?" he asked again. "I am still waiting for your prediction, you know. As a matter of fact that was the only reason which brought me here. I wasn't at all interested in the possibilities of either blondes or brunettes."

Madame Zylphara shook her head at him. The gesture held no hint of dubiety. Much more certainly it betokened duality. Coventry, undismayed, rallied her again. "Come on. If you aren't sure of anything—take a chance. I won't come back and reproach you if your prophecies go all to blazes. I promise you that."

She flashed a look of withering scorn at him which checked effectively his tendency to flippancy. "There is no need for you to make that promise. I know that you will not come back. But ask me no more questions. I can tell you nothing."

"You mean that you won't. Isn't that more like the truth?"

"Not at all. I can tell you nothing—because there is nothing to tell. How can I say more than that?"

Coventry seemed uncertain as to her meaning. He interrogated her more closely. "What do you mean exactly by that cryptic statement? It leaves me so much in the air, doesn't it?"

Madame Zylphara gazed at him stoically. "I do not understand what you mean by that expression 'in the air.' But what I mean is this. I cannot tell you of your future—because there is no future for you. That is all. Please do not ask me any more."

Coventry expostulated. "But if you'll pardon my saying so—that's wholly absurd. Look at it for yourself. There must be some future. It stands to reason. This present moment when I am talking to you was a future moment but a moment ago. It must be so. Past, present, and future are changing all the time. I'm not a scientific chap by any manner of means, but that's a simple matter for anybody to understand."

Madame Zylphara, however, remained adamant. "I know nothing of the things you talk about. But I know this. The past time was yesterday. The present is to-day. To-morrow and the days to come beyond to-morrow are the future. For you there is no future. I cannot say any more than that. Will you please go?" Madame Zylphara rose from her chair in an effort to indicate finality. Coventry shrugged his shoulders at her. If the woman wouldn't talk—well then, she wouldn't, and that was all there was to it. He accepted the inevitable with the best grace that he could muster. "In that case, then, I will wish you a very good afternoon and apologize for having troubled you."

The woman inclined her head as she dismissed him. Aubrey Coventry made his way slowly out of the tent. His principal emotion was one of confused bewilderment. A few minutes afterwards he met his wife surrounded by a cluster of laughing friends and carrying a bouquet of flowers. Everybody in the company seemed to be in the highest spirits.

"Wherever have you been, Aubrey?" she demanded of him. "We've been looking for you everywhere."

A second or so passed before he replied to her. He felt that it was incumbent upon him to pull himself together.

"We've been looking for you everywhere," repeated Mrs. Coventry. "Noel said that you must have got off with one of his Sunday school teachers. I defended you tooth and nail almost. Now you assure me and all these others that my confidence in you was justified." There was a general laugh at her demand. Coventry shuddered at his wife's suggestion.

"As a matter of fact I've been on a much more romantic expedition than that. I've been having my fortune told. It was all for the good of the cause."

Mrs. Coventry and her companions laughed boisterously. "How perfectly thrilling! You must tell us all about it. Who's my successor? A blonde or a brunette?"

Aubrey Coventry shook his head at her. "That's the peculiar part about it all. I'm afraid I haven't anything to tell you. So you must resign yourselves to disappointment."

As he spoke, the similarity of his second sentence to that of expression used by Madame Zylphara in the tent struck forcibly.

"Oh—what a terrible pity," responded his wife. "I was bracing myself to hearing the most sensational revelations and then you go and let me down like that. Still, never mind—take me over to the refreshment tent and buy me an ice. I think it will have to be a strawberry ice. And you can whisper in my ear all that did happen. Come along now."

She linked her arm in his rather imperiously and led him away— waving light-heartedly to the group of people she left behind. Coventry said nothing. He suffered himself to be led away. This, as has already been stated, was the second remarkable incident of the day's happenings.

Aubrey Coventry was expecting three men to arrive at his London house at half-past seven. He was attending with them a fancy dress ball at Dorset House half an hour later. The three men whom he expected to accompany him were his only son, Philip, his niece's fiancé, Peter Crayle, and Philip's bosom crony, Hubert Palmer. They were all frequently together under his roof. It was to be a stag party as far as they themselves were concerned, as neither his wife nor Valerie Moffatt, his niece, was going. Since leaving the Bazaar in the Vicarage grounds at Leyland, he had been the creature of many conflicting moods and emotions. Strive as he might to retain his normality, he was unable to put away from him the remembrance of the interview in the tent of Madame Zylphara. At six o'clock he was so disturbed that he went to his room to dress. His wife was returning from Leyland later. Duff was bringing her back. Six o'clock! A clock struck as he made his way upstairs. An hour and a half yet before the other three men were due to arrive. He was absurdly early. More early even than he had previously realized. He looked at the costume that he had arranged to wear that evening, which was there in his room already prepared for him. He feared as he looked at it that it was entirely unoriginal. A monk's robe with tonsure wig and sandals. He had let his wife choose it for him. Coventry, restless and preoccupied, looked at his watch again. Five minutes past six. Suddenly he decided that he would not change yet awhile. He would go into the park opposite to his house, smoke a cigarette to steady his nerves, and then return to the house about half-past six. This would still give him ample time to get ready and then to slip into his costume. He had no sooner considered the plan than he proceeded to put it into effect. He went briskly downstairs and out into the street. Crossing the road quickly he walked straight into the park. Coventry felt that he wanted to sit quietly somewhere and smoke a cigarette or cigarettes. He soon found a comfortable seat that was unoccupied and sat in the corner. His hand went to his cigarette case and he took out a cigarette. Then, to his utter dismay, he discovered that he had with him neither matches nor lighter. He remembered that he had put them on his dressing-table preparatory to changing.

He felt a strong feeling of annoyance not only with the circumstances in which he found himself, but also with himself for having contributed thereto. He looked up and down the path in the hope that somebody might be approaching from whom he could beg a match. His luck, however, was out. The path in each direction was empty of pedestrians. Coventry looked down the line of seats. His hopes rose. Two seats away to his left a man was sitting. To his relief Coventry saw that the man was smoking. He rose, therefore, and walked down the line of seats towards the smoker. Coventry reached the seat, and halted before the smoker. "I'm sorry to trouble you," he said, "but would you mind obliging me with a match? I seem to have come out with an empty box."

To Coventry's surprise, the man whom he had addressed deliberately hunched his shoulders, took a paper from his pocket and stared into it studiously. Of Coventry's request he appeared to be completely oblivious. Of Coventry's presence he seemed equally oblivious. To say that Coventry was amazed at this extraordinary reception is putting the matter too mildly. He looked at the man seated in front of him. He had greyish hair, a little unkempt, and wore a suit of blue dungaree. His boots were well worn and soiled. Coventry decided to put his request again. There was the possibility, perhaps, that the man on the seat had not properly heard his question. He repeated it therefore more loudly and in slightly different terms. "Pardon my troubling you . . . but I asked you if you could kindly oblige me with a match." If Coventry had been surprised at the manner in which his original request had been received, the reception of his second question absolutely astonished him. The man turned half away from him, and dropped the paper from his face, thrust his left hand into his pocket, and rewarded Coventry with a leer of diabolical malevolence. His lips curled back from his gums and he showed his teeth just as a surly cur would do if disturbed from the enjoyment of a bone. For a matter of many seconds Aubrey Daventry was too amazed to utter a syllable. Then he jerked himself together and said: "Thanks very much, old chap. It's a pleasure to meet such a thorough gentleman." The man on the seat snarled again and drew his shoulder farther away from the speaker. He appeared to be endeavouring to get as far away from Aubrey Coventry as was possible in the circumstances. Coventry turned on his heel and walked away. Some twenty yards from the seat he turned his head and looked back. His paramount feeling was one of complete disgust. The man was glaring in his direction as a citizen of the Republic might have gazed upon an aristocrat stepping from the tumbril to the waiting blade of the guillotine. Coventry walked slowly out of the park. All desire to smoke had left him. What in the name of goodness was the matter with the man? Was he an imbecile? This was the third of that day's remarkable incidents as they affected Aubrey Coventry.

Chapter II
THE BALL AT DORSET HOUSE

WHEN half-past seven came Coventry received the three anticipated visitors in a subdued mood. The day had held so much for him that had been exhausting and abnormal that his fund of customary spirits had departed from him. His three companions arrived together. He greeted them quietly. Philip was quick to detect that his father was not altogether himself. He immediately sought explanation.

"What's the trouble, father? Feeling a bit under the weather?"

"Got a bit of a head, Phil. That's all. Had a tiring day."

"Change for you. Where have you been?"

"To Leyland. To that wretched bazaar of Uncle Noel's: that I promised to attend some time ago, if you remember. I left your mother down there. She was having the time of her life."

Philip Coventry laughed. "Well—I ask you—if you must bring these things on yourself—" He was a tall, slim, fair-haired youngster of four-and-twenty. Poise and self-possession were his to the extreme. Life so far had been very kind to him and he had profited thereby. Peter Crayle, the second man of the party, and who stood behind him, was his antithesis. Short and dark with a strongly muscled neck and swarthy skin. Crayle joined in Phil Coventry's laugh.

"A church bazaar, sir, and a headache! Surely the two terms are synonymous and one of them therefore a redundancy."

This sally brought the third man, Palmer, into the conversation. He looked to be an older man than either of the other men who had come with him. Probably in the early thirties. Well-built and compact, he gave an immediate impression of strength and self-reliance.

"As a matter of fact," he contributed in a voice of exceptional quality, "it depends on the actual bazaar. There are Church Bazaars and Church Bazaars, you know. I'll tell you something that once happened to me. I actually attended one on four successive evenings."

"Good Lord," said Phil Coventry, "what on earth induced you to do a thing like that? Was she so very easy on the eye?"

"It wasn't a she as it happened," returned Hubert Palmer, with dry insistence, "it was something much more attractive. It was a steak and kidney pie."

Aubrey Coventry stared at him in bewilderment. "A what?" he demanded.

"A steak and kidney pie, sir," repeated Palmer. "Perhaps I had better explain myself. I was playing in a side-show at that bazaar. During my act I was expected to consume a portion of steak and kidney pie. The pie on the first evening was good. A real humdinger. I scoffed the lot. Result was 'one evening—one pie.' I don't mind telling you fellows that I thoroughly enjoyed and appreciated every evening of that particular Church Bazaar."

The others laughed at his story. Coventry began to criticize the costumes which they had chosen. Peter Crayle was attired as a discus thrower. Palmer made a magnificent buccaneer, whilst Philip Coventry, giving vent to his usual flair for originality, had come as Captain Kettle, that superb creation of Cutcliffe Hyne's.

"Not so bad," said Aubrey Coventry, after a moment or so's quiet assessment of the three costumes. "Although you're too tall for Captain Kettle, and Hubert looks on the fierce side."

"My dear sir," replied Palmer, "you are providing the sacerdotal element yourself. You must regard me as your natural foil. I take it that I shall pass muster."

"No need to worry about that." This from Peter Crayle. "You're the goods, Hubert. You'll be one of the most spectacular hits of the evening. Everybody falls nowadays for the he-man. In these days mere elegant Athleticism as represented by me is regarded as something very much like a floral excrescence."

Phil Coventry fingered the beard of Owen Kettle. "If you ask me," he said, "we're very nicely assorted. Nobody has gone up the other's street. And I'm certainly O.K. Which is all to the good. Well, how about making a move? Time's getting on."

Aubrey Coventry looked at his watch. "I ordered Greer to bring the car for ten minutes to eight. It should be here any moment now. So you can get ready, you chaps, and if I know anything about it we're due for a thundering good evening. The Seven Arts always do you well."

The car came. The three men went downstairs and got into it. Aubrey Coventry followed them. "I'm driving," he announced.

Within five minutes of leaving Danvers Gate they were at Dorset House. Dancing had already started. Aubrey Coventry and his three companions were soon in the swing of it. The fun waxed fast and furious. Coventry forgot temporarily the earlier troubles of the day. This was the third year in succession that he had attended this particular function of the Seven Arts, which meant that he knew many of the people who were present. He was hailed by several men and by even more women. Crayle came up to him soon after their arrival. "Pity the girls didn't come along—after all. We should have persuaded them. Plenty of people here whom they know."

Aubrey Coventry nodded his agreement. "I agree. I told Susanna that there would be. But she said she wasn't keen and I fancy her opinion influenced Valerie. You know how women hang together. Ah, well, Peter, you'll be able to console yourself for Valerie's absence, I don't doubt for an instant."

Crayle grinned at him in return. "I'll do my best—don't you worry. I caught sight of Nancy Brocklebank over there with Rufus Nelson a few moments ago. She looks marvellous as a shepherdess. I'll go and murmur sweet nothings to the back of her neck when Rufus is looking the other way. See you later." Crayle strolled off in the direction he had indicated. Coventry watched him go. He saw that Philip and Hubert Palmer had each found what seemed to be a singularly appropriate partner. They accosted him as they swung round close to him. Spirits were already running boisterously high. Coventry was introduced to a girl in a blue-black costume intended obviously to convey the title of ink. He danced with her twice in succession. Suddenly, whilst the second of these dances was in progress, he stopped. His companion rallied him. "What's the matter?"

She saw that her partner's eyes were staring fascinatedly towards a far corner of the big saloon. Her eyes followed his. "What is it?" she asked again, "seen a ghost or something?"

"Not a ghost," replied Coventry, "certainly not a ghost. All I've done is to see somebody whom I never expected to see here. Indeed, he is the very last person on earth whom I should have expected to find here. That's why it was a shock to me."

"Who is it? Who's the man you mean?"

"That fellow standing over there by himself. Greyish hair. In a suit of blue overalls." The girl looked curiously, for Aubrey Coventry had pointed out to her the man who had been on the seat in the park, and from whom he had attempted to obtain a match. As Coventry spoke, the man looked across the room full into his eyes.

"I've no idea who it is," said Miss Ink. "Have you?"

"No. But I'd give a good deal to find out. As soon as we've finished this dance I'll make a few inquiries. You won't mind?"

When the time came he piloted his partner to a seat and made his further excuses. It was his intention to find his son and the two others. He hadn't far to travel. As he had surmised, they were making their respective ways towards the bar. Aubrey Coventry joined them. He let them order drinks before he raised the subject that was uppermost in his mind.

"I want a word with you fellows," he said. "On a somewhat peculiar matter. You may think my question a strange one—but did anyone of you notice a bloke with grey hair hanging about within the last quarter of an hour, dressed in a sort of blue dungaree suit?"

Crayle and Philip Coventry shook their heads. Neither of them had seen the man. "Where was he?" inquired Hubert Palmer.

Aubrey Coventry took pains to describe the man's position. "When the band was playing 'Hurry Home' just now, he was standing by that cluster of big palms. He was standing absolutely by himself."

"Then I did see him," responded Hubert Palmer with a nod. "Although I'm afraid I paid but scant attention to him at the time. I took him to be one of the guests in a somewhat unusual costume. You know what atrocious garbs you do find at crushes like this. But why do you ask—what's the odds about him—anyhow?"

Coventry smiled ruefully. "Well—listen to this. I think it will interest you. It happened to me just before you chaps turned up at my place this evening. It's a ludicrous sort of incident, but it made a deep impression on me at the time and I haven't been able to forget it. When you hear it, you may think me all sorts of a silly ass. Still—I'll chance that. You just listen to what I'm going to say."

Aubrey Coventry thereupon told the story of the snarling man. To his intense relief the three others listened to him attentively.

"Lovely fellow," commented Palmer, "thorough sportsman. Real old school tie. One of the new nobility, I guess. How he must have hated your guts. And you meet him in the evening of the same day—fellow guests at Dorset House. Well-well-well! Incredible and amazing coincidence."

"But what I can't understand," contributed Peter Crayle thoughtfully, "after admitting all that Hubert has just said, is how the fellow happens to be here in any case. How on earth did he manage to get in? He must have gate-crashed—that's a certainty. How about making inquiries—discreet inquiries—from the chaps on the front? It's on the cards that they may be able to tell you something about him."

"That's an idea," corroborated Phil Coventry. "Seems to me very sound. Even though the whole affair may possess no real importance, it's pretty thin that a cove of that class should be allowed to barge in on a crush like this without being challenged in any way. Something wrong somewhere." He stopped and thought things over for a moment. "Wouldn't it be better," he urged eventually, "better than making inquiries at the front, if we pounced on the fellow next time we run into him and challenge him to produce his credentials? Bring him to a show-down? After all, the entire list of invitations here is by ticket. Brereton told me only the other day. I happen to know that for certain."

His father nodded as Phil finished speaking. "Yes, I think perhaps you're right, Phil. That would be the sounder course to adopt. And more practical. We'll have another round and then go back and look for the beggar. He must be somewhere about. Drink up, you chaps."

The three men obeyed him, another round went its way, and they made their way back to the main hall. But there no sign anywhere of the man in the blue overalls. Aubrey Coventry and his three companions looked everywhere for him—to no avail. He had vanished without trace. Just after midnight, Coventry stood with the three others on the spot. There he had caught sight of the missing man. "This is about the place where I saw the fellow. He was standing here just at the side of those palms, looking across the room—in that direction." Coventry indicated with his hand. "Do you know," he went on, "I feel rather worried about it. It's on my nerves. And if Hubert here hadn't seen the chap as well and quite independently of me, I should be beginning to wonder If I hadn't been seeing visions and dreaming dreams. It's all so damned odd—and—er—peculiar—no rhyme or reason about it."

Crayle nodded. "I agree with you entirely, Mr. Coventry. We should have done better to make inquiries at the front as I suggested in the first place. I'll tell you what happened, in my opinion. This chap, whoever he is, slipped in for a certain purpose which probably didn't take him very long and then, having accomplished what he wanted, slipped out again. It wouldn't be too difficult to do any one of these things. Very possibly he's a 'dip'—out to improve the shining hour. They get everywhere these days."

"A 'dip'?" queried Phil Coventry. "I'm not quite sure—a dip is a—"

"Pickpocket is what you and I would describe him as," returned Peter Crayle—"but in the actual profession they're known, I believe, by the romantic appellation of 'dips'."

"You don't read the best fiction, Phil," contributed Hubert Palmer, "I can see that—you're behind the times."

Aubrey Coventry looked at his watch. It had just come home to him again that he had an appointment with a certain Silas Montgomery within less than two hours. "Well—it's gone twelve, you chaps, and I'm beating it. If any one of you wants to stop on for a bit—he's welcome. But if any of you wants a lift back—he's welcome to that too. Well—how does it go?"

Palmer considered the question for a moment. "I think I'll stay on for a little while, if you don't mind. I want a word with a bloke who doesn't seem to have put in an appearance yet."

"That's all right, Hubert. What about you, Crayle?"

"If Phil's coming along with you, sir—then I'll join the pair of you. I might as well. The lift back will be a help to me. What are you doing, Phil?"

"Going back with Dad," answered Phil briskly. "I've had all I want of this show and there's nothing to keep me."

"That's all right then," concluded the older Coventry. "Good night, Hubert."

"Good night, sir, and thanks for the offer. Good night and all the rest of it." Palmer waved to them a few minutes later when they drove off in Aubrey Coventry's car. After that, he went back to the saloon. As he had told the elder Coventry, he particularly wanted to see 'Tubby' Atherton before he turned in. 'Why can't people be punctual?' he thought savagely as he entered the hall again.

Within a short space of time Aubrey and Phil Coventry were saying good night to Peter Crayle outside the Coventry residence in Danvers Gate. "Sure you won't come in for a spot, Peter?" asked Phil. "Won't take a second."

"No thanks, old man. It's latish and I can see your father's tired. Leave it for another time. To-morrow is also a night." Crayle shook hands. The two Coventrys, father and son, went in.

CHAPTER III
ENTER SILAS MONTGOMERY

PHIL Coventry had a 'spot' in company with his father and went to bed. To Aubrey Coventry's surprise, after he had changed into ordinary clothes, Rayner was waiting for him in the study. The secretary coughed apologetically. "I wasn't sure whether you would require my presence, sir, so I stayed up—just in case."

Coventry shook his head. Rayner was a secretary in a thousand. "You shouldn't have done that, Rayner. Although I appreciate the feelings that prompted you. But I shall be all right. Don't you worry about me. You toddle off to bed now and get some rest."

Rayner still seemed dubious. Coventry noticed his indecision. "I mean what I say, Rayner. I'm perfectly able to look after myself. Go along now—you get up to bed."

Rather reluctantly, Rayner rose from his chair to obey. "Very good, sir. If that's how you feel about things, I'll wish you good night, sir. I'm sorry if I appear over-zealous, sir, I suppose it's just my way."

Coventry smiled at him. "That's all right, Rayner. Good night."

"Good night to you, Mr. Coventry."

Aubrey Coventry watched him go and then sat in the swivel chair at his desk. He felt absurdly and most abominably tired. Ordinarily he was capable of a tremendous amount of exertion without feeling that the resources of his stamina were being unduly taxed. He had had a long day, it was true . . . and an unusually varied day . . . perhaps this latter was the main reason that lay behind his unaccustomed tiredness. Once again he looked at the time. Twenty-two minutes past one. Not over-long before his visitor was due. He had always wanted to meet the famous Silas Montgomery . . . or should it be notorious . . . and had more than once expressed this desire in words. Strange now, when the meeting was to take place, that the overtures had come from Montgomery and not from him. His thoughts rioted. Aubrey Coventry wondered . . . in the event of—at that moment his telephone rang. Just as it had rung, so it seemed to him, on the previous morning when he had ordered the faithful Rayner to answer it. On this second occasion, having sent Rayner to bed, he would be compelled to answer it himself. He took off the receiver.

"This is Aubrey Coventry speaking. . . ."

A voice with a strong nasal intonation answered him. It was the voice he had heard before. "Good evening. Silas Montgomery this end. As we arranged yesterday I shall be with you at two o'clock precisely . . . and it is important that I should speak to you alone. There must be nobody in the room with you. Don't forget that. Good-bye until two o'clock."

Before Coventry could find words to reply, Montgomery had rung off. Coventry pushed back his chair and ran his fingers through his hair. He noticed that Rayner had thoughtfully provided for a tantalus and syphon to be within his reach. He mixed himself a stiff one and drank it down at a gulp. Instead of reviving him as he had hoped, it seemed to aggravate his feeling of tiredness. Strange how this extraordinary lassitude persisted. It was so unlike him. He must be getting old. Come to think of it, he *was* getting on! Funny you didn't realize these things until something unexpected happened which threw you out of your stride and forced you to consider them. The minutes passed quickly while Aubrey Coventry was in this reverie. When he looked at his watch again he saw to his surprise that the time was five minutes to two. Silas Montgomery might be with him at any minute now. He must pull himself together in order to be at his best during the interview.

At two o'clock exactly the front door bell rang. Aubrey Coventry walked to the door. Before he could reach it, the bell rang again loudly and insistently. Coventry quickened his pace and opened the door. To his utter astonishment, there stood on the step the man in the dungaree suit. It took Aubrey Coventry a moment to recover himself.

"You are Silas Montgomery?" he asked in amazement. The man nodded.

"Come in then," said Aubrey Coventry.

The man followed him into his study. "Sit down," said Coventry.

<h1 style="text-align:center">CHAPTER IV
MURDER</h1>

CHIEF-Inspector Andrew MacMorran of the Criminal Investigation Department of New Scotland Yard sat opposite Sir Austin Mostyn Kemble, K.C.V.O., D.S.O., in the latter's room, overlooking the Thames, and wondered at the real reason behind the rather peremptory summons which had brought him there. It was early in the day for the Commissioner to send for him like this. Besides he was busy on the Gordon-Fitch forgery case. Sir Austin did not leave him long in doubt as to why he had been summoned.

"Morning, MacMorran, sit down, will you? Oh, you are sitting down—that's all right then." The Commissioner tilted his swivel chair and MacMorran recognized a somewhat ominous sign. "I've just had an urgent call from downstairs, MacMorran. There's somebody waiting to come up now. In Hemingway's office. I'd like you to be here. I've a special reason for that. I understand it's a case of murder. Almost on our doorstep too."

"Really, sir?" MacMorran was politely inquiring.

"Yes. There's no doubt about it, I'm afraid. I'll have the chap up here at once and then we can hear all about it. Ring down for me, will you, MacMorran?"

The Inspector picked up the telephone. "The Commissioner is ready to see the gentleman who's waiting . . . if you'll be good enough to bring him up, Hemingway. Thank you." MacMorran put down the receiver and looked across at Sir Austin Kemble. "Last night, sir, I dreamt of Mr. Bathurst. Funny that—wasn't it? As a matter of fact, I haven't seen him for months. And now this comes along."

"Don't be ridiculous, MacMorran. Indigestion! I'll be bound it was. What did you have for supper? Cucumber or something?"

"Quite light, Sir Austin. Just a kipper with a cup of cocoa. Nothing to trouble anybody in that. The missus has rather set her face against my supper beer, so I've been tryin' the old Cadbury. She says it's warm and nutritious. Here they are, sir."

Steps were heard outside and the door of the Commissioner's room opened. There entered to them the figures of burly Superintendent Walter Hemingway and of a thin-faced spare man wearing horn-rimmed glasses.

"Mr. Arthur Rayner," announced the Superintendent.

"Sit down, Mr. Rayner. Thank you, Hemingway. If I want you again I'll send for you."

"Very good, sir." Hemingway departed and made his way along the bare stone-floored corridor that took him back to his own room.

"Now, Mr. Rayner, what is it that you have to tell me?"

MacMorran saw that Rayner's face was twitching and his hands were trembling. His nerves were all to pieces—that was very evident. Suddenly he found his tongue. "It's murder, sir. My employer, Mr. Aubrey Coventry . . . the well-known Stock Exchange operator . . . has been murdered in the night . . . or rather this morning."

The Commissioner gestured to the Inspector. MacMorran understood what he was supposed to do. "Where?" asked MacMorran.

"At his house in Danvers Gate . . . number twenty-two . . . just opposite Hyde Park."

"Give me the full particulars, will you, please?"

"I came down this morning about nine o'clock. That's about my usual time, gentlemen. I always do. The maid isn't allowed to do Mr. Coventry's room until after I've been in there. I went into the study to put some papers in order that I had left over from the day before. Mr. Coventry was seated in his chair—dead. I could tell he was dead directly I clapped my eyes on him. From the look on his face, sir, it would appear that he had been garrotted . . . or something like that. I at once roused Mr. Philip Coventry, his son, and told him the terrible news. It was Mr. Philip Coventry who sent me along here. I wanted to call you on the 'phone, but he thought it would be better if I came along. I can assure you that I wasted no time in coming."

"Just a minute," intervened the Commissioner. "You made a rather curious correction of speech just now in your statement."

Rayner was cooler now, however, and more collected. "In what way was that?"

"You stated," remarked Sir Austin authoritatively, "that Mr. Coventry had been murdered in the night. But you immediately corrected that statement to 'this morning.' Will you kindly explain, Mr. Rayner, why you did that?"

"I intended to, sir. I made the correction deliberately. I knew that Mr. Coventry must have been murdered this morning because I saw him alive at a quarter to one this morning. That would be three-quarters of an hour after midnight."

"Where was that?" asked Inspector MacMorran.

"In his study."

"Rather late, wasn't it, for you to be up with your employer? Was that anything like a usual procedure?"

"No. Not at all. Last night Mr. Coventry attended a fancy dress ball at Dorset House. He returned home to his house in Danvers Gate shortly after midnight. I awaited his return. I may say that I had a special reason for doing so."

"What was that?"

"Mr. Coventry had an important appointment at two o'clock this morning. At his house in Danvers Gate."

"Go on," said MacMorran. "This is getting highly interesting—who with?"

"Yes," supplemented Sir Austin Kemble. "With whom?"

"Mr. Silas Montgomery . . . the well-known American financier and Wall Street operator." Rayner went on to describe the preliminary arrangements regarding the appointment Montgomery-Coventry. Sir Austin leant over towards him.

"And did Mr. Coventry keep this appointment . . . or rather did this man Montgomery keep it?"

"I don't know, sir." Rayner shook his head as he spoke.

"You don't know?" The Commissioner's voice held a tone of incredulity.

"No, sir. It was like this, you see. Let me explain. Mr. Coventry ordered me to go to bed. He wouldn't hear of me staying up with him. I was forced to obey. Mr. Coventry wasn't a man you could argue with. I wish now that I had disobeyed. If I had, Mr. Coventry might still have been alive." Rayner put his face in his hands. There were tears in his eyes. MacMorran put a question to him. "Do you mean to say that you have no knowledge of anything that took place after Mr. Coventry told you to go to bed? Do I understand that that's so?"

Rayner nodded again. "That is quite true. I went to bed as I had been told to do by Mr. Coventry. I was tired. I went to sleep almost at once. I almost invariably do. I did not wake until this morning. That means I heard no sound in the night. My first knowledge of the tragedy was when I found Mr. Coventry this morning in the circumstances I have already outlined."

"I find it somewhat difficult to believe," said Sir Austin Kemble, drumming on his desk with his finger-tips, "that your employer took this man Silas Montgomery so much 'on trust' as it were."

Rayner nodded his agreement.

"I made that point myself, sir, when the man telephoned on the first occasion. I was almost insistent on the point. I disliked the arrangement from the start. But I think that I can explain it like this. Mr. Coventry took Silas Montgomery for granted: let me make myself more clear. The man's reputation was enough. I think that Mr. Coventry was flattered by the thought that Montgomery wanted to see him so specially as you might say and even perhaps so mysteriously. Can you understand partly—even—what I mean?"

The Commissioner had no direct answer. Instead he spoke to MacMorran. "Get along at once to Danvers Gate, MacMorran. Mr. Rayner will accompany you. Make arrangements for the Divisional-Surgeon and the others to follow. They can be with you later. Let me have your preliminary report as soon as possible."

"Very good, Sir Austin." Rayner, MacMorran, and Doctor Sugden were at Danvers Gate within a quarter of an hour of the conclusion of the interview with the Commissioner of Police. Philip Coventry was there to meet them. Rayner explained matters to him. Philip nodded at what he was told. "Nothing has been disturbed in any way, Inspector. I have left everything as it was when Rayner made the discovery. But I have not told my mother the entire truth yet. All I've told her so far is that my father has had a seizure of some kind and that we've had to send for the doctor. I've asked her to remain in her room until I send for her. Come this way, gentlemen, will you, please?" Young Coventry led the way to his father's study. He unlocked the door for them. Andrew MacMorran noticed this fact particularly. Aubrey Coventry was seated in a chair drawn up to the table. His head had fallen and his mouth was open. Dr. Sugden went straight to the body. His professional reaction came almost immediately. "Death by asphyxia. The man's been suffocated by compression of the windpipe. Strangled, in other words. Judging by the marks on the neck and throat, a rope was tied round his throat and pulled tight. Observe, Inspector, the difference in the appearance of these marks from those which follow a judicial hanging. In that case, the mark of the noose on the neck is oblique. In a death from strangling such as this undoubtedly is, the mark is circular. Look here. Well, Inspector, it's a case of wilful murder all right. You may make your mind clear on that."

Phil Coventry stood by the doorway. "Close that door," said MacMorran, "and come in, please. This is a wretched job and I don't want any interlopers cluttering the place up."

Coventry obeyed silently and shut the door. MacMorran took a quick look round the room. He always liked to do this before the photographers arrived. There were several cigarette-ends in an ash-tray on the table. MacMorran examined them. They were all of the same brand. He turned to Philip Coventry. "I think that you can help me, Mr. Coventry. Has this room been disturbed in any way? I don't mean by you since your father's death was discovered. But before that? Is it as it would be ordinarily? You see nothing unusual about it? You get my meaning?"

Phil Coventry replied steadily and with extreme composure.

"As far as I can see, Inspector, and I have looked closely, the room is absolutely normal in every way. Nothing has been disturbed. That I can see. Nothing appears to have been taken from it. Nothing appears to have been broken into. All is orderly—in short, exactly as one would expect to find it. Indeed—but for my father's body there—" Phil Coventry stopped sharply with a gesture of helplessness and shrugged his shoulders.

"Valuable papers," commented MacMorran, "is it possible that any could have been stolen—say—from a drawer—and you be none the wiser?"

Coventry emphatically shook his head. "No—and I'll tell you why. For the simple reason that there were none here. My father always kept them at the bank. He was very strong on that point. Has done so for years."

"He might have had something of that kind in his possession," suggested the Inspector, "something that he had taken from the bank temporarily. That can be easily ascertained."

"He banked at the London and Home Counties, Victoria branch."

"H'm," said MacMorran, "well, we can look into that possibility later." At that precise moment the telephone rang. MacMorran gestured towards Rayner to answer it. The last named, who had been studiously filling in the background since his return to the house, stepped forward in response. He took off the receiver.

"It is for you, Inspector," he announced a second later. "From the Yard, I think."

The Inspector nodded curtly and took the receiver from Rayner's hand. "MacMorran speaking. Oh—is that you, Sir Austin? Yes . . . yes .. . well, that's a surprise, sir . . . I must say . . . very well, sir, any minute now, you say. Only too delighted, sir. I'll make the necessary arrangements, of course." MacMorran nodded several times more and replaced the receiver. He stood by the table in contemplation for a few seconds. The others watched him. Two minutes later there came a tap on the door. MacMorran motioned to Philip Coventry. The latter went across and opened the door and there entered, clad in a grey flannel suit of a pleasing elegance, the tall form of Anthony Lotherington Bathurst. MacMorran shook hands. Pleasure showed on his face. Sugden shook hands. It must be remembered that the three of them had worked before in treble harness. MacMorran brought Phil Coventry and Rayner into the circle. "The Commissioner wants me to have a look round," said Mr. Bathurst.

"There are two of us who think like that, sir," returned Chief-Inspector Andrew MacMorran.

"Thank you, Andrew," acknowledged Mr. Bathurst.

CHAPTER V
CERTAIN STRANGENESSES

ANTHONY Bathurst listened to Dr. Sugden. Sugden, as always, was completely explicit. "May I look at the body, Doctor?"

"Of course."

Mr. Bathurst went across to the chair which held death. He looked and nodded two or three times. Suddenly he bent down and called Dr. Sugden's attention to the left trouser leg. "Notice how that's caught up, Doctor? May be nothing in it, of course, but it's suggestive of a certain . . . by the way—have you looked at the wrists yet, Doctor?"

Sugden pushed back the sleeves of the coat. He and Bathurst bent down to look at the dead man's wrists. "Marked," said Sugden, with curt directness. "Yes . . . you're right. Been tied up."

"I thought there might be the chance of that. As I see it, he was tied first. Say—across the chest, round the wrists, and also round the legs. To render him helpless. That's how they wanted him. He was strangled afterwards."

"Two ropes—eh?"

"Looks like it to me. Extraordinary case though—altogether." MacMorran beckoned to him. "This is rather peculiar, Mr. Bathurst.

Young Mr. Coventry here has just brought it to my notice. There are two note-books on the table. See them? Each appears to have been used. Look here for yourself, sir." Anthony went to the table and looked. The note-books were of the type that has no top-cover of any kind. Mr. Bathurst looked at the one nearer to the position where the dead Aubrey Coventry was seated. The top sheet was blank. He picked it up and scrutinized it closely.

There were slight indentations on it. Too slight, though, to be decipherable. He shook his head. "A pencil was used on the sheet that lay on top of this. I feel pretty sure about that. Let me have a glance at the other note-book, Inspector—will you, please?"

MacMorran passed over the second note-book. "Much the same condition applies here. But a pen has been used for this writing. There is no need for indentations either, for me to make that assertion. Two of the words have been left behind. The top sheet was torn off carelessly and a fragment has been left behind in the book. The perforation at the top of the book was missed by the person tearing . . . just at the beginning. The two written words are . . . I think . . . 'your offer'."

Phil Coventry pressed forward eagerly. "May I look at that, Mr. Bathurst? I may be able to throw some light on it."

"By all means. Here you are!"

Philip Coventry took the note-book. "Those two words are in my father's handwriting, Mr. Bathurst. I can tell you that for certain. That was why I wanted to look—does that help you at all? They're written carelessly, perhaps, but well enough for me to recognize the fist."

"My dear chap! Of course it helps. All authentic information must help. But I'm puzzled at what you've told me, all the same."

"I think I can see your difficulty," interposed Rayner. "You are wondering why Mr. Coventry should have used two books for making notes of the interview. I must confess that the same point has been troubling me."

"Exactly—and our confusion increases when we realize that the note-book in which we know he had written was the one that was the farther away from him. That fact is certainly a strange one. I don't understand it at all. I suppose, by the way, Mr. Rayner, that

Mr. Coventry was in the habit of using note-books, such as these, for interviews?"

"Almost invariably."

"Good. That's as well to know. Normality always holds attraction for the investigator. All the same, these note-books still puzzle me. There's something about them that isn't right."

"I agree—entirely." Rayner nodded in corroboration. Mr. Bathurst inspected the pen-tray. There were two pencils lying in it. "Tell me more, MacMorran," he said. "Tell me all that you've managed to pick up since you've been here. Make your own limits—naturally. First and foremost—what's the motive, Inspector?"

MacMorran shook his head. Seeing this, the dead man's son took it upon himself to answer Mr. Bathurst's question.

"As far as we know—there's no motive. Absolutely none at all. That's the damned silly part about it. My father hasn't been robbed and he hadn't an enemy in the world. Not a single one! So it's up to you, Mr. Bathurst, to suggest something to us."

Anthony Bathurst looked across at the dead man's secretary. Rayner seemed to sense what was required of him. "I am able to endorse what Mr. Philip says, sir. Fully and faithfully. The whole business is an absolute mystery to us. It would be a sheer impossibility for me to hint even at a motive. I have been the late Mr. Coventry's secretary for over eleven years now. Nobody knew his business life like I did. Practically all his affairs were in my hands. He trusted me with everything. If ever the term 'confidential' secretary could be used justifiably of anybody it could be used with regard to me during my term of service with Mr. Coventry."

MacMorran thrust his hands into his trouser pockets. Things negative were going too far. He felt it was time that he projected criticism. "That's all very well as far as it goes, Mr. Rayner. You said yourself—his business life. That's only part of a man's life. What about his private life? This murder may have its origin there. Very probably, I should say."

Anthony Bathurst was listening carefully. He knew that these were vital and critical moments. Rayner and Philip Coventry answered the Inspector's point almost in unison.

Perhaps Coventry was ahead. Rayner seemed to think so because he stopped to let Philip go on.

"My father lived for his business, Inspector. He had scarcely any other interests in life. Beyond a little golf at occasional week-ends he was always at his work. He was very young when he became a member of the Stock Exchange, and bulls and bears have been in his blood ever since the day he started. You can take my word on all that, Inspector." Phil Coventry spoke with emphasis and conviction. Rayner had been punctuating the young man's remarks with nods of agreement.

"Again—I thoroughly endorse all that Mr. Philip has said, Inspector."

Mr. Bathurst commenced to pace the room. He could tell already that there was something altogether wrong about this case. Things must be made to fit better than they so far were fitting. He suddenly swung round and addressed Philip Coventry.

"That appointment your father had this morning. With this Mr. Silas Montgomery. The Commissioner of Police has told me of it. Were you aware of it?"

Phil Coventry shook his head. "I knew nothing at all about it. Even when my father said good night to me not long before this Montgomery was expected, he gave me no sign and I had no inkling of it. I thought that my father was going to bed."

Rayner intervened again. "That is perfectly true. Mr. Aubrey Coventry and I were the only people who knew of the Montgomery appointment. I am certain of that."

Phil Coventry grasped the opportunity to go on again.

"At the same time, Mr. Bathurst, you mustn't imagine that there was anything unusual in my not knowing about Montgomery. My father seldom discussed his business affairs with me. I have my own career—which is quite apart from my father's business . . . and we never bothered each other on such matters. I think that it would be as well if you knew that—in case you should be forming wrong conclusions."

"I see. Thank you, Mr. Coventry. That information certainly does clear the air for me."

MacMorran spoke to Dr. Sugden. "Very good. Doctor . . . if you will make the necessary arrangements."

Dr. Sugden nodded briskly and made his exit. Mr. Bathurst had conversation with the Inspector. The latter came over to Phil Coventry and Rayner the secretary. "I should like to have a look over the rest of the house . . . if you two gentlemen wouldn't mind. Will you accompany us, Mr. Bathurst?"

"Not for the minute, Inspector . . . if you don't mind . . . but don't be concerned about me."

"I'm at your service, Inspector," said Coventry. "Rayner and I will take you round with pleasure. Will you come along now?"

Coventry and Rayner ushered MacMorran from the room. Anthony Bathurst, as had been his wish, was left to the devices and desires of his own heart. Again he walked round the room. The use of the two note-books on Coventry's desk had puzzled him when he had first seen them and they still puzzled him. He went again to the dead man in the chair. An idea had occurred to him. He bent over the body to look for something. Something that should be there. Yes . . . there was a fountain-pen in the usual pocket of the waistcoat. The pen was Coventry's. Had Aubrey Coventry and Montgomery then changed places? Had Coventry sat elsewhere . . . close to the note-book that bore the, writing of the fountain-pen . . . and the other man been seated where Coventry's body was now? It was an idea . . . but if so, why? What credible reason could there be behind such an interchange of places? For the third time that morning Mr. Bathurst made a tour of the room. It showed in all respects obvious signs of comparative opulence. The furniture was of the finest quality. The carpet had been costly . . . all the appointments indeed were of the highest standard. Taste and refinement showed everywhere. Aubrey Coventry must have been an exceedingly wealthy man. The pictures, too, caught the eye. They were oil paintings, the two of them. Imitations doubtless of the masters. One was of a girl in a Tudor dress. The girl had red hair. Mr. Bathurst judged it to be an imitation of Holbein.

The other was a copy of a picture that he knew well. Rembrandt's 'Saskia at her Toilet.' Aubrey Coventry had evidently liked and intended to possess the next best thing. Mr. Bathurst went across to the bookcase. Coventry, he considered, had not been a reader. The books were too clean and in too meticulous an order. They stood in too precise ranks. He noticed that Coventry Patmore, de Maupassant, Dickens, and Anatole France were all represented. There were few moderns to be observed. Mr. Bathurst could find only Priestley, Rebecca West, and Somerset Maugham. He reflected that after all Aubrey Coventry had been a business man, and his sole interest had almost certainly been in the markets of finance. He could see the truth of what Philip Coventry had already told him. There was no disturbance in the room whatever. Two note-books and a dead man on a chair. Strangled by a rope. Tied in the chair, too, by another rope before he had been strangled. Beyond these indications—nothing. What a case! To all intents and purposes, scarcely a starting point of the slightest importance. Mr. Bathurst was unable to remember when he had been so baffled in the preliminary stages of the problem. He heard the sound of footsteps outside the door. It was MacMorran returning with Phil Coventry and the secretary Rayner. The Inspector entered the room briskly. Anthony looked at him with interrogation.

"Mr. Bathurst," he said at once, "young Mr. Coventry here tells me that he has just thought of something which he considers we ought to know. I suggested to him that it would be as well if you could hear it too. . . . So I've brought him back to tell the yarn in here."

"Very well, Inspector. That's good of you. To say nothing of being considerate. I shall be interested to hear it, whatever it may be. By the way, Mr. Coventry . . . your mother. . . . Have you . . . ?"

"Not yet, Mr. Bathurst. I'm a coward over that. I'm delaying the tragic business for as long as I possibly can."

"Naturally. I can understand your feelings. Tell me this, though. Was your mother in your father's company yesterday?"

"For part of the time. They were at a bazaar during the afternoon at Leyland in Essex—my mother's brother is the Vicar there. The Rev. Noel Duff. I expect you've heard him on the radio. He's an authority on slugs and beetles, and has broadcast several times. My father left his place, however, towards the end of the afternoon. He had an appointment with me and two other fellows. At a fancy dress ball at Dorset House. The Seven Arts. We go there every year. We left there just after midnight. Came on here."

"Your mother, I take it, stayed on at Leyland?"

"That's right. Some hours after my father. She came back during the evening sometime."

"Thank you, Mr. Coventry. I'll return to that later. Now tell me the story that Inspector MacMorran referred to when you came in just now."

"Well, funnily enough the two things mix up a bit now I come to think of them. My father told us the yarn while we were at Dorset House. I'll warn you, though, that to me it sounded pretty ridiculous. I'm afraid that you'll think the same as I thought. I'll tell it to you just as my father told it to Crayle, Palmer, and me." Phil Coventry paused and looked round the company. He seemed to be collecting his thoughts. When he started again he spoke slowly as though his mind were uncertain and dubious with regard to something and that he was groping for words. "I want to convey this to you, gentlemen. That my father regarded what I am about to tell you as undoubtedly serious. There was nothing ridiculous about it as far as he was concerned . . . whatever we may have thought about it. I want you to understand that first of all. It's important and must make a lot of difference to me as I tell you. Now for the story. My father came back from Leyland towards the end of the afternoon and, as I told you, he was expecting Crayle and Palmer and myself, and we were due here somewhere about half-past seven. He found that he had time on his hands before he need dress for the Dorset House show, and decided to go out into the park and smoke a cigarette. When he got there he found a seat and was just on the point of lighting up when he discovered to his extreme annoyance that he had no matches. Two seats away from him he happened to see a man smoking. So my father went along and as one smoker to another asked him for a light. To his utter amazement, the man made no reply. In my father's words 'he simply shrank away from me and snarled at me.' My father also made this rather eloquent remark. He said that the man reminded him of a citizen of the Revolution times denouncing an aristocrat . . . there was such blazing hatred in his face."

"Just a moment," put in Anthony Bathurst. "I find this story most interesting, Mr. Coventry. What was your father's immediate reaction to this most extraordinary reception?"

"Well, according to what he told us, he repeated his request and the same thing happened. Exactly the same thing. The man simply snarled at him. Then my father indulged in a little sarcasm and walked away. But that's not all, Mr. Bathurst. Incredible though it may be, there's an equally interesting sequel to come."

Mr. Bathurst rubbed his hands in pleasurable anticipation. "Please go on, Mr. Coventry."

"My father went home and dressed for the Seven Arts show. Put on his costume, etc., for the do at Dorset House, met us—Crayle and Palmer and me—and we all went down there in the car. During the evening my father told us the story I've just put across to you . . . and then, to our complete astonishment, said that he had just seen his friend of the snarl *in the ballroom at Dorset House* standing only a few yards away from us!"

Mr. Bathurst rubbed his hands for the second time. "Really, Mr. Coventry . . . this is most illuminating. Go on, please."

"According to my father the man was wearing a suit of blue overalls. Dungaree . . . you know the idea. Like electricians or mechanics wear. Which was exactly as he had been dressed when he snarled on the seat in the park."

"Just a minute, Mr. Coventry. I'd like a word in here."

The interruption on this occasion came from Inspector MacMorran. "Did you see this man yourself?"

Phil Coventry seemed a little taken aback at the Inspector's question. "No, I didn't. I only wish that I had. I was coming to that. After my father told us about him we all went to try to find the fellow. The idea was to pounce on him suddenly and challenge him as to why he was there. It's always an invitation affair, you know, at Dorset House. But our plan miscarried. We could do nothing. The fellow had vanished. There wasn't a trace of him anywhere. We searched everywhere. I'm certain that my father was upset by the incident."

A question from Anthony Bathurst. "What costumes were the members of your party wearing?"

"Crayle a discus thrower, my father a monk, Palmer a sort of pirate costume, and myself—Captain Kettle of fiction fame." MacMorran's impatience came at Coventry again.

"So that it amounts to this, Mr. Coventry. Your father seems to have been the only person who saw this chap! That's a pity, isn't it? You know what I mean—it's unsatisfactory—it leaves us somewhat in the air."

Phil Coventry dissented. He shook his head. "No, Inspector. You're not quite right over that. As a matter of fact, Palmer saw the chap as well. About the same time, too, that my father had seen him. My father asked us all and Palmer admitted it."

"He agreed with your father as to the man's costume?"

"Oh—absolutely. My father seemed relieved when he heard Hubert Palmer confirm his story. What worries me now is that we failed to lay our hands on the bloke. Now I come to look back on everything I can't help thinking that he may have had something to do with my father's death. The coincidence of his two appearances in one day is too strong to be overlooked."

Phil Coventry stopped. His face was shadowed. Anthony Bathurst fingered the ridge of his jaw. "A most unusual story, Mr. Coventry, and one which I frankly admit greatly intrigues me. The snarling man! I wonder what connection the gentleman has with our other friend, Mr. Silas Montgomery. I'm afraid that it may take us some time to discover that."

"You think I did right to tell you of the incident?"

"Oh, undoubtedly, Mr. Coventry. If I were you I'd break the news to your mother . . . before more of Inspector MacMorran's homicide squad put in their appearance. It's hard, I know . . . but it's harder to keep her in protracted suspense." Phil Coventry rose. He spoke to Rayner who had been silent for an unreasonably long time. Then he turned again to Anthony Bathurst.

"All right, I'll take your advice. I'll tell my mother now." Anthony made a sign to the Inspector. MacMorran went over to his side.

Chapter VI
SUSANNA COVENTRY

Anthony Bathurst walked into MacMorran's room at New Scotland Yard. MacMorran was expecting him.

"Well, Andrew," he inquired, "and what luck?"

Andrew MacMorran grinned. Mr. Bathurst sat on a corner of MacMorran's flat table. It was a favourite seat of his. Mr. Bathurst smoked and waited for the Inspector's grin to translate itself into speech. He did not have long to wait for the translation.

"I have news for you. News that will make you sit up and take notice."

"Tell me then, Andrew," urged Anthony, with gentle persuasion. "I was ever impatient."

"I fear it may shock you," said MacMorran, with mock solemnity.

"Shock me, Andrew. I'm wearing my bullet-proof undies. Put 'em on specially—in case. Knowing your savage tendencies."

MacMorran delivered himself of his shock tactics. Very carefully and slowly. "Consider these facts. Silas Montgomery is in New York. Hasn't been away from the U.S.A. for over two months. I've been in touch with the other side. Now—Mr. Bathurst!"

Anthony smiled at him sweetly.

"Pre-cisely as I expected, dear Andrew. I would have banked on it cheerfully. Come, come, you must do better than that, my dear old Frankenstein. Don't kid me that you were surprised when New York came over with that. Because even my natural simplicity will kick at the bare idea. I know you too well, Andrew mine."

"Well, I won't say that *I* was exactly flabbergasted. Does that satisfy you?"

"More or less, Andrew. Chiefly less. So it was impersonation, was it?"

"You've said it."

"Well—we're no worse off on that account. On the contrary, I think we're better. It's up to us to find the man who had the burning desire to identify himself with Silas Montgomery and have that early morning chat with Aubrey Coventry. Which may be a rather simpler matter than wasting time with a genuine Montgomery who might conceivably have had legitimate business with the aforesaid late Aubrey Coventry. See my point, Andrew?"

"Ay. And I think there's something in it. Because I've established the fact that the pukka Montgomery had no business with Coventry at all."

Anthony Bathurst slid from his table seat and prowled round the room. "Another thing," he declared. "It's going to be a Yard case from the start. Again—all to the good. It won't have been clotted up by the local police until that awful moment comes when they bellow for help."

"Yes, there's something in that. I'll tell you another thing I've done. Listen, Mr. Bathurst. How did this man who called himself Silas Montgomery get to the house in Danvers Gate? Did he walk? Did he have his own car? Or did he use a taxi? It seems to me that these three possibilities are the most reasonable lines to work on."

"You're convinced, I take it then, Andrew, that this pseudo-Montgomery is the murderer?"

"I am," returned MacMorran with grim emphasis. "Why shouldn't it be?"

"I won't quarrel with you, Andrew, but the theory isn't a hundred-per-cent watertight, is it now?"

MacMorran surveyed him gloomily. "Must you?"

Mr. Bathurst shrugged his shoulders. "Damn it all, Andrew—we must use our intelligences. Such as they are." Anthony lit a cigarette and handed the case to the Inspector.

"I was using mine," retorted the Inspector, selecting a cigarette. "And I look at it like this. If there's a convenient road made for you and on which you can see your way, why chase round the arches looking for side-turnings that are pretty well impassable, and in addition lead you nowhere? There's one answer for you, Mr. Bathurst—and there are others. But I won't bother you with more for the moment—that one will do to be going on with."

Anthony smiled at the Inspector's uncompromising attitude.

"Go ahead then. What were you going to say that you had done?"

"I've tried to get into touch with anybody who may have seen the murderer either on his way to Danvers Gate, or even actually arriving there. And I'm a wee bit optimistic concerning results."

"I wish you luck, Andrew. Now for a pudden-head question by a mere assistant sleuth. Have you had a chat yet with Aubrey Coventry's widow?"

"That's due for this morning, Mr. Bathurst. Perhaps you'd like to come along with me when I go?"

Again Anthony came with an interruption. "Yes. You can book me up for that. I am interested in that direction. Now another question. Crayle and Palmer—the two men who were with the Coventrys, père et fils, at the Dorset House affair—who are they? I presume you have checked up on them?"

MacMorran fluttered papers on his desk. "Peter Crayle. Aged thirty-four. Educated Radley and Cambridge. Announcer at the B.B.C. Spoken of as one of the most likely youngsters on the B.B.C. staff. Author of several radio plays. Engaged to Valerie Moffatt, niece of late Aubrey Coventry. Which accounts in the main for his association with the Coventry family. That goes for Crayle. Now, Hubert Palmer. Aged thirty-three. Author and script writer. Very successful. Big career predicted for him. Born in Halifax, Nova Scotia, and although comparatively young, has already lived in most countries of the world. Knows the Coventrys through Peter Crayle. Unmarried and unattached."

Anthony Bathurst blew a smoke ring. "I presume you've seen 'em—in addition to collecting these data? How did they strike you themselves? It's a better test, I think."

"Typical of their class and kind. Very self-confident. Sophisticated and all that. Men of the modern world—and very modern at that."

"Did you get their stories?"

MacMorran nodded. "Crayle drove back to Danvers Gate with the two Coventrys. The dead man invited him. That's confirmed by Philip. Philip also states that he invited Crayle in for a drink, but Crayle refused to accept the invitation. Crayle says he refused because it was getting late, and he could see that the elder Coventry was tired. Crayle went straight on to the 'Vermilion Lizard,' the night-club in Rothwell Street. He stayed there for about an hour and a half and then went home."

"Proved the alibi, Andrew?"

"Not yet. Haven't had time. Shall check up on it, of course. But I've little doubt that it's all above board."

"Right. Let me know when you do. Now for the other chap—Hubert Palmer. What about him?"

"Not quite so good." MacMorran shifted a little in his chair. Anthony thought that he had suddenly become a trifle uneasy. He found himself wondering why—exactly.

"Well—this is Palmer's story, Mr. Bathurst. I'll give it to you as I had it from him. Aubrey Coventry offered him a lift back from Dorset House along with Crayle, but Palmer was compelled to refuse it. He states that he had a sort of appointment with another man who was expected to be at Dorset House that same evening. This man's name is Rex Atherton. He's well known, I'm told, in the 'flick' industry. Palmer referred to him as 'Tubby' Atherton."

Anthony cut in. "Did this Atherton fellow turn up at Dorset House?"

MacMorran nodded—still on the doleful side. "Palmer says that he did. And that they were together until the affair broke up—about half-past four. I'm arranging to have a word with Mr. Atherton as a check up on that. That's to stop you asking me if I've already had it."

Anthony grinned at the crack. "How did Palmer strike you—particularly?"

"H'm! All right I should say, on the whole."

"What age did you say he was—thirty-three?"

"Yes, a trifle younger than Crayle, although he doesn't look it."

"What do you mean?"

"Just this. I mean that he looks older than Crayle, although actually he's younger."

"What's he like physically?"

"Good type. Well set-up chap. Strong shoulders. Muscular."

"Good looker?"

"To my mind, Mr. Bathurst—yes. But you mightn't agree. You've got funny ideas about looks. I should call you a man of likes and dislikes."

"I certainly prefer Ascot to Alexandra Park and champagne to cocoa, Andrew, if that's what you mean. I'll admit to those preferences with the utmost cheerfulness."

MacMorran's face changed. His gloom gave way to a grin. "Crayle and Palmer don't fill the bill, Mr. Bathurst. By any manner of means. We've got to look beyond them. They've been friends of the Coventrys for years. The fact that they were with them on the evening before the murder means less than nothing. It just happened out of normal associations."

Anthony assented. "I'm inclined to agree with you, Andrew. But knowledge of their movements helps us to assemble the various parts of the puzzle, and it is necessary that we should have that knowledge. That was the principal reason I inquired—concerning them. Now—this call on Mrs. Coventry. I'm ready when you are."

MacMorran went for his hat. His face twisted into a smile.

"I'll say you are, knowing you as I do. Come along then. We can be at Danvers Gate in a matter of ten minutes."

The Inspector and Anthony Bathurst entered a room that was heavy and oppressive with silence. After an interval of waiting, Susanna Coventry came to them. It seemed to Anthony when she first spoke to him, that there was a certain aggressive sense of possession both in her attitude and manner. She was certainly not vulgar . . . and her voice was well pitched. But there was an expression on her keen and somewhat worldly face which clearly betokened her intention of holding her own all the way with her two visitors. She was both well and tastefully dressed. It struck Anthony as he looked at her, that she was probably a willing victim of her own inspiration, and that when she was victimized it usually ran her, like the Gadarene swine, violently down a steep place. MacMorran saw to the usual preliminaries. Mrs. Coventry responded to them satisfactorily, if tearfully. MacMorran put a number of pertinent questions. Mrs. Coventry, shaking her head, was entirely unable to help him. She knew next to nothing with regard to her late husband's business activities, and nothing whatever concerning his appointment with Silas Montgomery. Other questions followed.

Mr. Bathurst listened attentively. Mrs. Coventry still remained totally negative. "You were with your husband during the better part of Tuesday afternoon, I understand, Mrs. Coventry?"

Here she was able to assist the Inspector. "Yes. At a bazaar at my brother's church. He's Vicar of Leyland in Essex. Aubrey went down there with me. It was my particular wish that he should do so. If I had only known . . ." More tears from Mrs. Coventry. Anthony felt that he was an unwarrantable intruder upon a private grief. He waited quietly for her to recover herself. MacMorran, however, hardened by professional experience, intervened with a further question.

"Was the late Mr. Coventry in good spirits during the time that he spent with you at Leyland?"

"Oh, yes. . . . All the way down to my brother's place he was full of good spirits and looking forward . . ." Mrs. Coventry suddenly hesitated, and put her hand to her cheek.

Anthony leant forward and made his first contribution to the inquiry. "You have remembered something, Mrs. Coventry. . . . I feel sure of it."

Mrs. Coventry, for a moment, seemed oblivious of her immediate surroundings, but she speedily collected her wandering thoughts.

"Yes . . . yes. You are right. I have thought of something. This other gentleman's words suggested it to me. My husband was obviously affected by it. He partly admitted as much to me. It was like this. I'll tell you about it. It will be better if I do. There was one of those Romany palmists at the bazaar, and my husband went to her entirely on his own. He didn't say anything to me, mind you, about going . . . he went, as I said, on his own. When he came back I was with a group of friends. They were making rather a fuss of me. They always do down at Leyland. They chaffed him . . . you know what I mean . . . wanted him to tell them what the palmist had said. He told them that he had nothing to say." Mrs. Coventry paused. MacMorran looked at Bathurst with pained resignation. The latter, however, was more concerned with the lady whom they had come to see than with the personal reactions of Inspector MacMorran. She went on:

"I took him away from the crowd. I did so deliberately. I wanted to talk to him alone. After a time . . . he was extremely reticent with me for quite a while . . . he told me that the interview he had just had with the palmist had been most extraordinary. The woman had refused to tell him anything! Not a single word. Said that there was nothing to tell him. In other words—that he had no future—that his life was, to all intents and purposes, finished and done with. Considering what we know to have happened afterwards—and looking back over everything—that seems to me now a most remarkable occurrence. Don't you think so, gentlemen?"

Anthony wondered whether his first assessment of her qualities of imagination had been an accurate one. All the same he was undeniably interested by her story, and it would have been idle to have pretended otherwise. "Do you happen to remember the name of this palmist, Mrs. Coventry?"

For possibly half a second the lady addressed stared at him almost blankly. Then she nodded. "Oh, yes, of course. My husband did tell me. It was a Madame Zylphara. I believe from what he said that she practises in the West End."

MacMorran nodded in his turn. "Been through our hands, I'll be bound. At some time or the other. A good many of 'em have. Although I can't say that I remember this particular name."

Mrs. Coventry went on. "My brother's Bazaar Committee engaged her, so there should be no difficulty in tracing her . . . if that was your idea."

"Dear me, no, ma'am," returned the Inspector. "Don't you bother."

Anthony adroitly concealed a smile at MacMorran's reception of the lady's remark. He turned and spoke again to Mrs. Coventry.

"Was this Madame Zylphara young . . . or the reverse? Did Mr. Coventry happen to mention it?"

"Middle-aged. She impressed him tremendously. In fact, I think he was almost shocked at what she said, if I may use the word."

"Badly shocked?"

"No-o. I don't mean near to collapsing . . . or anything at all like that. Perhaps 'shaken' would have been a better word for me to have used. What she had said to him, or rather—refused to say to him—was undoubtedly on his mind. It seemed to be all that he could think of as it were. It filled his thoughts, let me say, to the exclusion of almost everything else. I could see that plainly. Now have I made myself more clear?" There was a long silence. Mr. Bathurst leant back in his chair and regarded the view above him. MacMorran frowned uncompromisingly at several articles of furniture in turn. Anthony at length broke the silence.

"Yes, Mrs. Coventry, I think that you have made the position much more clear to us. Thank you very much."

"I am glad that I have been able to do that."

"Did you see your husband again . . . after he left Leyland in the afternoon?"

"No. He had that engagement to fulfil with my son at Dorset House that you have already heard about, so he left Leyland before me. I came up from there during the evening. I went to bed before my husband returned. I did not see him again."

It was evident that Mrs. Coventry's distress was returning. Anthony and MacMorran each felt that no good purpose would be served by prolonging the interview. They rose, preparatory to making their departure. "I may be going to Leyland to stop with my brother for a time. After the funeral. It will help me considerably. If you want to see me again I shall probably be down there. I haven't really decided yet when I shall go. Rayner will stay on here for a time . . . and there is also, of course, my son Philip."

MacMorran thanked her for the information.

"Well, Mr. Bathurst," he remarked, as they made their way back to the Yard.

Anthony interrupted him. "I don't know that it is, Andrew. A great many strangenesses are present in the problem. They tend to increase rather than to decrease. I'm tempted to do a spot of investigation on my own account. I'll tell you what. We'll make a bargain. You follow up the 'general' lines of inquiry and I'll have a dip into the 'particulars.' For I'll confess to you, my dear Andrew, that the woman interests me."

"Mrs. Coventry?" declared MacMorran, with surprise in his tone.

"No," returned Mr. Bathurst, "not Mrs. Coventry—on the contrary, this so-called Madame Zylphara of Leyland and the West End, mark you!"

Chapter VII
CLAIRVOYANTE

Mr. Bathurst rang the bell of a drab-fronted house in Fairfax Crescent, W. A particularly small brass plate was inconveniently close to his elbow. He felt that he would like to grimace at it. It bore the inscription in neat black letters on a gold ground, BIANCA ZYLPHARA, CLAIRVOYANTE AND PALMIST. Whoever was inside the establishment seemed in no hurry to answer Mr. Bathurst's summons. Mr. Bathurst promptly pressed the bell again. After a time, he heard the sound of approaching footsteps. An unusually sour-faced woman answered the ring. Mr. Bathurst was polite and explained the reason of his call. Had the gentleman an appointment with Madame? Mr. Bathurst intimated that he hadn't. At the same time he expressed the pious and reverent hope that Madame were not so surfeited with engagements that she had no time to see him. He smiled engagingly as he projected this hope. He was not entirely disappointed. The sour-faced woman suggested that if he came in, she would inquire regarding the possibility of Madame Zylphara granting him an interview. Mr. Bathurst at once accepted the suggestion and was shown into a tawdry room that had seen very much better days. He waited in the tawdriness for a longer period than appealed to him. To be precise, for close upon half an hour. A medley of sound assaulted his ears. Then the sour-faced woman appeared to him again. She looked as forbidding as previously.

"If you will come this way Madame Zylphara will see you now."

"Thank you," murmured Mr. Bathurst, "I shall be charmed."

He was led to an apartment that was as dark and sombre as the previous room had been cheap and tawdry. A deep voice greeted him as he crossed the threshold. It came so suddenly that it almost startled him.

"Sit down, please."

Mr. Bathurst seated himself on the only chair. He saw a dark woman with braided hair facing him. A woman of late middle age. She sat by a small oval table. None of the usual impedimenta of her trade was evident. The half-hour period, evidently, had been put to good use. Before he could speak to her the woman spoke to him. Mr. Bathurst heard what she said with some amazement.

"Let me tell you this before you choose to speak falsely, that you are not here as an ordinary visitor. I am aware of that, so that it will be useless for you to attempt to deceive me. You have come from Scotland Yard. What does Scotland Yard desire to know from Bianca Zylphara?"

In a flash it came to him that if he wanted results he must tell this woman the truth and meet her fairly. After all—why shouldn't he?

"You are right, Madame," he said quietly. "I do not come to you upon an ordinary errand. But you need have no fear that I am spying upon you for your ultimate hurt."

"You cannot hurt me," she replied disdainfully. "It is not in your power. I am Bianca Zylphara in the true line of the royal house of Milan. I am not a cheap fraud who empties the purses of curious servant girls. I am descended from the eighth Visconti. Tell me what you seek to know."

Mr. Bathurst accepted the situation for what it was worth. He chose his next words with care. "A man was strangled two days ago at his house in Danvers Gate, not very far from here."

She moved her head as though in assent. "His name," continued Anthony in an even tone, "was Aubrey Coventry."

"I read of it in the paper. What has it to do with me?"

"It makes a contact with you in this way. He had an interview with you but a few hours prior to his death."

"Where was that?"

"In the Vicarage grounds at Leyland in Essex. At a bazaar that was being held there."

He heard her sudden intake of breath. "So . . . so," she said, almost to herself. Then to him: "Yes, I remember the man well. His span had come to its end. He came to me with the request that I should read his hand. He wanted information concerning his future. So . . . he went away to die. Yes . . . that is what he had to do."

"You told him that he had no future!"

"That is true. How do you know these things?"

"The man told his wife. She is now his widow. The widow told me what he had told her. That is how I know."

"What is it that you have come to me for then, seeing that you already know so much? Neither you nor I can bring a dead man back!"

It sounded like a reproach, but just as Coventry had realized it at Leyland, so Anthony Bathurst realized, too, that there was dignity in her reproach.

"I have come for anything more that you may be willing to tell me."

She gave way to an impatient gesture. "Do not say willing. I have no desire to help you. It is a question of Fate—that is all. There was death in the man's hand. How could I, with generations of knowledge in my blood, fail to see its sign? There was death almost, as you English say, at the man's elbow. And—in a way—more than death itself." Madame Zylphara checked herself abruptly.

"Yes?" urged Mr. Bathurst persuasively.

Her black eyes stared straight at him. "Why should I go on? Whose servant am I?"

"Why not of Truth and Justice? There are worse allegiances."

Zylphara cupped her chin in her hands. "So be it then. The death that I saw in that man's hand was a tragic death. Not a natural one. I saw murder there, sudden and treacherous. But I could not tell him so. I could tell him no more than I did."

"But you can tell me."

"The influences seem sympathetic. I will tell you. I saw the end of things for him. That Time for him was almost at a standstill. I saw a room and the man who was sitting in front of me, dead within that room."

"And," murmured Mr. Bathurst again, "did you see anything else?"

Madame Zylphara seemed to have relapsed into something like a trance. She shook her head more than once. Mr. Bathurst waited patiently. "Oil," she said plainly. "I get oil from somewhere."

Mr. Bathurst thought of Mr. Silas Montgomery. Yes . . . it was understandable. The woman went on. "And yet it is not clear to me . . . it is obscure . . . yes . . . not altogether to do with this country . . . foreign . . . a ruler . . . a king. I am not sure—ah, the vision is clearing for me. There are two women . . . but they are not together

. . . friendly . . . there is no alliance between them, they oppose each other—it is because of these women. . . ." Zylphara's head went forward, and her voice began to dwindle away so that Anthony found himself unable to catch any of the words that she was saying. She began to whisper phrases in Italian. He watched her somewhat anxiously. It was the first experience that he had ever had of an affair of this kind, and he was bound to admit to himself that Zylphara had made an impression upon him. He saw her eyes slowly open again. She stared at him wonderingly. She shook her head at him. "I do not know why I have done this for you. It is unlike me to alter my first intentions. I did not intend to, when you first came in. . . ."

"It would be useless for me, I suppose, to talk to you of what you have just said?"

She shook her head. "I cannot remember it. It has gone from me. It was of the spirit. The mind can recall things, but the spirit cannot."

"I understand, I think. Thank you. Please let me leave this with you. You must know many who are suffering." Anthony handed over two currency notes.

Zylphara rose. "I cannot accept them. I am Bianca Zylphara. Of the royal line of Milan. Such things are beyond me. Do I vex my spirit and travail in my mind for money recompense? Leave them with my attendant in the other room." Mr. Bathurst took back the notes and had hard work to repress a smile. "She will return them to you?"

"She had better. If she forgets, it will be the worse for her," retorted Bianca Zylphara grimly. "Now will you please go . . . for I have an appointment within a few minutes, and I expect that my client is waiting now."

Mr. Bathurst bowed. "Certainly. I have no right to trespass any further upon your valuable time. I feel that I have blundered sufficiently already." He was shown into the room of the sour-faced attendant. In somewhat amused silence he handed over the financial consideration according to the instructions of Zylphara of a moment or so ago. The woman to whom he gave the money muttered a few remarks that, to Mr. Bathurst, were unintelligible. In some attempt to recognize and preserve the semblance of the gaiety of nations, Mr. Bathurst replied to her with cheery commonplaces.

Suddenly the woman seemed to lose her sense of his presence and to be listening to something in the distance. She sharply inclined her head, and then said: "You will please excuse me for a moment. But stay here, if you please—don't go." She made a hurried exit.

Anthony, surprised at the turn which affairs had taken, stayed put. Whatever this new development might turn out to be, he considered that he might as well see it through. Especially in view of the attendant's last remark. He looked round and selected an old-fashioned chair in the hope, it must be admitted, that he would not be destined to stay there over-long. Minutes passed. A loud-ticking clock upon the mantelpiece, which regularly produced a strange whizzing noise that suggested speedy dissolution, indicated the passage of time with a desperate certainty. The passing minutes soon amounted to twenty. Then Mr. Bathurst heard footsteps outside the door. Hurrying, and at the same time, irresolute footsteps. He left the chair and waited for the entrance of somebody. His judgment was accurate. The sour-faced attendant returned to him.

"I have a message for you from Madame."

Anthony nodded. "Yes, what is it?" His surprise was increasing. What could the message be that was coming to him now?

"She cannot see you again," said the attendant, "but she has entrusted the message to me. You are in her good books. I cannot understand why. I was to tell you that the client she has just seen was Mr. Morris Sere. I was also told to tell you this: that if the name of Morris Sere means nothing to you, it happens to be the name of a man who was closely connected with the late Mr. Coventry in several most important business ventures, and who is the man who married Vere Valentine the film star. That is all. You may go now."

Mr. Bathurst accepted this rather summary dismissal with feelings of even more bewilderment. When he found himself in the street known as Fairfax Crescent, he knew that the various matters which were at that moment occupying his brain must be sorted out into something like order. Oil. A ruler. Two women who apparently did not love each other. Nothing unusual in that! Mr. Morris Sere . . . at Madame Zylphara's. His wife—Vere Valentine of the picture world. And, of course, all of this, *according to Madame Zylphara!* Was the woman a fraud? Or was she gifted with certain powers?

Mr. Bathurst had heard of such cases. He would talk things over with Inspector MacMorran.

Chapter VIII
MACMORRAN DRAWS BLOOD

MACMORRAN listened to Mr. Bathurst with a trifle more than his accustomed gravity. Then he shook his head slowly. There was a certain amount of admiration in the shake.

"I think a great deal more of your story where it touches this man Morris Sere than of all the rest of it put together. Or, in other words, I infinitely prefer-r for-r-tune-teller's facts to their mystical tr-r-ances and flights of imagination. The first is definite. The second is not much more than an old wives' tale."

Mr. Bathurst suffered the implied censure with a good-humoured smile. "Yet I've known old wives, Andrew, to be extraordinarily eloquent. And come to that, both young and middle-aged wives also. But you ought to know that better than I do."

"That's all very well. That's just your way of jesting away what I just said."

"That so, Andrew? Well, have it your own way then. Anyhow, I've put you wise as to what I was able to pick up at the Zylphara studio. You're on equal terms with me. What I really think of it all can remain for another day."

"I won't argue about that, Mr. Bathurst. Because I've got some news for you. A *quid pro quo*, we'll call it."

"Good going, Andrew. What is it?"

"The murder of Coventry is a simple case. That is to say in its broad principles. I've been able to establish that. All that we have to do is to find a man in a blue suit of dungaree overalls. When we've done that, we're home and dry. Because he's the man that strangled Coventry."

"Sure of that?"

"Positive. Listen to this." MacMorran took a sheet of paper from a container on his desk.

"This is a statement I took this morning from a taxi-driver. Name, Gordon Lucas Sewell. Licence number 5485. Sewell states that at 1.50 on the morning of the murder, he picked up a fare at the corner of Valentia Street and Stafford Gate. Sewell had had a run out with a fare on the Bath road and was returning to his garage, which is in Clapton Square. This man he picked up hailed him and asked to be driven to Danvers Gate. He mentioned no particular number, you observe. Sewell accepted the fare and put him down just outside Coventry's house. This would be, Sewell says, about 1.58. That is to say within two minutes of the time fixed for Coventry's interview with the 'dud' Silas Montgomery. *And*, Mr. Bathurst, please note this—the man that Sewell drove to Coventry's house was wearing blue dungaree overalls. And there you have the reason for what I said just now." MacMorran gave way to self-satisfaction.

Anthony Bathurst made no immediate comment.

"Well?" inquired the Inspector. "Satisfied?"

Anthony flicked the ash from his cigarette. "Up to a point, Andrew, I suppose that I must be. I mean by that, that it would be absurd for me not to be. All the same, it's a bit blatantly obvious, isn't it?"

MacMorran frowned heavily. "How do you mean?"

Mr. Bathurst shrugged his shoulders. "Well—look at it for yourself. It's *all* blue overalls. *Blau über alles!* Consider his trio of sensational appearances—this gentleman in the dungarees. First on a seat in the park. Near the late Aubrey Coventry. Then at a fancy dress dance at Dorset House—the last place, mind you, where one would reasonably expect to find him—and again close to Coventry—and finally, on the way to strangle the same man! Good lord, Andrew, the man advertises himself all the way through. If his main desire had been to call attention to himself, he certainly did the job most thoroughly. Talk about banners and heralds and fanfares of triumph! He's used them all and then some." Mr. Bathurst shook his head and went on. "No—Andrew, it don't please me. It don't please me one little iota! Still—go on with the story of your friend Gordon Lucas Sewell. I presume that he was able to give you at least some description of his passenger?"

"He was. He is no fool, let me tell you. I'll read it to you. 'Medium height, not short, not tall.'"

Anthony grimaced. "As usual with these descriptions. Might fit anybody."

"You wait a minute. Wore a roughish-looking cap. Age—anything between thirty-five and fifty. Sewell didn't get a good enough look at the man to be anything like positive concerning his age. 'All his clothes'—these were Sewell's own words—'were in keeping with his general appearance.' Pretty vague, I admit—but I think I know what Sewell wants to imply. Then he went on to make two other remarks which I consider, perhaps, to be the most important of all. Here they are. I'll read them to you as I took them down from him. 'Had a pinkish complexion as though he had just shaved'— that's the first, 'and carried a large, square, brown paper parcel.'" MacMorran pushed aside the sheet of paper from which he had been reading. "I've taken the usual steps, Mr. Bathurst, and all the country is being scoured for this man in the blue overalls."

"You'll never run across him that way, Andrew. For the simple reason that he'll never wear blue overalls again. Sorry if I'm unsticking your theories and all that." Mr. Bathurst rose. "I'll tell you what, Andrew," he continued, "we're up against a murderer with brains. He's alert, he's confident, and, I think, not only able to see the step ahead, but also another step farther than that. That's a big thing, you know, in a criminal. What's the Governor think about it?"

"Sir Austin?"

"Ay, ay! What's he say?"

MacMorran looked a trifle dubious. "Oh—you know. The usual. 'But what are we *doing*, MacMorran? What you say is all very well as far as it goes—but what is being *done*?' You can guess the rest for yourself, Mr. Bathurst—you've heard it all before."

Anthony grinned at him. "I was afraid that's how it would be. By the way—tested those alibis yet?"

"That's one of my next jobs. I should have done it before, but this fellow Sewell coming in stopped me and put me behindhand. Then I'm putting in a call at Dorset House."

"Re the blue overalls."

"That's the idea."

"Yes, that's sound enough. You might be lucky and pick up something there. I think if I were you, Andrew, I'd reverse the order of your intentions and call at Dorset House first. After all, we haven't the slightest reason to suspect Palmer and Co., have we? I rather think those alibi checks can very well wait without much harm being done."

MacMorran caressed his cheek. "Perhaps you're right, Mr. Bathurst. I'm inclined to think that you are. I wonder if they have regular attendants on duty at Dorset House. I mean—I wonder if the same blokes are on duty now as were doing the job on the evening of that fancy dress stunt."

"Andrew," cried Mr. Bathurst, "the proof of the flunkey will be in the meeting. We will go along there and find out. You and I together!"

MacMorran nodded and spoke on the telephone. "Have my car ready for me in five minutes. Send Wade and Parsons up at once."

Within a few moments the men named came in. "Wade," instructed the Chief Inspector, "I'm going out with Mr. Bathurst. Take over for me until I come back. If I'm wanted, I shall be at Dorset House. I may be there half an hour or so."

"Very good. I understand, sir."

"Parsons," continued MacMorran, "you know what I've done with regard to that taxi-driver's story concerning the Coventry case. You were here when I took the man's statement. If anything should come in while I'm away—deal with it promptly." MacMorran reached for his hat. "At your service, Mr. Bathurst," he said, with something like a chuckle.

"You're a good scout, Andrew," replied Anthony. "Now for that chariot of yours that should be waiting for us."

At Dorset House MacMorran wasted no time. He made inquiries at the reception counter. "The evening of the 'Seven Arts' Fancy Dress Ball?"

"That's the ticket," replied MacMorran.

The clerk wrinkled his brows and then reached for a book. "Yes . . . yes . . . the usual staff were on duty. Our two regular footmen-porters. I can give you their names. Just a moment. Ernest Wood and Arthur McCorkell. Yes, they're our regular staff for that particular work. Been employed here for years."

"Are they available now? Because I want a word with them, please. If not with both of them now—well—perhaps with one of them."

The receptionist consulted his records again. "You're in luck. They're both on the premises. Wood's on duty upstairs and McCorkell's round the back somewhere. I'll send for both of them. Together—or singly?"

"Er—singly."

"Very good, Inspector—where will you see them?"

"That's for you to say. Where can I see them that's convenient?"

"I rather think one of the smaller committee rooms is unoccupied at the moment. I'll have a look for you. Now where are we . . . number ten . . . number eleven. . . . Yes, I thought so. There's nobody using number eight. I'll have you taken up there, Inspector, and then I'll send Wood up. You'll find him a very decent fellow. Send him back to me when you've finished with him and then I'll do the same with McCorkell."

"Thank you," returned MacMorran. "As soon as you like."

The clerk understood and used his telephone. "Ask Robbins to come to the vestibule, will you, please. Tell him at once."

Robbins, in uniform, came and received his orders and conducted MacMorran and Mr. Bathurst to committee room number eight. Wood, the first porter summoned, soon followed them. Tall, thin, with a bird-like eye, he looked a little surprised when MacMorran tackled him.

"The 'Seven Arts,' sir? That's right. I was on the front all the time with McCorkell. We usually work together on shows like that. Proper 'posh' do it was, too. More than once I said to my mate: 'Cor—look 'oos 'ere."

"I see. Remember the costumes, Wood?"

The man made a wry face. "Arskin' me something, aren't cher? Blimey, we went from Nero with his 'uke' to the bl—to the Virgin Queen 'erself."

Anthony grinned. This showed signs of being good. MacMorran, disdaining the humour, came to the porter's assistance. "I'm not expecting you to supply me with a complete list of the costumes. I am inquiring rather with regard to one of them. Do you remember—a man dressed, say, as a mechanic—wearing a set of blue dungaree overalls—arriving here during the evening?"

"Cor—no, Inspector. I should have thought twice about letting in a bloke like that. Would have been as much as my job's worth. I 'ave to be careful on my job, you know. Don't do to shut your eyes to things. Only sometimes." Wood winked solemnly at Mr. Bathurst. "Not that we get doubtful women in 'ere. Not by a long chalk. When they *are* a bit that way—they ain't what you'd call 'doubtful.' They're bl— er . . . blinkin' certs."

Mr. Bathurst coughed discreetly. MacMorran ignored the allusion. He kept to the main point at issue. "I see. Now, Wood, tell me this. During the evening of the 'Seven Arts' do, a man was seen in the dance-hall, by more than one person, dressed as I have just described. If you didn't pass him through—how did he get in? That's what I've come to find out." Wood's eyes opened wide at the Inspector's announcement. Anthony thought that his astonishment was genuine. "In the dance-hall? Cor—Inspector—you don't say!"

"I do. Most decidedly. I have been informed that at least two people saw him."

Wood shook his head blankly. "That's a new one on me, Inspector. And that's straight. He must 'ave got in through the back by the kitchen entrance. That's the only reasonable explanation. But I can't even believe that, Inspector—the kitchen staff had gone and all the back premises should have been locked up. I tell you what. 'Ave a word with Ronald—'e's the head cook and bottle-washer. He'll put you right with regard to that, Inspector."

"Thank you, Wood. I will. Anyhow, I can take it as Gospel that you neither saw this fellow nor passed him through?"

"You can, Inspector. As far as I'm concerned, you're on a stone bonker. Anything more?"

MacMorran dismissed him. Wood made his exit. McCorkell came in within a few seconds. He was dark and dour, whereas Wood had been fresh-faced and fair. MacMorran questioned him on similar lines to those he had used with Wood. McCorkell nodded that he understood. "Yes, I remember the evening of the 'Seven Arts,' sir. Yes, I was with Woody—er—Wood, sir." MacMorran put the question with regard to the blue overall costume. "No, sir. I can't recall ever seeing anything like that, sir, about the place. Of course, there's this you must bear in mind—there was all sorts and conditions of costume 'ere, as you might say—there always is on that particular occasion, but there was none of that kind. They was all more polite like, if you know what I mean—more of the romantic outfit. Still—before I say any more—let me ask you a question, Inspector. What time was this bloke supposed to 'ave crashed in on us?"

"He was *seen*," replied MacMorran, with strong emphasis on the past participle, "in the dance-room by two people somewhere about ten-thirty—dressed as I have described to you."

McCorkell came in with an almost triumphant certainty. "Then he never passed me or my mate, Inspector. I should certainly recall that costume. I'll give you my solemn word on that."

"How do you suggest he got in, then?"

McCorkell shrugged his shoulders. "I couldn't make a suggestion based on common sense, for I don't see how the fellow *could* 'ave got in. Still, as you say you know 'e was there, 'e must 'ave got in some way unbeknown to me. That's logic, ain't it?"

"Now, what about the back of the premises? Through the kitchen? Is that a reasonable possibility?"

McCorkell screwed up his face. "No—I don't think so, Inspector. Not in my opinion. You could inquire though, of course—if you wanted to make sure."

"Thanks, I think I will. So that's all you can tell me—eh, McCorkell?"

"I'm afraid that's the bundle, Inspector. Sorry I can't make it a trifle more satisfactory—but what's the good if you know you can't?"

MacMorran went to the door to show the footman out. Returning, he 'phoned at once to the reception counter. Anthony Bathurst heard him request the attendance of Ronald, the head cook.

"He'll be here in a few minutes," remarked MacMorran, as he replaced the receiver. "So our friend did not arrive from the front and by the presentation of a ticket," commented Mr. Bathurst. "I thought as much."

"Looks like it," agreed MacMorran grimly, "which means at the same time—which way *did* he get in? Perhaps chef Ronald may be able to enlighten us."

"A cook," quoth Anthony, "should confine himself to his cooking . . . but, of course, Ronald may not be a good cook. There is always that possibility."

When Ronald did appear, he was brought in by the reception clerk. The latter explained certain matters to him as a mere preliminary. MacMorran mentioned the man in the blue overalls. Ronald, whose other name was Morgan, and who was as Welsh as his name, shook his head emphatically at the suggestion which the Inspector made. His dark eyes flashed resentment. "It is a positive thing he could not have got in through the kitchens. The rear of the place was all locked up long before half-past ten—yes it was. Not only the inner doors but the outer ones also. The service for the 'Seven Arts' people was from the special service room at the side of the main dance-hall. So that you can take it from me, Inspector, that this man you speak of did not slink in through my kitchens—no indeed. I should have stopped him, to be sure, if he had."

MacMorran looked at Anthony Bathurst. The latter motioned to him to dismiss the indignant Ronald. Mr. Bathurst evidently considered that nothing more of value could be obtained from him. MacMorran acquiesced. He dismissed the chef with a nod and a curt expression of thanks.

Anthony consoled him. "Don't worry, Andrew. You'll get no more from him if you stay here an hour. Blue overalls didn't get in that way. It would have been too clumsy altogether. As a matter of fact—don't get too optimistic, you old scoundrel—I'm beginning to glimpse just a ray of light. We'll call it the beginning of the ghost of an idea. But who knows—it may develop into a really healthy affair before we get very much farther."

"We needn't stay here," said the Inspector, "there's nothing more to be learned—and we have other things to do."

"Too true," said Anthony airily. "You have a positive flair, Andrew, for saying the right thing."

Chapter IX
ALIBIS

MacMorran gave orders to his chauffeur. He was in his curt mood. "The 'Vermilion Lizard'—Rothwell Street. It's on the right-hand side." The chauffeur grinned at the instruction. The Inspector and Anthony entered the car.

"One thing, Andrew, in connection with the Coventry problem that we mustn't forget. I'm mentioning it as a signpost of warning. That the blue overalls made their appearance into a fancy dress ball."

MacMorran chuckled suddenly. "Not their *first* appearance, Mr. Bathurst. Don't forget that. Coventry had seen the man before then. Which, with all due respect, I suggest makes all the difference."

"I don't think that it does, Andrew. Yet awhile. There may be a factor there which has so far eluded us. Thinking matters over very carefully, I'm inclined to the belief that there is. What sort of place is this 'Lizard' outfit?"

"Not too bad. Conducts itself pretty well. Not one of the hottest places by a long way. We haven't had any serious complaints so far." He peered out of the window. "We're only a minute or so away from it. Rothwell Street is the next turning."

MacMorran was right. The car stopped almost immediately. MacMorran went straight in and Anthony Bathurst followed him. It was comparatively early and there weren't many people present inside. MacMorran played for safety. He made his way to the bar which was in the corner of the first large apartment. The counter had been cunningly arranged to fit neatly and conveniently into an alcove. The bartender, picturesquely and patriotically attired in a jacket trimmed with red, white, and blue, was short, dark-skinned, and jovial. MacMorran leant across the counter and spoke a few words to him in an undertone. Anthony, a few paces away, listened to the conversation attentively. MacMorran proceeded to explain his errand. "The 'Seven Arts' Ball was on the evening of the eleventh. Were you on duty here?"

The man nodded. "I was, Guv'nor. I'm always on duty. I'm never supposed to want an evening off. Not even on Coronation days. They didn't ought to have a steward here, they ought to have a perishin' robot."

"Are you acquainted with a Mr. Crayle? A Mr. Peter Crayle?"

"Can't say I am. Perhaps, though, if you described him to me I could answer your question with more certainty."

MacMorran added a short description of Crayle. "It may help you," he went on, "if I tell you of the costume he was wearing at the time in question. Mr. Crayle at the time I mention would have been wearing the costume of a Greek discus-thrower. In case you don't understand what I mean, I'll tell you within a little what the dress would have looked like."

MacMorran gave the bar steward the necessary details. The man nodded briskly. It was clear that he harboured no doubts on the matter. "That's O.K., Inspector. He was here all right. You needn't spill any more. I remember the gentleman quite well. Came in about a quarter-past one. Sat down just there. As a matter of fact I served him with several drinks. Half a dozen at least, I'm sure. Directly he came in, I reckoned as how he'd been along to the 'Seven Arts' do at Dorset House from the look of him. Several of 'em had dropped in here at various times. Usually do those nights. They made quite a splash of colour here, I can tell you. Usually we begin to drop off a bit round about two o'clock in the morning, but the 'Seven Arts' crowd caused us to be quite busy that evening. Is that all you wanted to ask me?"

"Just a moment. What time did Mr. Crayle leave?"

The steward considered the question. "I should say he left here about 2.45, Inspector. That would mean he was here about an hour and a half. Yes . . . that's about right. I can tell that pretty well by the number of parties I served while he was here."

MacMorran turned to Anthony Bathurst. "Did you hear that? It's almost exactly consistent with what Crayle himself told me."

Anthony nodded. "I thought so. And it seems pretty sound. Do you mind if I ask him a question, Andrew?" MacMorran grinned. "Ask away. I've been waiting for some of your questions ever since we came in. Couldn't make out what had come over you."

Mr. Bathurst leant over the bar counter. "Did Mr. Crayle sit here all the time . . . can you remember?"

"He did, sir. All the time. In that chair—just about there." The steward indicated one of the seats close at hand. "He just ordered his drinks . . . gin and lime chiefly . . . one after the other . . . and sat there enjoying them. And very nice, too! One of these days I hope to be in the same position, if my Littlewoods rolls up one Saturday night. Gor blimey—what a lump of fat!"

"I see. Do you happen to know Mr. Crayle well?"

"No. I wouldn't say that, sir. I know my place, I hope . . . and I try to keep it. Never push myself on anybody. Nobody can accuse me of not knowing how to behave." Anthony nodded as though he completely understood the steward's point of view. "Is he a frequent visitor here?"

"Oh, no! By no means. Just drops in occasionally like. Certainly doesn't overdo things and can take his liquor like a gentleman. All the same, I should put him down as a bit of a lad."

"Thank you," returned Anthony. "I don't think that either the Inspector or I need trouble you any further."

Outside the 'Lizard,' MacMorran turned to Mr. Bathurst. "That clears Crayle's story. Now we'll bowl along and have that word with that fellow Atherton."

"Where's his place? Close at hand?"

"Not too bad. The chauffeur knows. I primed him beforehand. 122 Studholme Gardens. A quarter of an hour's run should do it. I know where the place is, roughly."

For the first few moments of the car's run, Anthony was silent. The Inspector saw that he was thinking deeply. Then he put his hand on MacMorran's arm. "Tell me, Andrew, what does Sugden say about Coventry's death? I take it you've had his complete report by now."

"I had the p.m. report yesterday. Death by strangulation as we knew, of course. According to Sugden, Coventry had been dead 'at least seven hours' when he first saw the body, which puts the time of the murder at about half-past two. Sugden saw the body about half-past nine. At any rate before ten o'clock. I had a chat with him when he brought me the report. There were one or two points I wanted further information about. He's pretty certain that Coventry died shortly after two o'clock."

Anthony thought over the information. "Which," he said, "being interpreted, means very soon after the presumed entry of the man calling himself Silas Montgomery."

"Exactly," returned MacMorran, "and there you have the thing in a nutshell."

"H'm," said Anthony, "but I wouldn't go farther than to say 'perhaps.' Although I admit it clears the air somewhat." He looked out of the car window. "I rather fancy we're turning down Studholme Gardens, Andrew. I recognized one of the landmarks. Let's hope that we find Mr. Atherton at home."

"He will be," responded MacMorran. "I saw to that. I made an appointment with him. For one thing, I didn't want your valuable time to be wasted."

"Good! You're improving in your old age. Hullo—the car's stopping. Here we are."

MacMorran got out and spoke to his chauffeur. Then he accompanied Anthony to the front door of No. 122. The Inspector rang the bell. As he had stated to Anthony, Mr. Atherton was in. They heard his voice in the distance. "Let the gentlemen in, Rigby. I'm expecting them. Come in, Inspector."

MacMorran and Anthony went into Atherton's room. "As I promised you on the 'phone I won't detain you very long, Mr. Atherton," opened MacMorran, "but I've called in connection with the Coventry murder case. You're a friend of a Mr. Hubert Palmer, I believe."

Atherton was casual and nonchalant. "Sit down, Inspector, and you, too—er—"

"My name's Bathurst. Thank you." Anthony and MacMorran seated themselves. Atherton, in his own time, answered the Inspector's question. "Yes, I know Hubert Palmer well. Very charming and reliable fellow. Script writer for the B.B.C., you know. Doing very well quietly. If I'm any judge got a big future in front of him. At least, that's my opinion. And I'm not often wrong in these matters."

"Thank you. I understand that you were in Palmer's company on the evening of the 'Seven Arts' Fancy Dress Ball. Perhaps I should say 'on the morning after,' rather than the evening."

Atherton nodded his corroboration of MacMorran's statement.

"You're right, Inspector. I can confirm that. I was with him by definite arrangement. Hubert rang me up two or three days before the 'Seven Arts' do, and asked me if I intended to be there. I told him that I did. He said he wanted to see me. I can tell you why. It was about a new series of talks that he's thinking of putting over to the B.B.C. Rather quaint idea, too. On English surnames and their origins right back to the year dot. As it happened, I was a bit late turning up at Dorset House . . . well . . . come to that a good deal late, and old Hubert had to wait for me. I was detained on a special job of work. . . . I was actually down in Surrey, and didn't arrive at Dorset House until about a quarter-past twelve. Luckily he knows I'm not the best of time-keepers, so he stayed on and waited for me."

"You were with him then for some time, I take it?"

"I was, Inspector. From about a quarter-past twelve until about a quarter to three, I should say, at a rough estimate. We discussed Hubert's idea in pretty extensive detail to see whether it was likely to be a money-spinner. I can vouch for that all right." Atherton's tone was still nonchalant, and his entire manner the epitome of casual self-confidence. Anthony Bathurst listened without comment. MacMorran asked a further question. "Were you and Mr. Palmer together for the entire period that you have mentioned?"

"Absolutely. For every damned second of it. We just strolled off to the buffet directly we met, found a nice little table where we could gossip in peace, and made the most of our opportunity. Actually, I hadn't seen old Hubert for some little time, and naturally we found a good deal to say to each other. Apart from his special stunt." Atherton laughed easily. He was pink-faced and plump. There was good and ample reason for his nickname of 'Tubby.' Anthony decided to take a turn in the conversation.

"Mr. Atherton's story seems to be quite satisfactory, Inspector." Then, as though the result of a sudden afterthought, he addressed Rex Atherton himself. "Just as a point of interest, Mr. Atherton, what costume did you wear?"

Atherton seemed surprised by this question. "What costume did I wear? Well, if it's important and you must know, I went as Napoleon Bonaparte. Le Petit Caporal. It rather suits my figure, you know. But I expect that you can tell that at a glance." Atherton smiled again with comfortable assurance. Anthony returned the smile.

"I won't argue that it's important. The thought came to me to ask you, that was all. There was nothing unusual about Palmer's manner, I suppose?"

"Certainly nothing that I noticed. Old Hubert doesn't vary very much in the ordinary way. He's a consistent sort of cove. Rarely out of temper and as steady as the best of 'em. Takes a lot to ruffle him, I can assure you. I think the world of Hubert Palmer. I'll let you into a personal secret. I always say that his telegraphic address should be 'Reliability, London.'"

It was at that precise moment in the conversation that Anthony Bathurst seemed to take a chance with Mr. Atherton. A certain point had flashed through his mind. "Can you tell me, this, Mr. Atherton? Did Palmer refer in any way to the 'Seven Arts' dance itself?"

Atherton seemed puzzled at the inquiry. His eyes showed it. "I don't quite follow you. Can you make the question a little plainer?"

"Yes, I can do that for you with pleasure. Did he refer to any incident that had occurred at the ball that evening?"

Rex Atherton shook his head decisively. "No. And I'm sure of that. We never discussed such a thing. When you first asked me, I wasn't quite sure as to what you meant."

"Thank you, Mr. Atherton, that's quite clear. I have no more questions to ask, Inspector."

"I don't think that I have either," supplemented MacMorran. "So that, with thanks to Mr. Atherton for his information and general assistance, we'll wish him good day."

Atherton rose to see them off his premises. "Anything I can do, Inspector, at any time—don't you hesitate. Just give me a tinkle and I'll be only too pleased. Good day, Inspector, and to you, Mr. Bathurst."

Anthony and the Inspector returned to the car. Mr. Bathurst rubbed his chin. On the journey back, the former was strangely silent. MacMorran rallied him.

"Well—we haven't done too badly. We've at least clarified the situations as regards Palmer and Crayle. You know what I mean. We've cleared the internal complications of the case. We can start straight now, as it were, on the externals of the case. I like to be in that position. I always feel more satisfied in my own mind when I'm able to tackle the externals. . . ." Anthony rubbed the ridge of his jaw. "I'm going to tell you frankly, Andrew, that I don't like any of it."

"How do you mean?"

"I've a strong suspicion at the back of my mind that we're running round in circles. You and I, laddie. MacMorran, Bathurst, and Co. And when I feel like that I always feel thoroughly uncomfortable. At the same time damnably suspicious."

MacMorran showed disagreement. "You're seeing difficulties where they don't exist."

"On the contrary, I'm seeing obviousness which I'm equally certain doesn't exist, and what's more—shouldn't exist. Now that's a damned sight worse, Andrew."

MacMorran shook his head again. "Get away with you. You're deliberately going out of your way to meet trouble. Why? What's the point in it? I never do that. I used to years ago when I was in the green stage—but I soon learned that nine times out of ten it got you nowhere, and all you did was to waste your time."

Anthony chuckled. "How about the tenth time?"

"Wait till it comes along," returned MacMorran, "and then, when it does come along, count carefully to make sure that it *is* the tenth time and not one of the ordinary number."

This time it was Mr. Bathurst's turn to shake his head. "No, Andrew. You can please yourself, but I'm far from satisfied. I'm not beating about the bush. I shan't gain anything by doing that. I'm telling you straight."

"Oh—cut the warnings! It's a moderately simple case, which resolves itself into this. All we have to do is to find the man who wore the blue overalls. As I keep on saying. Which will be equivalent to finding the murderer of Aubrey Coventry. There you are. That's my summing-up." MacMorran spoke decisively. From Anthony there came a quiet interruption.

"All right. Give me the motive then, Andrew—do you mind? I could bear to hear that immediately."

"Motive? Well . . . er . . . anything . . . come to that, what's it matter? Particularly? Say revenge for something that occurred between the two men in business. That will do to go on with."

"No! Don't like it. Too makeshift altogether. Not worthy of you, Andrew. I want to get my teeth into something more substantial than that before I'm feeling satisfied."

"Tell me this, then." MacMorran was out for argument. "Why did the murderer choose the alias of Silas Montgomery? To me, that plainly indicates that there was a business side to the crime. Surely you'll agree with that?"

"I haven't yet admitted that the man who made the two o'clock morning call on Coventry in the guise of Montgomery must *ipso facto* be his murderer. And, even conceding that point for the purpose of discussion, there may yet be more than one reason why he hit upon the sobriquet of Silas Montgomery. We just don't know."

MacMorran gestured his disagreement. Anthony, unperturbed however, continued to outline his point of view. "And it may be our task, Andrew, mind you, I say 'may be,' to find that possible *other* reason and drag the truth out of it. For instance—answer me this. What was the large parcel which the taxi-driver mentions as having been carried by your blue-overalled murderer? Why did he take it—presumably to Coventry's house? Again—did he bring it away with him? If not, what did he do with it? Candidly, I don't know. And I don't like not knowing. It disturbs me. I'm sorry, Andrew, if I appear to be throwing cold water on your attractive theories—but there you are! That's how I feel about the case. I shall have to get right down to one of my concentration exercises in intensive thought."

"Don't you worry, Mr. Bathurst," said MacMorran, with good nature. "I'll have my man within the week."

"Very likely, Andrew—but will it be the right man?"

CHAPTER X
MESSAGES BY PROXY

WHEN the car reached Scotland Yard, Anthony accompanied MacMorran on to the premises. For one thing he had plenty of time on his hands before he need return to his flat, and for another, he wanted to see if any more information had turned up out of MacMorran's many inquiries. In this second connection, his luck happened to be in. Almost immediately upon their return, the irrepressible Superintendent Hemingway buttonholed the Inspector.

"Glad you're back, sir. As a matter of fact, there's been somebody waiting to see you for over half an hour. I've already had a couple of chats with him. Says he has important information with regard to the Coventry murder case. I guessed you'd be back about this time so I told the chap to wait. I've got him in my room."

"Who is it, Superintendent?"

Hemingway scratched his cheek. "All I know about him is his name. John Austin. I managed to get that much out of him. Bit of an oyster. The rest, I understand, is for your ear alone. Shall I bring him along to your room?"

"That's the idea, Hemingway. Just give me five minutes or so to get settled. Then I'll have a word with him. Come along with me, Mr. Bathurst."

"I think I will, Andrew, if you can bring yourself to put up with me. Naturally, I'm interested to hear what this fellow has to say."

"That's O.K. then. We'll get up to my room at once and hear the story."

A few minutes later, in strict accordance with MacMorran's instructions, Hemingway brought the man up to the Inspector's room. He assumed his best official manner and introduced him in a few words. "Good. Sit down, Mr. Austin." MacMorran took a good look at the caller. He saw a thin, white-faced man seated in front of him. A man whose watery blue eyes were restless, and whose nervous fingers seemed to be never still. Lines on his face and round his mouth suggested that he and prosperity had long been strangers. Much stubble was on his chin and cheeks. His clothes were cheap and rapidly approaching the threadbare condition. One of his shoes showed a large gap between uppers and sole. In his hands he carried a cloth cap which he plucked at nervously when the Inspector spoke to him. He answered MacMorran: "Thank you, sir."

MacMorran, having attempted rather unsuccessfully to size the man up, got to grips with him at once. "Now what is it you want to see me about?"

"The Coventry murder case, sir." The man's voice was harsh but cracked.

'Good food and better drink,' commented Mr. Bathurst to himself, 'would do you a world of good, old chap. That's impression No. 1.'

"And what do you know about the Coventry murder case?"

"Not much, sir—but just a little that may prove valuable to you." Austin coughed behind his hand. "Certainly well worth knowing."

"In that case, then, let's hear it."

"I read the papers, you know, sir, although I might seem to be pretty well down and out. I know what's going on. That's how I've got to hear of this murder the other night at Danvers Gate. But p'raps, first of all I'd better tell you a bit about myself—who I am, so to speak. My name's John Austin. A packer by employment, which isn't too often. At the moment, I regret to say, I'm out of a job. On the dole. Fourteen months of it I've had. But there's little doin' these days for the likes of me—so there you are. I suppose I've got to put up with it. Just one of many similarly situated. Now I'll tell you what I know. The morning before the Coventry murder I was sittin' in the park—opposite that row of houses in Danvers Gate where the late Mr. Coventry used to live. Sittin' in the park is one of the ways I 'ave for passin' the time. It don't cost nothin'. Gentleman of leisure me—oh, yes, says you! Well, I was sittin' there, as I say, when up comes a bloke dressed in a suit of blue engineer's overalls. He sits down next to me on the seat and says all of a sudden: ''Ow would you like to earn an Oxford, mate?' I said I would—you bet—provided it was all fair and square and above board, and nothin' crooked. Dollars don't come my way so often that I can afford to refuse 'em—or even sniff at the way they're comin'.'" Austin paused to lick his thin lips. Anthony watched him carefully. This was even better than he had expected. He determined to let the man tell his entire story before he questioned him. He hoped fervently that the Inspector would do the same. MacMorran was sitting quiet. Austin licked his lips twice and then proceeded. "I said to 'im, straight out like—'what is it you want done?' and he tells me as slick as you like. 'Quite simple—and absolute money for chocolate.' I was to 'phone up Mr. Coventry from the call-box and give 'im a message. Easy as kiss your 'and it was. The bloke said as 'ow 'e would come into the box with me and tell me what to say to 'im. Mind you, Inspector, I'll admit I thought it was 'phoney' at the time, but it didn't seem to be doin' no 'arm, did it—and an 'Oxford's' an 'Oxford' any old day— say what you like about it. Well, we walked into a 'phone-box, that one on the far corner of the park, and I did what the bloke told me to do. Fixed up an appointment with the little old fellow at 2 a.m. I was supposed to be a Yank—by name Silas Montgomery, some moniker that. The bloke told me 'ow he wanted me to talk. Well, it began with old Coventry not standin' for it. But my bloke wrote down what my replies were to be every time, so I shoved 'em down the little old mouthpiece in as posh an American voice as I could manage. In the end, old Coventry come over all sweetie-pie, as the bloke in the overalls wanted 'im to."

Austin stopped in his recital for a second time. More lip licking followed. Again Mr. Bathurst and MacMorran waited on his pleasure. Neither of them interrupted him. "Then I got a surprise, sir." Austin was speaking again. "The bloke 'anded me over the five bob and then showed me another coin. Blimey, it was a sight for sore mince-pies. He 'eld it up in his 'and for me to look at. There it was—waitin' for me to shove it in my sky. A proper old cart-wheel— solid and 'eavy. 'Would you like to earn this one as well?' says 'e to me. This time I scents a bit of trouble, p'raps, and I am not taking any chances. So I put the shutters up a bit. 'What do you want this time?' I asks my nibs. To my surprise, sir, the second job of work was just as easy as the first had been. No more in it at all. I was to 'phone old Coventry at half-past one on the following morning. This time the bloke wrote out the message for me. Sort of confirmin' the appointment with him. Also, I 'adn't got to wait for any answer. Well, I thought to myself, I'm in the dirt already up to my bushel. I might as well be 'anged for a sheep as a lamb—so I says to my fellow: 'Right-o. I'll do it.' He 'ands me the second Oxford then and there—and Bob's your uncle."

"Five, surely," murmured Mr. Bathurst.

"So you 'phoned Mr. Coventry at half-past one in the morning— eh?"

"Yes, Guv'nor, I did. At one-thirty Ack Emma on the dot. I took the 'bees' and I followed out the instructions."

MacMorran caught Mr. Bathurst's eye and nodded his understanding.

"You say that this man who employed you to send these telephone messages for him, *wrote* the second one out for you?"

Austin assented with eagerness. "Yes, sir. On a piece of paper. Plain it was. I've got it with me now if you'd like to have a 'butchers.'"

"We most certainly would," replied the Inspector eagerly. "Let me have it, will you, Austin?"

Austin felt carefully in an inside pocket. At last he seemed to find what he wanted, and produced for their inspection a long, thin strip of paper such as might have come from a tape machine. "There you are, sir—there's what you want—the identical bit."

Austin handed it over to MacMorran. The moment he looked at it, the Inspector uttered an exclamation of disappointment. Instead of having been written, the words had been printed in capital letters. He read the message. 'SILAS MONTGOMERY THIS END. AS WE ARRANGED YESTERDAY I SHALL BE WITH YOU AT TWO O'CLOCK PRECICELY. AND IT IS IMPORTANT THAT I SHOULD SPEAK TO YOU ALONE. DON'T FORGET THAT. GOOD-BYE UNTIL TWO O'CLOCK.'

MacMorran passed it over to Anthony Bathurst. "Nothing to go on there. The damned thing's been printed like a kid in school might have done it. They teach it to 'em in school these days. My kid used to bring it home with him. Call it script, I believe."

Anthony nodded and turned the paper over to get a better look at it. Then he returned it to the Inspector. "H'm! As you say—not much to go on here. Still—there might be something in this." He indicated the word 'PRECICELY.'

"What about it?" said MacMorran, frowning.

"I was drawing your attention to the spelling."

"What—only one E?"

"No—the two c's."

"That's all right, isn't it?" asked MacMorran doubtfully.

Mr. Bathurst shook his head.

"Oh—I see," returned the Inspector rather doubtfully, "it certainly is a point, I agree. But it doesn't give us a lot to work on, does it?"

Mr. Bathurst looked towards Austin. "This man who gave you the money, could you give us any details of his description? Beyond, of course, those that you have already given us?"

Austin nodded briskly. "About forty-five years of age, I should say at a rough guess. Medium height. Unusual way of speaking. Might be a foreigner, but I wouldn't be sure of that, Guv'nor."

Anthony, however, pressed for more definite particulars. "Did you happen to notice the man's complexion?"

Austin looked a little surprised. "Not particularly, sir. I should say as 'ow it was just ordinary. Very much the same as yours and mine might be. You know what I mean, sir—not pretty-pretty, pass in a crowd."

Anthony smiled. "I don't know that I referred to anything of that kind. My inquiry really concerned the colour of the man's complexion. Not the quality. Would you, for instance, describe it as 'pinkish?'"

"No, I wouldn't. Not on any account, sir. I know what you mean. 'E wasn't no 'Pansy,' believe me. Oh, no—very different."

"Note that, Inspector," remarked Mr. Bathurst, "because I regard it as having a distinct importance."

MacMorran, thinking in terms of Sewell, the taxi-driver, saw Mr. Bathurst's point and readily understood. Anthony put another question to Austin. "You haven't seen the man since, of course?"

"No, sir."

"Or ever before?"

"No, sir."

"And you haven't the slightest idea as to who he was?"

"No, sir. Don't know 'im from Adam. Although I should be able to recognize 'im again, all right, if I happened to drop across 'im."

"Did he have any mannerisms that you were able to observe?" This from MacMorran.

"No. Couldn't put a name to any."

"What about his hands?" asked Anthony. "You must have noticed his hands particularly, when he printed the second message that you were to send to Aubrey Coventry. Were they the hands of a mechanic as you would expect to find them? In harmony with his clothes?"

Austin exhibited doubt. "I don't think they were, sir. They were too white, perhaps—in fact, like a swell's. Not rough enough round the palms and finger-tips."

"You had a good look at them, then?"

"Oh, yes, sir."

"Where did the man print the message for you? In the 'phone-box?"

"Yes, sir. On the ledge at the corner, where the directories are usually kept. Now I come to think of it, I believe he used one of 'em to write on. Not that I use the 'phones very much myself. Still—I know that."

Anthony tried him again. "Tell me this, Austin. When you 'phoned to Coventry on the first occasion, did he appear to understand the reason why a Silas Montgomery should be speaking to him? Or did he seem surprised?"

"I'm not sure, sir. But let me tell you this. 'E didn't answer me first of all. It was his secretary—or somebody like that. I got put on to old man Coventry afterwards. And the bloke in the blue overalls told me what to say each time. I was to mention 'big money.' Dangle a sort of bait in front of 'im, although I said nothing particular. For my own part, I was talkin' boloney, and—if you want my opinion—I'll swear on my dyin' oath old Coventry didn't know the first word about it." Austin rubbed his nose with the back of his fingers.

"And yet he agreed to making the appointment?"

"Yes. Not at first, though. After a while, 'e did. But he took a rare lot of persuadin', I can tell you. It wasn't easy to convince 'im. It was my charm of manner did the trick." Anthony, who had made a shrewd assessment of Austin's psychology, had by this time decided that the man was by no means a fool.

"Why do you think you were able to persuade him? Seeing that Silas Montgomery—the genuine Silas Montgomery, that is—was a complete stranger to him?"

"I figure it out that there was two things what really turned the scale, Guv'nor!" Austin assumed an air of cunning appreciation. "Human curiosity, which we all suffer from—and the idea that there might be 'big money' for 'im knocking about somewhere. That's my opinion—and I don't think you'll better it in a 'urry."

Anthony nodded, almost as though he were disposed to accept Austin's conclusions.

"Seems to me that's quite feasible," supplemented MacMorran.

"More than feasible, Guv'nor," contributed Austin, with a leer, "it's natcheral. And we all know what natcher is. She will 'ave 'er way—old Mother Natcher, whether we like it or not." He gestured with a motion of superb finality.

"Leave your address with me, Austin," said MacMorran, "in case I should want to communicate with you again."

"Right, Guv'nor—only too pleased. But don't forget you've got it, round about Christmas time. I can do with a nice York 'am or a real Norfolk bird. I fancy a 'en myself. They eat more tender. Post early and you won't be disappointed. Number Eight, Katherine's Court, Shield Street. And you spell Katherine with a 'K.'"

MacMorran noted the address on a slip of paper. "Thank you, Austin. That's understood, then. I'll let you know if I want you again."

Austin rose as the Inspector finished. "'Ow do I go for a little dough before I scram? 'Bees-and!' Don't I draw for all the trouble I've been put to?"

MacMorran winked at Mr. Bathurst. "And I'll let you know about that later, too. You mustn't be in too much of a hurry, Austin. We have to take our time, you know, the same as everybody else has to—and you must fall into line."

Austin shrugged his shoulders. "Very well, sir. I'll take you at your early-bird and 'ope for the best. But you won't forget that *talk* don't put nothin' on the table. You've got the address—that's okay with me."

Austin went to the door and shuffled out. MacMorran stood up and jingled the coins in his pockets.

"Well, Andrew," remarked Anthony, "and how do we go now? What do you make of that lot? Things getting clearer—or more obscure? Made up your mind?"

"Supposing I ask you that? How would you answer the same question?"

Anthony took the retort in good part. "Oh—clearer without doubt. Definitely clearer."

"Glad you think so. Wish I could share your optimism."

"What troubles me, though, Andrew—as I said before—is the question of *motive*. As regards that—we're no nearer. At the moment, I'm damned if I can get anywhere near it." Mr. Bathurst selected a cigarette. MacMorran took another from the case held out to him. Anthony lit it for him. Then he lit his own. Tossing the match away, he looked at the Inspector whimsically. "Permit me to call your attention, Andrew, to the incident of the 'snarling man.'"

"The snarling man? What—when the dead man asked him for a match, do you mean?"

"Exactly," replied Mr. Bathurst. "Consider the incident of the snarling man in close relation to the subsequent incident of the proxy telephone messages. I find the entire programme most eloquent."

MacMorran stared at him with bewilderment. Then he slowly shook his head. "Sorry—but I don't get it."

"Neither do I, Andrew—all of it. There's a link missing somewhere, and the name of that link is motive. I'll give you a look up to-morrow, Andrew. All the best." Mr. Bathurst took his hat and his departure.

Chapter XI
DETECTION BY DISSECTION

Anthony Lotherington Bathurst was a creature of habit. For some hours, now, it had been in his mind to assemble the main features of the Coventry problem and analyse them as intensely as possible. When he left MacMorran and returned to his flat, he lost no time in commencing this exercise in analysis. In distinction from his usual practice, he was inclined, first of all, to detail the various happenings that had marked the affair rather than to consider the reactions of the different personalities concerned therein. Mr. Bathurst found his most comfortable arm-chair, filled his pipe, lit the tobacco, and pulled a note-book towards him. He determined, as far as possible, to list the relevant incidents in some degree of chronological order. After some slight hesitation, he produced the following points for his own examination.

(*a*) The proxy appointment made with Aubrey Coventry by the pseudo-Montgomery on the telephone through the agency of Austin. (Uncorroborated.)

(*b*) The interview of Coventry at Leyland with the palmist Bianca Zylphara. (Corroborated by the palmist herself.)

(*c*) The episode of the snarling man on the seat in the park. (From Philip Coventry, who states that he had the story from his father.)

(*d*) The ball at Dorset House, and the second appearance of the snarling man clad exactly as he had been before. (This, according to Philip Coventry, *seen* by Aubrey Coventry, and (uncorroborated) by Hubert Palmer. Palmer must be asked about this.)

(*e*) Sewell, the taxi-cab driver's, story of the man whom he drove to Danvers Gate. Pinkish complexion. Wearing blue overalls. And carrying a large, square, brown paper parcel.

(f) The death itself of Aubrey Coventry. The murder rather! Strangled by a rope. Found in his own room by Rayner, his secretary, after the early morning appointment.

(g) The two note-books on Aubrey Coventry's table. In presumably wrong places. (Not only wrong—but inappropriate.)

(h) His own visit to Madame Zylphara. The coincident visit of Mr. Morris Sere. (Coventry's business associate, who has a most attractive wife, the film star—Vere Valentine.)

(*i*) The strange story of John Austin on the dole. Here Mr. Bathurst paused in his writing. It came to him, as he surveyed the various items seriatim, that he had brought the history of the Coventry affair almost up-to-date. He frowned as he looked at the items which he had been able to collect. Not much here—in all conscience! Nothing really definite. Once again, the barrier to everything assailed Mr. Bathurst's brain and mocked at his ineptitude. Motive! *What* was the motive? *Where* was the motive? Nothing stolen! No papers taken! Revenge? Hatred? For what? And why? Anthony Bathurst tapped his teeth with the butt-end of his fountain-pen, and shook his head with dissatisfaction. There must be something tucked away somewhere in one, at least, of these events that should put this all-important thread in his hands. He considered again with infinite care the various incidents that he had listed one by one. With regard to the two proxy appointments, there was attendant there the risk of Austin not having told the truth. Or again—not having told the entire truth. *Suggestio falsi?* Or *suppressio veri?* Or even a portion of both? Mr. Bathurst thought of the interview which he and MacMorran had had with Austin. On the whole, he considered that Austin had told the truth. There seemed no sound reason why he should have done otherwise. Unless—there was a confederacy between Austin and the murderer of Coventry which went beyond the limits of sending messages by telephone. There was a possibility here certainly. Mr. Bathurst passed on. Madame Zylphara. At Leyland with Coventry. In her own establishment with himself. Bianca Zylphara who claimed direct descent in the true line of the royal house of Milan. What had she tried to tell him? Oil. Something foreign. A king. Two women. Unfriendly. Opposition to each other. Mr. Bathurst shook his head rather impatiently. The vague vapourings of a professional palmist. A woman employed to sit in a tent at the church bazaar. And a village church at that. Good lord—where was he getting to? If he used his common sense, he must discard entirely what the woman had told him. And yet—deny it as he might—he knew in his heart that the woman had impressed him. Why? Her personality? Perhaps! Rather more than perhaps. Almost certainly. Then to point number three. The snarling man. The first appearance of this sinister figure. Two seats away from Coventry on a bench in the park. Blue overalls. This, in connection with the proxy messages, most important as he had pointed out to MacMorran. Mr. Bathurst began to smile. For the first time since he had started his process of analysis. He had two incidents that could be linked together intelligently. What came next? The 'Seven Arts' affair at Dorset House. The snarling man again. Anthony shook his head. Frankly—this second appearance puzzled him. Nothing there that satisfied him! Then Sewell's statement. Two important points. The pink complexion and the parcel. Pink complexion—strange! And why that parcel? Why? Mr. Bathurst beat his head against the bars of this question. This insistent and persistent question. Why was the parcel taken *to* Coventry? It would have been so much simpler and more understandable if the man had been seen going away from the house in Danvers Gate with the parcel. Then the conditions of the murder. Rayner. The secretary. He had answered Austin when he had first spoken on the telephone. The two note-books. To all appearances in the wrong places. Coventry's not where Coventry had seemed to be sitting. Could there be a real significance in their changed positions?

What was the reason behind it? Anthony brought his best brains to bear upon the point. There was the writing. Coventry had used his fountain-pen, which was all in order, and exactly what one would reasonably expect to have occurred. But why write? Why use the *written* word for the communication of ideas instead of the ordinary *spoken* word? Two men in one room. Close to each other. At two o'clock in the morning—why, *then*? Mr. Bathurst suddenly sat stock-still! He felt that part, at least, of the truth had come to him. The man in the blue overalls was dumb! Austin had held back a vital part of the truth. He had lied when he said that the man had spoken to him. Of course, of course! Anthony reviewed with an almost feverish eagerness the various incidents of which he had knowledge that had to do directly with the blue-overalled man. When Aubrey Coventry had approached him in the park, and had made to him the commonplace request for a match, he couldn't reply—for the simple reason that he was unable to speak. He had drawn away, super-conscious perhaps of this infirmity and had mouthed an apology. From this movement, in Coventry's imagination, there had been born this fantastic idea of the snarling man. So far, so good! Mr. Bathurst rubbed his hands. Now for a closer examination of the incidents which had followed the encounter in the park. Austin's story of the proxy telephone messages was a mixture of truth and falsehood. The man in the overalls had not spoken to him when he had first explained his desire, he had conveyed the message of what he wanted done by some other means, and paid Austin to keep back the information that he was dumb in the event of Austin ever being questioned on the matter. Then—Mr. Bathurst's agile brain was now racing ahead—that would account for the second telephone communication having been printed for Austin to send. Anthony nodded to himself. Yes . . . that was feasible. And—here Mr. Bathurst felt intensely pleased with himself—there certainly followed the reason for the two note-books and their relative positions on Coventry's desk. The man was in all probability deaf as well as dumb. What Coventry wrote in the book that he was using had to be placed, of course, in front of his companion, so that the dumb man might be able to read that which had been written. Mr. Bathurst rubbed his hands again. He felt that he was beginning to fit together some of the pieces of the puzzle. Yes. That was how he saw things. Austin must have lied because—Anthony began to hesitate to develop the theory with which he was at the moment coquetting. Why should Austin tell part truth and part falsehood? For what sane reason? Anthony began to harbour doubts. The fact that he had come to the police with his story was sufficient indication that Austin had no qualms on the matter of betraying his associate. If he were prepared to give part of the scheme away, why should he have concealed such a vital factor that the man who had employed him was dumb? Anthony's previous idea that he had been paid not to reveal this latter fact now failed to satisfy him. The man who had used Austin would have had no guarantee as to how far Austin could be trusted. Mr. Bathurst rose from his seat and began to pace the room. He was afraid now that his theory of the deaf and dumb man would not hold water. He was surely missing something somewhere. Something absolutely vital at that. He went over the ground again, retracing his steps one by one, but with infinite care and patience. The idea of dumbness allied to deafness suited two of the incidents—those of the snarling man and the pair of note-books—but if Austin had told the entire truth it could not be possibly fitted into the conditions existing in the arrangement of the telephone messages! Mr. Bathurst's teeth bit hard on to the stem of his pipe. If Austin had told the truth! There was the rub. Who was Austin? Curse Austin! Mr. Bathurst decided to allow his thoughts to take another direction. What was there that was different in the three incidents? Two concerned direct contact with Coventry, the murdered man—the third incident didn't. If Austin had told the truth, was it possible that the intention was for Coventry to be tricked in some way? In what particular way could the deception have taken place? And for what particular motive? Anthony's mind cast in a variety of directions, but no satisfaction came to him from any of them. Irritation and annoyance sat at his elbow. He felt now more than ever that until he hit upon something like a feasible *motive* for the murder, he must of necessity be plough-ing the sands. He determined therefore to go to bed and to let the problem rest for a time. This constant reiteration of considered incident was doing him no good and tiring his brain at the same time. Mr. Bathurst therefore closed his note-book, screwed the top on his fountain-pen, and sought the seclusion that the bedroom granted. And—such was his power of detachment—within a very few minutes Anthony Bathurst was asleep.

CHAPTER XII
MR. BATHURST PERSEVERES

WHEN Anthony Bathurst was shown into the presence of Phil Coventry he discovered, to his surprise, that the young man was not alone. For Mr. Bathurst had understood that he was. With him were his mother, Peter Crayle, Hubert Palmer, and his cousin Valerie Moffatt, fiancée of Peter Crayle. Mr. Bathurst murmured an apology for his intrusion, but pleaded urgency and anxiety as his primary excuses. Mrs. Coventry introduced him to those of the company whom he had not previously met. She was cool and collected. Her eyes had become tranquil although her face was still worn and tired. There followed the usual, almost incoherent, conventionalities. Valerie Moffatt was a slim, vivacious, dark girl of great charm and personality. Her face was long, but the features held to a proper proportion. Her eyes, perhaps, were her most arresting feature. They were large and most unusually dark. Her hair, very dark, too, was closely-cropped. Her mouth was scarlet and provoking, and—to most men it must be admitted—eminently attractive and desirable. Crayle's eyes followed her, Anthony noted, wherever she went and indeed whenever she moved. She was inclined towards tallness and moved gracefully, and her body in no way belied the ripe promise of her face. When Mr. Bathurst was presented to her she almost swept the tips of her cool fingers across his hand. Anthony was given a chair next to Mrs. Coventry. Phil Coventry, as he looked towards him, was inclined, Mr. Bathurst considered, to raise his eyebrows. But a smile broke through the tired sadness that showed on Susanna Coventry's face.

"Well, Mr. Bathurst," she asked quietly, "you haven't come to worry us for nothing at this time of the day, I'll be bound. Won't you tell us what we can do for you?"

"My visit," returned Anthony, "need be but a short one. I wanted to make sure that the position with regard to the death of your husband had not changed at all."

Phil Coventry looked impatient at Anthony's statement. He approximated annoyance. "What exactly do you mean by that, Mr. Bathurst? I should like to understand it better—before I answer it."

Hubert Palmer, judged by the look on his face, was in sympathy with Coventry's expressed point of view.

"I mean this," replied Anthony quietly, "has anything happened since I was here last to affect, say, the question of the motive underlying the crime that caused the death of your father? You will remember, I'm sure, how the possible motive for the murder baffled the intelligence of all of you. Of all of us, if you would prefer me to say that."

Valerie Moffatt leant forward, her chin cupped in her hands. Anthony saw that she was listening to the conversation with intense eagerness. "Mr. Bathurst," she said, in a low voice of extreme quality, "I am both thrilled and interested to hear you ask that. If you want to know why—particularly—Mr. Crayle here will tell you."

"Just a minute, Valerie," put in Phil Coventry. "Let me answer Mr. Bathurst's question before we turn to what are more or less personal side issues. He asked me about 'motive' again. All I can tell him is that we know no more than we did. Nothing! My mother and I have racked our brains to try to think of a reason why my father was murdered. We can think of nothing. We meet a blank wall all the time. Nothing was stolen, as we told you before. No 'enmities' have occurred to us. My father was on the best of terms with everybody with whom he ever came in contact. Both socially and in his business life. Mr. Sere, with whom he worked very closely, feels just as we do about it. He says that my father hadn't an enemy in the world and he knew my father as well, if not better than anybody."

Anthony felt that here was the appropriate moment to ask a question.

"What exactly was your father's business, Mr. Coventry?"

"He was on 'Change, Mr. Bathurst. He knew the markets inside out. Touched anything that took his fancy. He was both shrewd and lucky. As I said, ready to have a cut in on almost anything. Morris Sere used to be his great rival. But that belongs to the past—in latter days they had, to all intents and purposes, joined forces."

Crayle made a contribution. "Morris Sere and the late Mr. Coventry made an ideal combination. I know that for a fact. Mr. Coventry himself has told me so more than once. Sere, he said, had a bump of caution which was missing from his own make-up. Sere makes few mistakes—financially, that is."

Valerie Moffatt tried again. It will be remembered that her cousin had side-tracked her a few moments previously. She spoke quietly but firmly. "Tell Mr. Bathurst, Peter, what I asked you to tell him a moment or so ago. In a way, I look upon him as my best friend."

Crayle flushed with annoyance. Anthony saw that he was more than a little embarrassed. Crayle shook his head. "It's nothing, Val. Mr. Bathurst doesn't want to be bothered with our private troubles."

"Oh, but he does. And I insist that he shall be. Go on now—tell him."

Crayle looked towards Palmer and then to the two Coventrys, as though he expected help from at least one of them, to extricate him from the situation towards which Miss Moffatt was deliberately urging him. The help wasn't forthcoming. Crayle shrugged his shoulders with a helpless gesture and surrendered to the inevitable. He addressed himself to Anthony. "Well—what Miss Moffatt means is this. She's rather put a pistol to my head. It's with regard to our wedding. It should have been in September. Somewhere about the 9th. Now she says she won't go through with it until her uncle's murderer has been found. Don't ask me why. I've tried to reason with her and argue her out of it—but she's tough about it and won't give way. There you are. Now you all know."

"And I mean it, Mr. Bathurst," added Valerie Moffatt with quiet certainty. "I mean it so much that I haven't the slightest intention of going back on it. Peter knows exactly how I feel about it. And he also knows that when I say a thing I mean it. I've told him quite plainly."

"I've pointed out to Val that it's not only damned hard on me—but also ridiculous. Quixotically ridiculous perhaps—but ridiculous all the same."

Valerie set her attractive lips. "You may think so, Peter—as it happens, I don't! I have a very real reason. I'm perfectly certain that I shouldn't be happy—that *we* shouldn't be happy—if we married with this awful cloud hanging over everything. Call it a woman's whim if you like. Or a hunch, even. But there it is—that's how I feel about it. Sorry, darling—and all that." She leant over to him and rather charmingly pressed his hand. Crayle flashed a grateful smile at her in response. Mrs. Coventry spoke.

"I think I understand how you feel, Valerie. In a way I appreciate your thoughtfulness. But there—I am a woman like you. We are two women surrounded by men. Perhaps we feel differently over these things. I hope Peter will try to understand both you—and me."

"I'll try to, Mrs. Coventry. You know me well enough to trust me in matters like that. But I'd been looking forward so intensely to being married in September—that Val's decision came to me as a bit of a blow."

"That's very nice of you, Peter," continued Mrs. Coventry, "and I'm perfectly sure that we all sympathize with you, and hope that your happiness even now won't be delayed."

Anthony thought that he would take the opportunity to have a word with Hubert Palmer. "May I ask you a question, Mr. Palmer? Concerning the evening you spent at Dorset House?"

"Certainly," returned Palmer. "What is it you want to know?"

"I understand that you saw a certain man in the dance-room, during the evening, dressed in a suit of blue overalls?"

Palmer nodded. "That is quite true, Mr. Bathurst. Mr. Coventry senior mentioned the matter to me. Said he had seen the chap there. Then I remembered that I had seen him as well. Mr. Coventry described to me what he was wearing. As a matter of fact, you see, I *had* spotted the chap, and directly he mentioned the dress to me I remembered the incident."

"That's most interesting, Mr. Palmer. Now I wonder if you could tell me this? When the late Mr. Coventry pointed this man out to you at Dorset House did he seem *perturbed* at all by the man being there?"

Palmer wrinkled his brows. "Perturbed? No! I wouldn't say that he was perturbed. No—certainly not that. But he was—I can't think of the word that I think *is* the word. Let me see now. Perhaps I shall be able to think of something that will fit." They all waited in silence while Hubert Palmer considered the matter. Suddenly his face seemed to clear. "I've got it. Or at least I think I've got it. The word is 'shamefaced.' He seemed ashamed to mention to me what, after all, might turn out to be the most trivial matter in the world. He told us about his previous meeting with the man 'shamefacedly,' as though he were putting over to us an absurd cock-and-bull story only fit for kids to listen to. I am sure that Peter here will agree with me." He broke off with almost a hint of apology. "I do hope that I've made myself clear . . . because I'm frightfully afraid that I may not have."

Anthony Bathurst hastened to reassure him. "On the contrary, I think that your explanation has been admirable. I feel that I know the tone almost in which Mr. Coventry spoke to you."

Valerie Moffatt was nothing if not direct. "Mr. Bathurst," she said deliberately, "do you attach any importance to this man with whom my uncle seems to have had these strange encounters? Surely it's all too fantastic to be regarded seriously?"

Anthony was mindful of the story of Sewell the taxi-driver, to say nothing of the curious history of Austin and the proxy telephone messages. Both of which facts he naturally intended for the time being to keep to himself. "I'm afraid I do, Miss Moffatt. Not only an importance, but a really considerable one at that. I can't get away from the fact that I find this strange figure popping up most surprisingly at several turns. Whichever way I look at the problem. Don't you agree with me yourself?" Crayle intervened and answered Mr. Bathurst's question on behalf of the lady of his choice.

"You must do, Val. You can't get away from it. Mr. Bathurst's point is clear. The continued presence of this man in the blue overalls is far too momentous to be overlooked. It's a vital clue, in all probability. And once the police get their hooks in him you can bet your boots they won't have to look any further for your uncle's murderer. At any rate, that's my opinion. And the sooner they pinch him the better, for all our sakes. Not to mention Val and myself."

Anthony felt that no value could come from prolonging the interview. Even though he had failed to learn what he had hoped to learn, he had more detailed information as to how Hubert Palmer stood in relation to the Dorset House incident. His statement thereon had been both frank and convincing. "Thank you all very much for listening to me," said Mr. Bathurst, as he rose from his seat. "Although you haven't been able to help me over the matter of the motive, you have provided me with much valuable information. It's up to me now to use it. Good-bye, Mrs. Coventry . . . and you, Miss Moffatt."

He shook hands with the three men. Philip Coventry seemed inclined to talk. Anthony listened in patience to a lengthy statement. Coventry appeared to be acutely critical of police methods in general. Anthony expressed sympathy with him. "I'll bear in mind what you say, Mr. Coventry, and I may be able to have a word with Chief-Inspector MacMorran who, as you know, is in charge of your case."

"I hope you will," returned Philip Coventry rather ungraciously. "Because I feel strongly about it. I assure you that I'm not thinking of myself. In any shape or form. I'm thinking of my mother."

"That's very charming of you," returned Anthony Bathurst, "and I entirely appreciate how you feel about most things."

Chapter XIII
UNDER THE SEAT

THE telephone in Mr. Bathurst's flat rang insistently.

"All right. Have a heart," he muttered to himself, as he strode towards it. Mr. Bathurst had a lengthy athletic stride. So unusually long was it that Stratton, the quick-tongued English master at Uppingham, had nicknamed him in due deference to Macaulay, 'the great Lord of Luna.' Anthony had borne the infliction with patience and sang-froid despite its unhappy possibilities. He reached the strident instrument and lifted the receiver. "Hallo! Mount 228. Bathurst speaking."

As he had half expected, it was Andrew MacMorran at the other end. "I want you to come to the Yard. Now! Pronto! Got a hell of a surprise for you."

"Sure?" returned Anthony, with a grin.

"Positive! Even for you, Mr. Bathurst. And that's paying you a compliment."

"That's about all you ever do pay me. What have you got for me besides the surprise?"

"You come round and have a look. Don't be so impatient. I'm not telling you over the 'phone. But take it from me—it's something big."

"I will sit up and take appropriate notice. Coventry case?"

"You've said it. And the most important development so far that's come our way. I tell you—we do things at the Yard."

"Yes, I know you do. Each way I expect, as a rule. Still, I won't deny that you've whetted my curiosity—I'll be round in a couple of shakes. Put the red carpet down, Andrew, it'll deaden my footsteps—and get out the Montrachet."

MacMorran chuckled as he finished the conversation. He put down the 'phone and turned to Hemingway, who was standing at his side.

"Expect Mr. Bathurst in about a quarter of an hour. I reckon I've 'revved' him up good and proper by what I told him. He was never one to resist a tickle in the right place . . . if it was put across properly. I know him, you see, and that makes a world of difference."

Hemingway assented with a clicking noise of his tongue. MacMorran's estimate of the time of Mr. Bathurst's arrival was commendably accurate. Hemingway opened the door of Mac-Morran's room to admit him with an air of pleasurable anticipation.

"Come this way, Mr. Bathurst. The Inspector's expecting you."

"What you want in here, Andrew," said Anthony, as he took his seat, "is a pink rug and a bowl of flowers on that ledge over there. Get your typist to push the boat out. If I'm any judge, she'll jump at the opportunity. You've got 'S.A.,' Andrew. How I envy you."

"Never mind about that. Take a look at that parcel on the table there. Then you can forget all your pink rugs and all your purple pansies."

"Andrew," murmured Anthony, "you've got me all wrong. I'm far too fond of you for that. I wasn't personal. Well—what about this parcel? On the table, you say?"

"Ay, Mr. Bathurst. On the table over there. The parcel's already been undone once. So you'll have no difficulty in opening it. The string round it is only loosely tied. As usual, I've unravelled the knots for you." MacMorran's eyes twinkled. He was in high feather at the moment. Anthony went to the table and pulled aside the paper of the parcel. The look in his eyes at once betokened his satisfaction. "So the blue overalls have come home at last, have they? Ah, well, I can't say that I'm surprised. Where did you pick this lot up, Andrew? Rathbone Street—Canning Town?"

MacMorran chuckled. "No! Where do you think? Have another shot and I'll tell you whether you qualify for cigars or nuts."

Anthony grinned. "Giving me a pretty wide field, aren't you, for selection? All the same, I'd bank on somewhere that's distinctly public. Like a park . . . for instance . . . or a lavatory." He paused again. "Well . . . how do I go, Andrew?"

"You don't," returned MacMorran. "So far you're an 'also ran.'"

Hemingway, who was listening to all this with the greatest interest, coughed discreetly. Anthony was unperturbed at his non-success. "All right. I'll have another shot. On the top of a bus—L.P.T.B."

MacMorran shook his head. "Wrong again. Three shots—three misses. Poor shooting for you, Mr. Bathurst. Proper Chelsea form."

"It is, I admit. And more like your own form, too, Andrew. Let me have one more attempt."

"It's our duty to encourage perseverance in the young. But I warn you this must be your last—or you'll keep on keepin' on."

Anthony thought hard over the problem. "I'll still stick to my publicity idea, and have the last shot down the same avenue. Under the seat of a first-class compartment of a railway carriage. But I won't attempt to nominate the exact train."

MacMorran turned to Hemingway with a glint in his eye. "What d'you think of that, Hemingway?" Then he rose from his seat and extended his right hand to Mr. Bathurst. "Put it there, sir . . . you've clicked. In four. And not sae bad considering everything."

"Am I right, then?"

"You are that. And I'll tell you the line."

"I should love to hear the full story, Andrew. Told in your dulcet tones."

"D'ye know a small branch line that runs between East Ham and St. Pancras?"

"I do, Andrew. Serves Leyton, Tottenham, and Harringay. There's about one train an hour if my memory serves me correctly, and that's very often a 'goods.'"

"That's the idea. You're right. It isn't used over-much in the middle of the day. I used to live at Walthamstow when I first joined the force, so I know it fairly well. The station I used was Black Horse Road. The trains run to East Ham, where there's a single line that enters the station. It then runs out a little way for the engine to be reversed and glides back again into East Ham station. Now listen. When the 12.50 arrived at East Ham to-day and the passengers (both of 'em) had cleared out, a porter noticed our parcel under the seat in an empty first-class compartment. Now here comes a rather singular thing." MacMorran paused and cocked a sapient eye in Anthony's direction. "I'm listening, Andrew . . . and in case you don't feel certain about it, you're the berries."

MacMorran grinned at the compliment.

"By a wee bit of coincidence this porter happens to have a brother who's a police constable. Stationed at East Ham. K Division. Name, Bernard Adams. Through his brother having mentioned it, the porter Adams, when he opened the parcel and spotted the blue overalls inside, immediately thought of the 'Coventry murder.' We've been in touch, of course, with the police everywhere, and they've all been on the lookout. Porter Adams at first thought he'd found a dead baby (he's in the Salvation Army and his mind dwells on those things), so he told the station-master, but when the parcel was opened, the blue overalls made him jump to it properly. 'There's the result . . . on the table there."

Anthony went across and looked at the parcel for the second time. He took out the suit of overalls. "Neatly folded, I observe—did you notice that?"

"Ay. That's how they're supposed to have been when Porter Adams first undid them."

Anthony shook his head with every sign of disappointment. "What do you think about 'em, Andrew? The same as I do?"

"If you mean that there's absolutely nothing to distinguish 'em from thousands of similar suits sold in every 'in and out' shop all over the blessed country—then I do! Is that the idea?"

"They're my sentiments, Andrew, to a nicety."

"But just a minute—there's one other little matter. Look at the bottom of the heap."

Anthony obeyed the Inspector's instructions. At the bottom of the heap of clothes, lay a black cloth cap—of the kind that the artisan is wont to wear on occasions. "There's more hope from that, Mr. Bathurst, I'm thinking. D'ye agree with me?"

Anthony nodded. "Certainly I do. Although again I wouldn't be too frightfully optimistic. As a cap, it's not exactly in a class by itself, is it? I remember that I went to Highbury once on a certain Saturday afternoon, and I should say that there were quite half a dozen of these behind one of the goals." MacMorran grinned at the remembrance. Mr. Bathurst continued: "And when the Arsenal scored—one of their forwards fell over in the area and there was a penalty awarded—at least three of the half-dozen were temporarily removed from their wearers' heads in celebration of the event." Hemingway gave way to a boisterous guffaw. Anthony looked at him in surprise. "Why—were you there as well, Superintendent?"

Hemingway shook his head with an almost indignant denial. "No, Mr. Bathurst, I'm no Arsenal fan, thank you. I support the 'Ammers myself. Down at Boleyn Castle. Good boys, too. A very nice little team, thank you. Though we may be in the Second Division, I reckon that if we had a class outside right—"

MacMorran cut him short ruthlessly. "Never mind now, Hemingway. You can discuss that with Mr. Bathurst some other time. This cap now. We must go thoroughly into the question. Get into touch—"

A sharp exclamation from Anthony Bathurst arrested his attention. "Hallo—hallo, Andrew! What have we here? Is it possible that there's something here which has escaped your notice? Or rather, as I should say, *temporarily* escaped your notice?"

The Inspector rose and went to Anthony Bathurst's side. "What have you found, Mr. Bathurst? Trust you to get your claws into something!"

He saw that Anthony was examining two small slips of paper. "These were under the peak—-just inside the cap, Andrew. Not tucked there exactly. What do you make of them yourself?" He handed the slips to MacMorran.

This is what the Inspector saw.

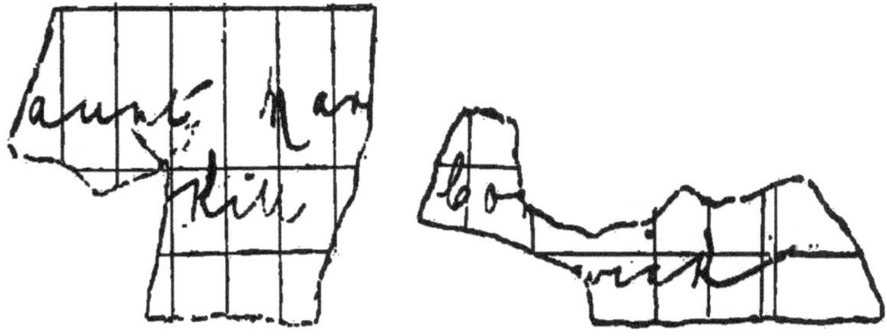

As he took in their significance, MacMorran whistled.

"By Jove, Mr. Bathurst. We're on to something here and no mistake. This message doesn't take a deal of reading, does it?"

Anthony shook his head. His whole attitude implied doubt and misgiving. "Why—how do you read it, Andrew?"

"Well, I reckon it's verra simple . . . on the face of it, that is. These two bits o' paper are parts of a letter that's been torn up . . . and the words . . . of which the parts are here are 'Aunt Mary,' 'kill Coventry.' And . . . er . . . 'quick.' Of course, I'm without the context. . . . I know that perfectly well. . . ." Mr. Bathurst began to pace the room. For a time he made no audible comment on MacMorran's expressed opinion. Superintendent Hemingway watched him with a certain amount of fascination. Suddenly Mr. Bathurst shook his head again.

"Don't like the 'Aunt Mary' business, Andrew. Not a little bit. Somehow. Don't get it—sorry."

Hemingway was looking at the two torn pieces of paper. His face was creased in doubt. "It might be Aunt Maria . . . or even Aunt Margaret," he remarked hopefully.

"True," said Anthony solemnly, "and conceivably Aunt Martha. Indeed, I have a profound sympathy for the Marthas of the world, Superintendent." He swung round on to MacMorran. "Look here, Andrew . . . the fellow that pushed these clothes under the seat knew they'd be found, didn't he?"

"He did that. Why, what's the point?"

"Well, then, these slips look to me like a plant. Deliberately put with the overalls for us to bash our heads against. What do you say to that, Andrew?"

"You mean we were meant to find them?"

"That's how it looks to me."

"If that's the case," argued MacMorran slowly, "and I'm not saying that I altogether disagree with you, mind you—why not make the thing clearer? Easier to read? As it is, it would be quite possible to interpret the words incorrectly—wouldn't it? And then where would the plant be?"

Anthony went and looked again at the two torn slips. "Yes," he conceded. "That's a good point, Andrew. I'll hand it to you for that. If we were meant to find them, there would be a *certainty* as to what we should make of it. Yes . . . yes . . . I think you're right."

Anthony nodded to himself. Then he came back to MacMorran.

"Work for you, Andrew. Quickly at that. Flood the papers with facsimiles of these two fragments, Andrew. Ask for the handwriting to be identified. There's a chance we shall pick up something in that way."

"I agree. I've already made the preliminary arrangements. I'll tell you what I think. When our friend the snarling man made up his parcel to be left under the seat, he tore up a letter. An incriminating letter. These two pieces fell into the cap, unbeknown to him, which means that they weren't meant for us to find. This is the murderer's mistake, Mr. Bathurst. They always make one—as I've told you many times before." MacMorran's eyes glinted with pleasure. Nothing pleased him better than to get Anthony Bathurst guessing.

"You may be right, Andrew," commented the latter, his eyes still on the torn scraps of paper, "but you say an 'incriminating letter.' These don't look to me as though they've come from a letter. Certainly not from an ordinary letter. Come over here and I'll try to show you why."

MacMorran went over to him. Hemingway, although uninvited, followed suit. This was far too good for him to miss.

"In the first place," declared Anthony Bathurst, "look at the rulings on the paper. Of the lines. The paper looks to me as though it had come from something like an account-book. Torn from it. It's certainly not ordinary letter paper. Look at the double line at the end of the word which you take to be 'quick.' See what I mean? There are horizontal lines as well. I repeat that this paper has undoubtedly been torn from a book of some kind. Do you agree with me, Andrew?"

"Yes. I think I do. But where does it get us? Candidly, I don't see. People, especially of the lower class, write letters on all sorts of paper. On any old paper they can pull from their pockets, you know."

"I wonder. I know what you mean, though. But I wouldn't say that I'm altogether satisfied. When paper is torn hurriedly from a book, I think the more likely purposes behind the action are to send a hasty message or to jot down a piece of valuable information. From which you will gather, Andrew, that I deprecate your idea of the incriminating letter."

MacMorran was not in the mood to accept Mr. Bathurst's views without argument. "Yes . . . I know all about that . . . but what you call a letter is different from what Bill Jones and Jack Smith call one. In other words your 'sending a message' is the equivalent to them of 'writing a letter.' You're better aware than I am of the average man in the street's vocabulary strength. I still think I'm right."

"You may be, Andrew, but I don't know. Anyhow, I won't dogmatize on the point. We'll agree to differ. We shall have to leave it at that until we know more. Possibly we shall pick up something in the handwriting identification direction. I'll candidly admit that I have hopes."

MacMorran turned and addressed Hemingway. "Tell the photographing people to put a jerk into it, Superintendent. It's time they got a move on. I gave them my orders quite an hour ago. Speak to Bowden himself. Then make all the Press contacts I was mentioning when Mr. Bathurst came in. By thunder, that reminds me. I promised Sir Austin a report this morning on this Coventry case. This latest development will make a difference."

"You've had inquiries made, I presume, between East Ham and St. Pancras?"

"Yes, Mr. Bathurst. I've been promised a detailed report this evening from every station. Including Junction Road. If I get a squeak worth anything I'll let you know at once."

"Thanks, Andrew. That's good of you. I'll be waiting for it."

Hemingway bustled off to attend to his various instructions. Anthony Bathurst's eyes held a far-away look.

"Penny for 'em, Mr. Bathurst," said Chief-Inspector Andrew MacMorran.

"I was just thinking, Andrew," remarked Mr. Bathurst quietly, "that despite all our efforts we still haven't the slightest idea as to why Aubrey Coventry was strangled by that length of rope."

MacMorran rubbed the tip of his nose. "Perhaps, Mr. Bathurst, when we lay hands on our man, *he'll* tell us all about that. It's quite on the cards, you know." His eyes twinkled.

Anthony ignored the sarcasm and shook his head. "I'd much rather be in the position of telling him," he replied.

"You want too much," remarked Inspector MacMorran good-humouredly.

"I certainly prefer too much to too little," returned Mr. Bathurst.

CHAPTER XIV
ANOTHER SENSATION

MR. BATHURST read his copy of the *Morning Message* with even more than his usual interest. On the front page, and in that part of the paper which for some days had been devoted to the Coventry murder, was a facsimile reproduction of the two pieces of paper that had been found within the peak of the discarded cap. Above the facsimile was printed Inspector MacMorran's appeal to the general public with regard to the identification of the handwriting. Anthony nodded his head in approval of MacMorran's appeal. It was extremely likely, he considered, that this appeal would produce gratifying results. The circulation of the morning dailies, taking them in the aggregate, was immense. Many thousands of eyes would read MacMorran's appeal. Many thousands probably had already read it. Perhaps indeed, included in these thousands, were the particular eyes from which would come the all-important recognition. In fact, MacMorran might even be moving already. Mr. Bathurst put down his copy of the *Morning Message*, and began to toy with a certain theory. Before he could get very far with it, he heard the outside bell ring and the footsteps of Emily as she went downstairs to answer it. Then he heard a medley of footsteps ascending, and the voice of Emily serving as an accompaniment. She came to the head of the stairs and tapped on the door of his room.

"Two ladies to see you, Mr. Bathurst. A Mrs. Coventry and a Miss Moffatt."

Mr. Bathurst felt a certain amount of surprise. He rose. "Bring them in, Emily. By all means. Even though they may be unexpected."

Emily turned away to usher in the two ladies whom she had escorted upstairs. "This way, if you please."

Anthony went forward to greet his two visitors. Emily, trained by tradition and experience, found chairs for the two ladies, before making a discreet departure. Anthony told his two visitors of the honour that they were doing him. Miss Moffatt's dark eyes flashed in quick recognition of the compliment. Mrs. Coventry surrendered the leadership to her. Miss Moffatt then opened fire. "No doubt you are extremely surprised to see us here, Mr. Bathurst. I'm sure you are. I could read it in your face as we came in. But we have come deliberately. My aunt was anxious to come to you rather than to go to Inspector MacMorran at Scotland Yard. I will admit candidly that I was doubtful of the wisdom of the course. But I allowed myself to be persuaded—which is unusual in my case. So here we are." She smiled rather charmingly.

"I am all attention," returned Anthony.

"Tell Mr. Bathurst, Valerie, what I want you to tell him, and then he can be the judge as to whether I am being wise or not."

There was determination in Mrs. Coventry's voice. Anthony was pleased to hear it there. He looked across at Valerie Moffatt—waiting for her to proceed.

"It's with regard to the notice in the Press this morning, Mr. Bathurst. You've seen it, I've no doubt. Your friend, Inspector MacMorran, is appealing for assistance. He wants the handwriting identified, on a certain two pieces of paper, that are showing on the front pages of the various newspapers this morning. That is so, isn't it? You do know about it? I haven't made any mistake?"

"You are quite right, Miss Moffatt. In all your details. Please go on."

"Good. I will. And this is where my aunt comes in—comes in first, I should say—before me. Now, Aunt—will you go on from here, please?" Valerie Moffatt set her lips tightly.

Mrs. Coventry gave every indication that she would. "I will, Valerie. Very willingly. And I feel first of all that I have a really big surprise in store for Mr. Bathurst."

Anthony smiled. "Let me have it then, Mrs. Coventry, will you please?"

"The handwriting that Inspector MacMorran wants identified, Mr. Bathurst, *I* can identify."

Mrs. Coventry's tones were even and steady.

"You can? Whose is it?"

"My late husband's, Mr. Bathurst! You weren't expecting me to say that, were you?" Mrs. Coventry leant over towards him, but retained her nonchalance. She watched Anthony Bathurst's face to see the impression that she had made on him. Valerie Moffatt did the same thing. Susanna Coventry's statement of a few moments ago that he would be surprised had certainly been a true one. Mr. Bathurst paused in the act of putting a hand to his forehead. He whistled at what he heard. "By Jove! Is that so, Mrs. Coventry? Well—you *have* given me a jerk. I'm perfectly willing to admit it. You're absolutely certain of what you say, I suppose?"

Mrs. Coventry was acidity itself. "Please don't be absurd, Mr. Bathurst. Your last remark almost goads me to impatience, at least."

Mr. Bathurst was imperturbable under the censure. He had endured experiences of this kind before. "Perhaps my question may not be quite so absurd as it sounded, Mrs. Coventry. It's possible, you know, for people to be deceived. I have known it happen before now. Handwriting may be *copied*. Copied with a degree of perfection that makes the forgery almost flawless. Very few people—and they would have to be experts almost certainly—are able to detect these absolutely first-class forgeries. I wanted to feel quite sure that nothing of that kind had happened in this case under our notice. You see my point, Mrs. Coventry?"

Mrs. Coventry remained in her condition of acidity. "The handwriting is my husband's, Mr. Bathurst. You need waste no time in wondering about it. I'm telling you. I know it as well as I know my own. Have you a copy of one of this morning's papers? I'll demonstrate to you if you'll be good enough to lend me one."

Mr. Bathurst reached for his copy of the *Morning Message*.

"There you are, Mrs. Coventry. Show me what you mean, will you, please?"

Mrs. Coventry spread the paper across the table. "Take the first fragment, Mr. Bathurst. Look at the capital letter 'M.' There are two features of it that are unmistakably Aubrey's. Note the long tail of the third stroke and the unusual distance between it and the letter which comes directly after it. See what I mean?"

She pointed to the newspaper. "You can't mistake things like that."

Anthony bent down for a more careful examination. "Yes, Mrs. Coventry," he nodded. "I do see what you mean."

"Good. I thought you would. Now look at the two 'K's'. The one in the word that appears to be 'kill,' and the final letter of what seems to be the last word of all. Notice the unusual, almost exaggerated tops of the letters and the backward inclination. Aubrey invariably made his 'K's' like that. As a matter of fact, I used to chaff him about them and call them antlers, you know—like a stag has. See them here on the paper?"

Anthony looked as he had looked before. "Yes. Again I see your point—and they're good points, too. Thank you very much, Mrs. Coventry."

Mrs. Coventry pressed her finger-tips together. She seemed very satisfied with what she had set out to do and had done. She looked across at the girl who had come with her. Valerie Moffatt intervened with a contribution. "If it's any help to you—I can thoroughly endorse my aunt's statement with regard to Uncle Aubrey's capital 'M's,' Mr. Bathurst. I have often noticed the capital 'M' on an envelope which he has sent to me. Both the long tail and the distance from the 'o' in the word 'Moffatt.'"

"Do you happen to have one of those envelopes with you, Miss Moffatt? It would help."

Valerie Moffatt looked dubious at the request. Then she seemed to think of something and began to fish in her bag. After a time, her face cleared. She produced an old envelope from the bag for Mr. Bathurst's inspection. "Yes. Here's one. I was afraid that I hadn't one. This is a comparatively old one, though. It must have been in my bag for months." She handed the envelope to Anthony Bathurst. "Look! Compare that 'M' there with the 'M' in the paper this morning. You can't make any mistake about it—this is the same handwriting. It's as plain as plain can be." Anthony made the required comparison. He placed the envelope at the side of the column in the piper. It was quite true what Valerie Moffatt had pointed out to him. He turned to Mrs. Coventry. This news that had been brought to him put an entirely different complexion on matters. Especially as far as he himself was concerned. He determined to use the gifts that the gods in their goodness had sent him. Mrs. Coventry was here in his flat. She might be of even further use to him.

"Mrs. Coventry," said Mr. Bathurst, "have you tried to make anything out of these words or fragments of words in your late husband's handwriting?"

"Make anything?"

"As to their meaning? Anything coherent? Can you interpret any part of it?"

Mrs. Coventry picked up Mr. Bathurst's copy of the *Morning Message*. "Let me look again." She carefully studied the printed words. There was a silence for a period that seemed like minutes. "My husband had one aunt living, I believe. He saw her but little. Indeed, I don't recall that I myself have ever seen her. She certainly didn't attend our wedding. She lives, I fancy, at Shrewsbury. Oddly enough, he always referred to her as Aunt Marley. Marley was her surname. Her husband used to keep a baker's shop. But I refuse to believe that she has anything to do with these pieces of paper found in an old cap. It's too ridiculous for words."

Anthony was interested in Miss Coventry's first reaction . . . more interested perhaps than the lady talking to him realized. He put a further question to her. "Who benefited under Mr. Coventry's will?"

"Everything was left to me," she returned coldly. "At least . . . it's as good as that. There were one or two small legacies as well. Amongst others—one for Valerie here. With regard to the main issue, when my turn comes to go, the estate will revert to my son Philip. All normal provisions—you see . . . just what might be expected . . . and nobody can reasonably cavil at any of them."

"I see. Thank you, Mrs. Coventry. Well, I must pass on your information concerning the handwriting to Inspector MacMorran. It's his pigeon much more than mine."

"Thank you, I shall be glad if you will. But I wanted you to know about it first. The police don't seem to have made much headway in the case, Mr. Bathurst."

The tone of her voice suggested inquiry rather than a statement of definite opinion. "I don't know that I altogether agree with you, Mrs. Coventry. One or two important matters have already turned up, you know. The police are sound, quietly efficient, and eminently thorough. Neither brilliant nor spectacular, I admit—but they usually get their man."

"I hope you're right and that your optimism is well founded." She began to pull on her gloves.

Valerie Moffatt shrugged her shoulders. "Now we'll get back, Aunt, if you don't mind. I've an appointment with Peter for lunch at 'Quantocks.' And I detest being late." She held out her slim hand to Anthony.

Mrs. Coventry lingered for a moment. "I often wonder,' she said dreamily, "about Rayner. He seems different lately."

"Shucks," retorted Valerie. "Rayner couldn't say 'Boo' to a goose. He's of the tame cat variety. Puffs at you like a train, and is cultivating a stutter."

"He *was* quiet," returned Mrs. Coventry, "but I don't know that he is now. He's changed considerably since the murder. And that's just what I've been trying to say for a long time. Good-bye, Mr. Bathurst. Tell the Inspector what I've told you, won't you? Thank you so much."

Mr. Bathurst put his visitors in Emily's care again. Then he stretched his arm and reached for the telephone. "Put me through to Chief-Inspector MacMorran," he said eventually. He waited patiently for MacMorran to come on at the other end. MacMorran came. Mr. Bathurst began to speak quickly but deliberately. More than once he distinctly heard MacMorran whistle.

Chapter XV
RAYNER AS ESCORT

WHEN MacMorran had heard all that Mr. Bathurst had to say he immediately sent for Superintendent Hemingway. When Hemingway had heard all that MacMorran had to say he sent for Chatterton. The last-named answered the call with some trepidation. As a rule, a summons of this kind meant work, more work, and work after that. Chatterton was not in love with work. As he often complained to his confrères Evershed and Bagshaw: "Old Walter knew how to farm it out when there was a bit of hard graft to tackle."

"Sit down, Chatterton," said Hemingway, upon Chatterton's entrance.

"Very good, sir."

"Inspector MacMorran wants some special work done on the Coventry case. Asked me to see to it for him. But he was emphatic that it should be given to one of our best officers. I'm handing it over to you, but don't flatter yourself on that account. It just happens that nobody else suitable is available."

"No, sir. I shouldn't think of it. What's the job that I've got to take over?"

"Wait for it! Wait for it! Don't be in too great a hurry—and I'll tell you."

"Thank you, sir. I'm sorry, sir."

"Now listen. Do you recall that fellow that called here on the first morning with regard to the Coventry murder?"

"What—that little old tramp fellow? What was his name—Austin?"

Hemingway shook his head in contempt. "Good lord, no! Not him. Where's your memory? Didn't I say that fellow that called here first of all, and gave information about the murder? He found Coventry dead in his room, remember? Rayner's his name. Arthur Rayner. Used to be old Coventry's secretary. Meek and mild sort of fellow."

"I never saw him—but I know the fellow you mean by name. Well—what about him?"

"The Chief wants an eye kept on him. And that eye's going to be yours, Chatterton. It don't matter if it's your right or your left. It's one of Mr. Bathurst's stunts."

"Got a photograph of the fellow?"

"No. But you'll have no difficulty. He's still at the Coventry house in Danvers Gate. But he often goes out for a stroll. The idea is that you shadow him for a few days and find out what he gets up to." Hemingway made a significant movement of the eye. "Perhaps he isn't the good boy he's supposed to be. You never know, Chatterton."

"Describe him to me, will you, sir? I'd like a picture of him in my mind to work on."

"Well—there's plenty of room for it."

Hemingway did the necessary. "Report to me, Chatterton," he concluded, "directly there's anything worth talking about."

"*If* there's anything, Super."

Hemingway glared at him.

"All right—have it your way."

Chatterton went to his own room and made certain notes. He always liked to be sure of what he was supposed to do. Within half an hour he was on his way to Danvers Gate. In plain clothes. He felt certain that if Rayner came out he would be able to recognize him from the description Hemingway had given. When Rayner did come out he felt certain that he would not lose sight of him. From years of experience he was familiar with this game. He hung about. An hour and then another passed all too slowly for him. Chatterton walked. He lounged. He stopped in his tracks and turned. He crossed roads. He hid himself round corners. At times—such was his skill—he almost effaced himself from the public gaze, but he always contrived to watch the front door of the Coventry house in Danvers Gate. Just as he was beginning to think that he would spend a profitless day as regards the man in whose movements he was interested, the door opened and there emerged the slight, clerical form of Arthur Rayner. Chatterton identified him at once without the slightest difficulty or hesitation. The time was eight minutes to four. Chatterton made particular note of it. Rayner looked round rather nervously, thought Chatterton, from his coign of vantage on the other side of the road, and made off in the direction of Palatine Street. He walked briskly, but the plain-clothes man was easily able to keep pace with him. Rayner walked for about ten minutes. All the time Chatterton was but a few yards away from him. Suddenly Chatterton saw him stop. At the corner of Ebor Street, Chatterton lounged past and crossed the road about the length of a cricket pitch ahead of him. Then Chatterton turned and came towards him again. To the plain-clothes man's surprise, Rayner was joined at the corner by a remarkably attractive woman. Chatterton whistled between his teeth. "Some bird!" He watched her carefully as she stood at Rayner's side. That they were on the most intimate terms was obvious to everybody. "Well I'm blessed!" muttered Chatterton to himself. "Some of these old 'uns are as bad as the young 'uns. All the same, I admire the old boy's taste. Some bird—I'll say. What a lovely drop of homework!"

Rayner, with the lady, turned and began to walk in the direction of Lindrum Street. Chatterton was soon in their tracks and following them at what he considered was a discreet distance. They crossed Ebor Street, turned down Palatine Street, which was the route by which Rayner had come and headed straight for Lindrum Street. Chatterton maintained his place behind them at a distance of about ten yards. At this stage of the journey, Rayner and his attractive companion were talking animatedly. Chatterton could see her even better now. She had flame-coloured hair and was on the tall side. When she turned, as she did every now and then to look at her companion or to speak to him, Chatterton could see her face. It was undeniably beautiful. One of those faces which many men will turn to look at a second time after they have passed the owners. She was pale, but her eyes would have demanded attention anywhere. Chatterton had an eyeful and realized, as he looked, that Hemingway might well have detailed to him a much more unpleasant duty. It was certainly an ill wind. He was still watching the lady's face when Rayner and she turned abruptly down a smallish side-turning which Chatterton at once noted bore the name of Faulkner Street. Chatterton made the turning a mere half-dozen yards behind them. He had already satisfied himself that neither Rayner nor his lady friend was in the least conscious of being followed. Half-way down Faulkner Street they stopped and went into a shop. Chatterton passed the shop at a leisurely pace. Looking up he saw that it announced itself to the passing public as 'The Nonpareil Tea-Room.'

Chatterton allowed a reasonable interval of time to elapse, and then he entered the tea-room himself. It was a small place, containing, at a quick assessment, about eight tables. From the corner of his eye, Chatterton saw that Rayner and the lady of his acquaintance had chosen the table in the far left-hand corner. Chatterton promptly seated himself so that he had his back to Rayner and the lady, but could avail himself, at the same time, of a large mirror which was placed upon the wall to his own immediate left. He gave the girl who came to him a commonplace order for tea and toast. He was now able to detect that the woman with Rayner had a soft deep voice. Chatterton could distinctly hear it. Sometimes he could even hear words in the Rayner conversation. Then the well-trained eye of Chatterton noticed something else. The woman's clothes were exquisite in every detail. Once she put a hand to her scarlet mouth and yawned. There came a miniature blaze from the rings which covered her fingers. Rayner certainly could pick 'em out, thought Chatterton again. He heard her say: "You, too?" Rayner replied to her in a low voice, but the tone suggested worry and anxiety. Chatterton heard the name "Morris." The lady pouted petulantly and shrugged slim shoulders. Then she leant over the table to Rayner and lowered her voice to the level of his. Chatterton was now able to catch nothing of what was being said. He saw that Rayner was nodding his head slowly as she spoke.

As though she were instructing him or he was taking her advice. Suddenly and for no reason that Chatterton could explain, she spoke to Rayner and every word she said sounded plainly across the tea-room. "If you think that he'll do that I'm afraid that you don't know Morris Sere. And I should have thought that you would have known him by this time." Chatterton almost held his breath. He knew enough of the Coventry case from Hemingway to know that Sere was the name of a man who had been in many ways Coventry's business associate. As he was thinking this, the woman turned in her chair, and through his convenient mirror Chatterton saw her full-faced for the first time. Rayner was asking the attendant for his bill. The lady began to put on her gloves. They were preparing for departure. Chatterton thought that she looked beautiful, supremely sure of herself, disdainful, and even insolent. Considering these things, therefore, what hold could Rayner reasonably have upon her? While he was thus meditating, the two of them passed by his table on their way out. Rayner was quite cool and collected. He showed no sign of nerves whatever. They went out. Chatterton contrived to follow them within a few seconds. When he reached the pavement, he saw that his double quarry had turned in the reverse direction to that from which they had come, and were already many yards ahead. Chatterton hastened his steps in an effort to catch them up, but an ill-timed traffic light held him up for some moments. At the same time, a large limousine also obscured his view. The result was that when Chatterton did eventually make the other side of the road, there was no sign of Rayner or his lady companion. Chatterton swore under his breath at the unlucky break and quickened his pace. But to no avail. Rayner and company had vanished. Chatterton almost ran to the next turning. His luck was still out, however. He stood on the pavement for a second, irresolute, and wondered as to his next step. Several possibilities occurred to him. Then, from the tail of his eye he caught sight of a fast-disappearing taxi. Chatterton knew that from his particular point of view at that moment, the worst had happened. He looked wildly round for another taxi. The horizon was beautifully clear of such vehicles.

As he stood there on the corner, it was borne upon Chatterton of New Scotland Yard that he was sunk. He stuck his two hands into his pockets and cursed. There was nothing for him now but to return to Hemingway. He had, at any rate, accomplished something. He struck down a side-turning into Kidd Lane, which, at the end of it, would bring him out into Plantagenet Street. Arrived here, Chatterton crossed to the north side. This route brought him directly opposite to a shop which was half-stationer's and half circulating library. Recent best-sellers by Priestley, Cronin, and Ruff, prominently displayed in a window, caught Chatterton's eye and arrested his attention. He allowed his gaze to concentrate for a moment upon the window itself. Besides books and magazines it held a row of most attractive picture post-cards. Chatterton's eyes wandered towards them. Suddenly he received something very much like a blow from a fist between the eyes! For there, in the middle of the row of photographs, was the face of the woman whom he had just been following. Chatterton went quickly to the window for a closer inspection. Above the cards was the caption presented in coloured inks, 'Famous Film Stars of the Moment.' Chatterton looked at the name under the card which held the special interest for him. 'Vere Valentine.' "Blimey," he muttered, "and I never recognized her! I must be nuts. Saw her, too, a fortnight ago in *The King's Proctor*. Well—I'm blistered! Wait till I tell the old woman." Chatterton entered the shop, and for the majestic sum of three denarii purchased a dazzling photograph of Vere Valentine. At least, it would be evidence of a kind for the delectation or otherwise of Superintendent Hemingway. He could feast his bloodshot eyes on the ruddy card! Chatterton made his way back to the Yard. When he reached there, he reported forthwith to Hemingway. Hemingway put aside his immediate job and at once arranged to see him. Chatterton went in to him with a certain amount of misgiving.

"Hallo!" said Hemingway. "Well—did you get anything?"

"Yes, Superintendent, I did. I'll tell you." Chatterton described the incidents of his activities up to the entrance into the 'Nonpareil Tea-Room.' Hemingway nodded encouragingly.

"So you went in, too—eh? Good work, Chatterton. Now tell me what you heard in there."

"Not a lot, Superintendent. Although I did my best. Just fragments of conversation here and there, and now and then. Still—what

I did hear was pretty nifty. Cast your mind back a bit—to the first part of the Coventry case. Ever heard of the name 'Sere' in connection with the affair? Morris Sere? You think, Super! Wasn't he mixed up in business in some way with old man Coventry?"

"He was, Chatterton! You're quite right. I remember it. What was said in that direction?"

Chatterton supplied the details.

"Good! Now what happened after all that?"

"Well—they went out and I lost 'em, Superintendent."

"What?" roared Hemingway. "What the hell were you doing to allow that? Standing at the corner of the street with your mouth wide open catching flies?"

"No, I wasn't, Superintendent! I was blinkin' unlucky—that's all there was to it."

Chatterton in his desire to justify his failure had raised his voice.

"Pipe down," cried Hemingway. "You've made a pretty mess of things. Why don't you admit it?"

"I don't admit it, Superintendent," returned Chatterton sullenly. "I just got caught on the wrong foot. Listen to me for a moment longer . . . before you sum up and send me to 'jug.' There's more for you to hear. Take a dekko at that." Chatterton handed over the photograph of Vere Valentine. Hemingway's eyes bulged.

"Easy on the eye, Chatterton! Very easy, I must say! But how long have you been collecting picture post-cards while you're on duty? Is your stamp album full up as well?"

Chatterton snorted. "That, Superintendent, is a photo of the bird who was with our friend Rayner. Now—shoot!"

Hemingway let go a low whistle. "'Struth!" he exclaimed.

Chapter XVI
CROSS TRAILS

"You can say what you like," urged MacMorran to Mr. Bathurst, "but Rayner has no alibi for the time of the murder. And you'll never convince me that he has."

"No," conceded Anthony. "I'll grant you that. Develop your case then."

"Well," went on MacMorran, "supposing that Rayner and Sere were working together against Coventry, with regard to some business proposition—which might be anything for all we know. At this stage of the case it doesn't really matter what it was. Where was Rayner when Coventry was at Dorset House? We don't know. What's to prevent him being the man in the blue overalls who came up in the taxi? Nothing at all, as far as I can see. There you are, Mr. Bathurst. There's my case with the bones out of it."

"That's dead easy to dispose of. What about Austin?"

"What about him?"

"Merely this, Angel-face. Blue Overalls employed Austin for the phoney 'phonings. Rayner answered them. Rayner, therefore, can't be Blue Overalls. Ergo and also Q.E.D."

MacMorran was sarcastic. "How do we know that it was Rayner who took the call? That merely belongs to Austin's story. And it's Rayner's, too, of course! The only man who could testify to it is Coventry himself, and he's stiff."

"I agree, Andrew. But even there, you're presuming a good deal, aren't you? Don't like an over-plus of mere presumption. It don't please me." Anthony shook his head. "Another thing, Andrew. According to your man Chatterton, Rayner is meeting the wife of M. Sere . . . not necessarily clandestinely but surreptitiously, we'll say . . . and murmuring soft nothings to her over teacups and toast. . . . You know what I mean. Nice and quiet like, with precious few listening. That, to me, savours much more of 'contra' Sere than of 'cum' Sere, or even 'pro' Sere. Get me, you old moustache?"

Anthony saw that he had shaken MacMorran's confidence in his own theory. He followed up his advantage. "Damn it all, Andrew— there's far too much working in the dark in this case for my liking already. Have you interviewed Morris Sere at all?"

"No. Why should I have done? What real approach can I make to him? We know all what there is to know about him. There isn't the slightest reason to connect him with the Coventry murder. Again, on the other hand, if there were any boloney about him, the more I keep away from him the less likely he will be to keep on his guard. Are you with me there, Mr. Bathurst?"

"Perhaps. It's possible, I suppose. But as I said just now we're groping far too much, which means that nearly everything is unsatisfactory. I don't like it. Leaving Rayner and his circle, suppose we cast in another direction? What do you make of the handwriting business? When did Coventry write it, and how did the pieces get inside Blue Overall's black cap?"

"Does it matter? We know now that Coventry *did* write the words and also that, barring accidents, he must have had contact with Blue Overalls. Which all goes to prove conclusively that my theory—the theory that I've held throughout—is the correct one. Namely—that Blue Overalls is the murderer. I don't see how you can get away from it."

"Ah? Then I've got you, Andrew, got you where you'll know all about it. Where the hair is short."

Anthony pointed at him a cigarette of scorn. "If Coventry wrote the word-fragments that we found—they can't mean what you made them out to mean in the first instance. Your 'Aunt Mary kill Coventry quick' business becomes pure Auntie Moonshine. Never mind about Aunt Mary." Anthony chuckled at the Inspector's discomfiture. "And there's something else you can pick the bones out of. Or try to!"

MacMorran coughed. "Yes,. I'll grant you you've scored there. Still, make allowances. I made a quick shot at the solution of the scribble—-just took what you might describe as the marrow of it. There's no doubt now that I was wrong and that the words mean something else."

"Nary a doubt of that, Andrew. I'm glad that you're prepared to concede me that much. It means that we're progressing. By Jiminy, that reminds me, Andrew. Let me have another squint at those bits of paper—will you? I am in the mood for them. I want to get them thoroughly fixed in my mind's eye."

MacMorran went to his safe and produced the torn fragments. "There you are, Mr. Bathurst. There are the identicals. You can take a good long look at them."

"I'm going to do even more than that, Andrew. I'm going to provide myself with an exact copy of them. Shove me over a piece of plain paper—do you mind?"

MacMorran did as requested.

"Thanks, Andrew." Anthony made a careful copy of the written word-parts. "Now—let's get down to this little problem, Andrew, more intensively than we have so far. Suppose we concentrate on the first word. The word that looks like 'Aunt.' Seeing that it's undoubtedly a small 'a' with which it begins, what letter or letters can we put in front of the 'a' in order to construct a reasonably sensible word?"

MacMorran grunted at the question. Anthony went on to answer it himself. "I suggest that we can reasonably include in our word-list daunt, flaunt, gaunt, haunt, jaunt, and taunt. I think that we may dismiss 'avaunt' as entirely unlikely. You're with me, Andrew?"

"Ye-es, I suppose so."

"Right. We'll leave those words standing, then, for the time being and pass on to the last word."

"Why?" inquired the Inspector somewhat curtly.

"For the primary reason that what we have of it interests me. I think, Andrew, when I come to consider it carefully, that it intrigues me more than any of the other words."

"Why? What's particularly remarkable about it?"

"Nothing remarkable about it, but something decidedly interesting."

"What?" MacMorran was growing impatient.

"You took it to be part of the word 'quick.' I don't think you're right. I think you were off the track. I don't think the first letter is a 'u.' I rather fancy it's a 'w.' I almost want it to be a 'w,' Andrew, because if it is I'm well on the way towards establishing three important points. Three! Do you hear the good tidings, you old sinner?"

"Oh—what are the three?" asked the still inquiring Inspector.

"Why these! If it is a 'w,' as I strongly suspect it is, the word or part-word becomes 'wick.' That's the first of my three points. Now 'wick' is an exceedingly frequent termination of English place names. Without taxing my memory in the slightest degree, I can mention offhand, Smethwick, Hawick, Warwick, Canwick, Southwick, Painswick, Berwick, and . . . er . . . Giggleswick. I really must have Giggleswick. How many's that?"

"Eight."

"Then I can go on again with Alnwick, Keswick . . . but there is no need for me to proceed any farther. *Place*names, Andrew—and that's the second of my two points."

MacMorran nodded. There was approval in the nod. "I think I begin to see, Mr. Bathurst."

"Wait. I haven't finished yet. I'm coming to my third point." Anthony answered MacMorran's slow smile with one of his own. "I want you to note my third point, Andrew, carefully. Because I feel that it's going to give you something of a shock. If our part-word is 'wick,' and 'wick' is, as we have seen, the ending of so many names of places, then those semi-sentences we picked up from the old cloth cap are extremely like an address. Do you hear that? An address it is to us, Andrew, an address—and nothing more."

MacMorran rose from his chair and clasped his hands behind him. He found words of congratulation. "Mr. Bathurst . . . sir . . . I think you're right."

"So do I, Andrew—though I sez it what shouldn't."

MacMorran nodded again . . . a slow, almost benevolent nod. "And if that's so—"

"Exactly," said Anthony, "if that's so—"

"We may be on to something."

"If we go all Poirot and use our little grey cells—we shall be—undoubtedly. What do you say?"

"Let's get down to it then." MacMorran, ever practical, was eager for the chase.

"Big field, Andrew. Worse than the 'Cambridgeshire,' or even the 'Stewards' Cup'. And no form to go on—to help us."

"I suppose we should take the bigger towns first."

Anthony considered the point. "We might, but I don't know that there's much in it. An address might be anywhere—come to that. Just as likely to be in an obscure country village as in an industrial centre. I'm afraid that our motto has got to be patience—illimitable patience. That's the one thing we can regard as certain."

MacMorran began to write down the names of the various places which Anthony had previously mentioned.

"Just a minute, Andrew, before you start anything. I think that I can help you. If we're dealing with an address, as we think we are, the first word or words is almost certainly a name. In that assumption, therefore, I'm banking on the first word itself being 'Gaunt.' At the moment 'Gaunt' is the only name I can think of which has the right ending. If I were you, Andrew, I'd concentrate on 'GAUNT.'" Anthony tossed off the information to him with the air of a juggler dexterously manipulating a set of Indian clubs. MacMorran blinked his eyes at the rapidity of the speech.

"By Jove," he said softly, "that *is* a help." The blink broke into a slow smile as though he had already found a solution. "I'll put Kingsley on to this at once. He's as smart as they make 'em on jobs of this kind. Best chap I've ever had in the department. Wait a minute, Mr. Bathurst. I'll send for him." MacMorran used the telephone on his desk. A smart fresh-faced young fellow answered it. MacMorran explained in a few curt sentences what he wanted. Two pertinent questions from Kingsley were quickly answered. The latter nodded his understanding to his superior and disappeared with alacrity.

Anthony left his chair and took up his favourite position on the corner of MacMorran's table. He hoisted his long body adroitly and regarded MacMorran urbanely. Minutes passed in silence. MacMorran showed signs of nervousness. Periods of inactivity nearly always affected him in this way. He seemed to put his thoughts into words. "He's a good chap. I've got a lot of confidence in him. He'll have it if it's there to be had."

"It's there all right, Andrew—don't worry." There was a glint of good humour in Anthony Bathurst's eyes. "Might take him a devil of a time though," went on MacMorran, still the victim of his own thoughts and anxieties.

"Must give him a break." Anthony took a cigarette. "Here you are. Soothe your throbbing nerves, Andrew."

MacMorran took a cigarette almost mechanically. Anthony held a lighted match for his use. MacMorran smoked nervously. Anthony's suggested elucidation of the two fragments had excited him. For the first time since the problem had presented itself, he felt that they had come to grips with something definite and . . . more than that . . . with something that he was able to understand. He continued to smoke quickly. Anthony swung his legs from his coign of vantage on MacMorran's table. MacMorran began to chew his cigarette-end. Shreds of tobacco began to show at a corner of his mouth. Anthony raised an eyebrow.

"Andrew . . . Andrew," he chided.

MacMorran tossed his cigarette-end into an ash-tray with a question on his lips. "Supposing we find this address, Mr. Bathurst, where do we go to from there?"

"Gertcher," returned Anthony. "You're travelling too fast for me. Hold your horses. He tires betimes who spurs too fast betimes. Don't forget that piece of excellent advice. The drunken clown of Stratford."

MacMorran looked up at him. "Shakespeare," added Anthony. *"Richard the Tooth."*

MacMorran nodded—something like a man just emerging from a bad dream, and shook his head impatiently. He looked at his watch. "Twenty-two minutes since Kingsley went. He's usually a fast worker."

"No good ever came from rushing fences," commented Anthony, as he selected another cigarette, "as I said just now—hold your horses."

He got down from the corner of the table and walked across the room. "We've certainly accomplished one thing, Andrew . . . if nothing else. We've pushed your friend Rayner out of the picture."

"Not for long," growled the Inspector. "He'll be back there good and proper, never fear. Rayner's a cute 'un—unless I'm very much mistaken."

Anthony was just beginning to smile again when there came a tap on the door. MacMorran called the invitation with eagerness. Kingsley, the fresh-faced, was in the room like a flash. Anthony was quite touched by the gleam of triumph in his eyes. He waited expectantly for Kingsley's news. "Well?" said MacMorran.

Kingsley handed him a slip of paper. "There you are, sir," said Kingsley, "there's the address you wanted. In full. Sorry if I was a bit slow. But my first two shots were duds and I wasted my time on them. I clicked, though, on the third. There's no doubt that's the right address, Inspector. It's the only one that fits."

MacMorran read eagerly from Kingsley's slip of paper before beckoning Anthony to his table. Mr. Bathurst went and read what Kingsley had written. 'Gaunt, Marston and Co., Brunskill Corner, Southwick.' Anthony rubbed his hands at what he saw. His grey eyes gleamed with satisfaction. MacMorran, recognizing the signs, looked up at him and slowly smiled. "Your trick, Mr. Bathurst. All yours. Thank you."

Anthony grinned and drooped his right eyelid in acknowledgment.

MacMorran turned quickly to his subordinate. "How did you get it, Kingsley?"

"I worked on 'Gaunt,' sir, as you suggested. 'Phoned the biggest places first. 'Phoned the G.P.O.'s. Warwick and Smethwick were stumers, as I said. Southwick, though, turned up trumps."

"Good work, Kingsley. I shan't forget it."

Kingsley flushed with pleasure at the Inspector's praise. MacMorran made certain notes. His pen scratched hard on the paper. Anthony came at Kingsley. "What are these people, Kingsley? Messrs. Gaunt, Marston, when they're at home? Any idea?"

"Yes, sir. Directly I got them I made full inquiries for you. The firm's main business, so I understood, is to do with antiques. I should say from what I've heard already, that they're pretty big people in their way. In fact, I was told that in their particular line they're amongst the leading half-dozen firms in the country; know their business, sir."

Anthony whistled at the news. "Antiques, eh? That's a new one on me, Andrew. I wasn't expecting that. This is a nice case, this is."

MacMorran repeated the important word. "Antiques! What has that to do with Coventry? I don't get it."

"That's what we have to find out. Also—why did it interest the pseudo-Silas Montgomery? Deep waters grow deeper, I fear, Andrew."

With a few more words, MacMorran dismissed the triumphant Kingsley. Anthony thought aloud.

"Gaunt, Marston and Co., Southwick. In Sussex, Andrew. Sussex by the sea. Well, there are worse places than Sussex. Now why was the address of these dealers in antiques—or part of it, to be precise—found in Blue Overalls' black cap? Why—oh why—oh why? It's a poser, Andrew. An absolute poser. We must give our best brains to its consideration."

"You're tellin' me."

Anthony walked to the window and looked out across the liver. Suddenly he turned. "There's a village green at Southwick, Andrew, that has known the sweetness of the game of cricket and a cottage nearby in which Charles the Second is reputed to have spent at least one night."

"You will go down there?"

"I shall go down there," replied Anthony gravely. "Tell Sir Austin for me, will you, Andrew? I shall go down there to-morrow. Though I'm not too sure that my visit will bring us much."

"Why not?"

"We don't know *why* Coventry wrote this address. That's the point that worries me. It's in the dead man's handwriting. There's always the odd chance that it may mean nothing. If it had been written by somebody else whom we were attempting to identify—"

MacMorran regarded him thoughtfully. "It's not like you to be pessimistic."

Anthony shook his head. "It wasn't like Coventry to have his fortune told."

Chapter XVII
ANTIQUES

When Mr. Bathurst reached Brighton station via the Brighton Belle out of Victoria, he crossed to a side-platform and boarded a train which announced itself as destined for Portsmouth Harbour. This train went through the stations of Hove and Portslade, and in surprisingly quick time landed him at Southwick. Arrived here, he first of all passed under the railway arch and walked to the water-front. Here the prospect he considered was surprisingly unattractive and uninviting. Though perhaps not so entirely industrial in character as its near neighbour Portslade, Southwick, on the whole, disappointed him. He walked a hundred yards or so in each direction before deciding to turn back from the foreshore into the town itself. Improvement soon manifested itself. Little inns there were in plenty. Striking inland, Mr. Bathurst found himself facing the green where cricket has been and can be played in the real Sussex spirit. Near by, he found a football field with yet another inn on the opposite corner. Mr. Bathurst entered this establishment, ordered a tankard of bitter, opened a conversation with the stout man who served him, and eventually, when the time had become ripe, inquired of his host as to the whereabouts of Brunskill Corner.

"Brunskill Corner, sir?"

Mr. Bathurst nodded.

"Brunskill Corner's a good mile walk from here. Every bit of that. Towards Shoreham. Turn right when you leave here, cut across the far corner of the green, then turn right again, and carry straight on along the front. You can't miss the turning. There's a pretty big building yard just by it. You'll be bound to see that, sir."

Mr. Bathurst thanked his informant and set off for Brunskill Corner. Twenty minutes hard walking brought him to it. There was the boat-building yard that the landlord of the inn had specially mentioned and there, too, but a few yards distant, was the 'antique' shop of Gaunt, Marston and Co. Mr. Bathurst, without hesitation, made his way into the shop. A bell announced the fact. Behind the counter stood a tall young man. The chief features of his face were his abnormal height of cheek-bone, sandy hair, and a wealth of freckles. His arms, too, were unusually long and thin. His mouth was slightly open. "Yes," he said rather eagerly, "do you want to look at anything?"

Anthony gave a comprehensive glance round. The shop held glass of all kinds, old coins, old books, old pictures, old furniture, old candlesticks, old time-pieces of many types, old silver, and old pewter. Every inch of the place seemed to be filled with something which spoke eloquently of the tale of the years. Anthony thought that he could never have seen a shop so full to overflowing of the genuine 'antique.' He smiled at the young man with the high cheek-bones.

"As a matter of fact," he said, "the boot's on the other foot. I want you to look at something. But first of all I'll introduce myself." Mr. Bathurst handed over his card, endorsed by Sir Austin Kemble.

The suspicion of a frown crossed the young man's face.

"I don't know that I quite—"

"You will in a moment," urged Anthony, "because I'm going to help you." He took from his pocket a cutting from the *Morning Message* of a few days ago. It was MacMorran's appeal to the public concerning the identification of Coventry's handwriting. Anthony smoothed it out and presented it to the young fellow behind the counter. "Take a good look at this. Have you ever seen it before?"

Cheek-bones took the cutting and glanced at it curiously. His features underwent a change. "Why—yes. This appeared in the morning papers one day last week. I remember seeing it."

"Ten out of ten," remarked Anthony. The man frowned at him. Mr. Bathurst went on at once. "Did it cause you any particular reaction?"

Cheek-bones shook his head rather slowly.

"No reaction at all?"

Another head shake. "No reaction at all. But I don't understand. Why—should it have?"

Anthony slowly nodded his head. "I think so. Let me demonstrate to you." He took the part-words of the cutting, and with his pen filled in the missing letters. "There," he said, "there you have the card up to the fall of the last wicket. Full score and bowling analysis. Gaunt, Marston and Co., Brunskill Corner, Southwick. This is Southwick and also Brunskill Corner and you, I take it, represent Gaunt, Marston and Co. Hence my suggestion concerning a possible reaction."

"My name is Alec Marston, certainly. My people have been in this business for generations. I can honestly say that our name is respected everywhere. I haven't the least idea what you mean by writing this." He looked again at the fragments from the *Morning Message*. Astonishment still remained on his face at the transformation which Anthony's additional letters had brought about. "Astonishing," he murmured. "I should never have dreamt of such a thing." He looked up at Anthony again. "This is to do with the Coventry murder case, I presume?"

"Entirely."

"Well, you have me at a complete loss. In fact, I'm absolutely bewildered. I don't mind admitting it."

"You don't recognize the handwriting, then, as the late Mr. Coventry's?"

The astonishment on the young man's face was increasing. "Certainly not. How can I? I don't know for certain that I have ever seen it."

"He has never used it, then, in any of his transactions with you?"

"Transactions with us? Say—I don't get this at all. I don't get any of it as far as I know. I have never seen Coventry. He has had *no* transactions with us. Until he was murdered and his name appeared in the Press I can safely say that I had never heard of the man or of his existence. That is why I am at such an utter loss to understand this and why you're here." He tapped the cutting from the *Morning Message*.

Anthony was brought up with a jerk. It is beside the point to say that he was surprised. Young Marston's statement had gone a long way towards destroying a theory which he had begun to build up. His calculations were completely undermined. A question rioted through his brain unceasingly. One, perhaps, to which he should have given closer consideration before. *Why* had Coventry written this address? It would be absurd to think that Mrs. Coventry and Valerie Moffatt had told him anything but the truth. He saw that Marston was watching him carefully. Suddenly he thought he began to see a little light. An explanation occurred to him. "The real point is, I suppose, that whereas you have never heard of Coventry, Coventry had heard of you. Which, also, was a point I had overlooked."

Marston looked a little puzzled. "Well, sir, as I said just now, we're well known throughout the trade and to almost everybody interested in our particular line. I'll grant you all that willingly. But I don't know that the ordinary person—what you'd call the man in the street—would have heard of us."

"He hadn't in my own case," returned Anthony with a grin.

"Well, there you are, sir, you see what I mean. That's exactly my point. To the experts in our game we're almost a household word. To the ordinary man in the street—well—we're an also ran. I don't think I can put it more plainly."

"Exactly—and that's just what I'm beginning to be afraid of." Anthony had begun to understand the dimensions of the barrier in his way.

Marston nodded. "So I suppose that I shan't be able to help you in any way, shall I?"

"Well, we'll see about that. Let's have a closer look at things. Suppose we assume for the sake of argument that Coventry *was* interested in your line of business. Granted that—he *would* know of your reputation! That follows logically. *If* he knew of your reputation, it is conceivable—going a step further—that he may have written your name down for somebody as a recommendation. That's a reasonable possibility, isn't it?"

"Definitely," replied Alec Marston. "That actually does happen. Often! We find that many of our regular clients recommend us to others. Coventry, through knowing *of* us, may well have done so. I expect we may even have been recommended to him in the first place."

"Now think of this, then. You can recall nothing that has happened recently in your business which would connect up with Coventry in any way? Any delivery to an address you may have made near to him, for example? He lived in London, you will remember—at Danvers Gate."

Marston shook his head with complete certainty. "Nothing at all, sir."

"You are quite sure of that? You will pardon my persistence, I know."

Marston reached for a book. "I can easily confirm it." He turned over several pages. Anthony kept silent. "No delivery from here to the West End of London for several weeks. Most of our customers live in the country or by the sea. In the better residential districts."

"I see. That's unfortunate. Well—I'm sorry to have put you to so much trouble."

"No trouble at all, sir. Only too pleased to help. Afraid I haven't, though."

"Not your fault. You did your best." Anthony felt completely baffled. There must, he reasoned, be a clue here of some sort, but how in Hades was he going to put his hand on it? Marston seemed to sympathize with him in his difficulty.

"I can tell how you're thinking. You're all burned up as to why Coventry wrote our name down. I reckon I should be, too, if I were in your position and had your job to do."

"Thanks." Anthony looked round again. "You've got a wonderful collection of stuff here."

"Yes," returned Marston, with a touch of professional pride, "we take a bit of beating in our line. You see, sir—there's what I should describe as two classes of custom in our trade. First of all there's the bread-and-butter stuff—people see something in the window or in the shop itself that they fancy—and they pop in and buy it over the counter. Sometimes, for example, they set their minds on a special piece that catches their eye—in they come, ask the price—and if it's too dear for them to pay for it at once, they'll leave a small deposit on it. Say a dollar, or even half a dollar—and I'll put the article on one side for them. They'll usually come and collect it the next day or the day after."

"Really! I should hardly have expected that."

"Oh—yes, it's quite a common occurrence in our trade. I can give you an instance I had only the day before yesterday. I'll give you the full facts. I had three very fine old pewter tankards in the window of the kind you don't run across every day. Picked 'em up at a sale near Horsham about a month ago. Came from an old Sussex farm-house. A lady spotted 'em, going by, had a closer look at them through the window and came in here to inquire the price. When I told her what I wanted for 'em, she found she hadn't enough cash with her to complete the purchase. So she left a dollar deposit and popped in to pick 'em up later. And who do you think she was?"

"I haven't the foggiest," responded Anthony.

"Wife of one of the 'tecs at Brighton—Claude Salter. I should have thought you would have known him. The fellow that arrested Torlani, the murderer."

"Interesting—very."

Marston warmed to his subject. "Well—that's one class of custom we get. The other's what I should describe as our 'expert' trade. The stuff with the jam on it. Requests come to us from all quarters of England, Ireland, and Scotland. I'll give you examples of it. One gentleman will want a medallion traced. Another may ask for a pair of genuine Elizabethan candlesticks, a third may require a copy of a well-known or valuable picture, a fourth may want a special piece of Sheraton or Chippendale furniture, and another might send to us for certain glass or china or even a valuable coin, such as a William and Mary halfpenny. Only a month ago I matched some exquisite Crown Derby for a gentleman in London named Bretherton. Gaunt, Marston and Co. stand for all that. I hope that I have made myself moderately clear to you, sir."

Anthony saw by this time that the heart and soul of Marston were in his business . . . the business to which he had succeeded through a line of ancestry. Anthony again let his eyes take in most of what the shop held. Marston quickly became his guide and counsellor. "That brandy glass there, sir, with the 'N' and the coronet, was given by Napoleon Bonaparte to the skipper of the *Bellerophon*. When the Emperor was on his way to St. Helena. Those cruets and the piece of black bread close to them, are relics of the siege of Paris. No, sir, that picture's not a genuine Rubens—it's only a copy. Oh, excellent, I grant you. We know where to place commissions for that sort of stuff. I can undertake commissions for copies of Raphaels, Rubenses, Titians, Giorgiones, Van Dycks, Murillos, Tintorettos— anything you like. Done by the smartest men at the game in Europe. It's the blending that counts. The canvases are cut . . . it takes time, of course, because they have to be submitted to the ageing process before being mounted on well worm-eaten wood."

Anthony nodded.

Marston went on: "Those two egg-cups belonged to Charles and Mary Lamb. This sampler was worked by Florence Nightingale. Now—here's an interesting curiosity—these two pairs of gloves belonged to one of the Popes of Rome. I forget which one it was. Early in the nineteenth century. This old lute is supposed to have been the property of Mary Seaton, one of the Queen's Marys—you remember, sir, the companion of Mary Queen of Scots. Those things will give you some idea of the class of our business."

Anthony assented. "As you observe—extremely interesting. I'm glad I came to Southwick, Marston. I have learned a great deal."

"Although you have failed in your primary object?"

"Yes, although as you say. Still"—Anthony laughed as he spoke—"there is always this to it—I can go away and have another 'think,' can't I?"

Marston smiled. "Have you got another think coming already?"

"Don't know yet. Not sure. That remains to be seen."

"Yes, I suppose so. That sort of thing's part of your job. You know your difficulties—just as I know mine when they come to me. Our experience teaches us. Experience more than anything."

This time Anthony smiled. "As it happens, I have another think already. One while you wait, so to speak. Tell me if you have ever done any business of your special class with anybody of the name of Rayner?"

"I shall have to refer to my books. Never mind—no trouble. Half a second." Marston assembled three or four account books in front of him. He began to search.

"A *Mrs*. Rayner. Living at a private hotel in Riverhead, near Sevenoaks, Kent. An inquiry re an old pack of Bezique cards. That was over three years ago."

"Nothing since then?"

"No. Nothing since then."

"Try again. Take the name of 'Sere.'"

"S-E-A-R?"

"No—S-E-R-E."

Marston looked. "No. Never. I've no one of that name in a period of the last ten years."

Anthony thought hard. He might as well, while he was here, be as thorough in his inquiries as possible. "Crayle?"

Further search by Marston. "No—no Crayle at all."

"Moffatt?" Marston flicked more pages. "I've a Moffatt who wrote to me from Rutherglen in Scotland. Again, over three years ago. An inquiry concerning a Jacobite medallion. I supplied it."

"Try 'Palmer,' do you mind?"

"Palmer! I think I *did* have a 'Palmer.' Yes—about fifteen months ago. An elderly gentleman, I think it was."

"What address?"

"Ealing. 22 Hanger Avenue."

Anthony made a note of the address. "Now try 'Austin,' will you? And then I think I needn't bother you any more."

"Certainly. 'In' or 'en?'" asked Marston.

Anthony couldn't reply with certainty. "Either or both," he compromised.

"Yes." Marston nodded his head. Eventually he ran across the entry. "We did business with a 'J. Austin' three months ago almost to the day. Provided a set of old-fashioned champagne glasses."

"Address?" said Anthony hopefully.

"11 Stannard Road, Wimbledon."

Again Anthony made a suitable note.

"Austin," said Marston, "is a fairly common name."

"Austin," replied Anthony gravely, "is, I'm afraid, an exceedingly common name."

CHAPTER XVIII
MUCH ARGUMENT

ALL the way home from Southwick Anthony argued and wrestled with himself. In this fashion. The man who murdered Coventry must have had a fairly intimate knowledge of him and his habits. In the first place he must have known that the name Silas Montgomery would be something like a talisman of interest as far as Coventry was concerned. In the second place, and here Anthony was inclined to concentrate, Coventry must have written down for him, for *some reason* or another, at some *time* or another, the name of the firm 'Gaunt, Marston and Co.,' and the address 'Brunskill Corner, Southwick.' Now why—this latter especially? Between Brighton and Victoria, Anthony Bathurst cudgelled his brains for a satisfactory answer to the question. "Who was it that wanted the address and why had he wanted it?" Yes—that was the most important side of it. *Why* had he wanted the address? If Anthony could but put his hand on the purpose behind the giving of that address, he felt that he would be a long way towards the ultimate solution of the problem. Rarely had he had a case in which he had run round, as it were, in so many circles. It seemed to him that for Coventry to have passed on the name and address of 'Gaunt, Marston and Co.,' he must have had more than the ordinary man's knowledge of the firm's existence, and peculiar reputation. *Despite* the statement of young Marston! In what particular direction, therefore, had Coventry been interested in 'Gaunt, Marston and Co.'? There, it seemed to Anthony, as he sat thinking, lay the kernel of the problem. He thought again of Austin's story. The interview that had been fixed between Coventry and the fake 'Silas Montgomery.' At two o'clock in the morning in Coventry's private room. In Coventry's room. That was the venue. The man had gone to kill Coventry in his own room. Extraordinary, that! Might it not have been easier to have decoyed him in some *way* from his own room and done the job somewhere else? Why beard the lion, as it were, in his own den? Put your head in his mouth almost? Was the *venue* important? Coventry's room! It began to appear to Anthony that it was. That it must have been! Then his heart missed a beat. That parcel which the presumed murderer had taken there? What was that? He hadn't left it behind him . . . or even the contents of it . . . whatever they might be . . . because the room after Coventry's death, according to Rayner, *and* Philip Coventry *and* Susanna Coventry (all three of them), was just as it had been before Coventry's death. Singular, that. Damned funny—whichever way you looked at it. Thus, in constant repetition—Anthony's thoughts in the train—between Brighton and Victoria. Nothing had gone *from* the room—almost universal testimony to that. Nothing had gone *into* it—similar testimony. The room was just as it had been. Normal in every particular. Anthony decided emphatically at that moment that he must look at the room again. There was the chance that he had missed the vital something. He was so impressed by this exercise of thinking that he determined to drive to the house in Danvers Gate immediately he arrived at Victoria. He looked out of the window. He saw the red roofs and miscellaneous housing variety of Purley and its intimate country. Not long to go now. Anthony looked at his watch. What he saw satisfied him. Yes—he would be able to get to the house in Danvers Gate in nice time. He trusted that he would have the good fortune to find people in. He picked up a taxi almost immediately and told the driver Danvers Gate. As the vehicle gathered pace, Anthony thought of Gordon Lucas Sewell, licence number 5485, and how he had turned his taxi in the same direction on the morning of the murder. Carrying a chance fare he had picked up at the corner of Valentia Street. Mr. Bathurst thought that he would look out for the corner of Valentia Street. He would be able the better then to calculate times and distances . . . questions that had interested him for some considerable time. Questions of possible importance, too. When he passed Valentia Street, Anthony checked on his watch. Later on he noted the interval that had elapsed between then and his arrival at Danvers Gate. Almost exactly ten minutes. Ten minutes within a few seconds. Anthony remembered that Sewell had given the time as eight minutes. From 1.50 to 1.58. That variation would be accounted for, probably, by the difference in traffic conditions. The road would be much clearer at the time when Sewell drove than it was now. Anthony paid his driver and went straight to the Coventry house. He was pleased to hear that Mrs. Coventry was in. With her were Crayle, Palmer, and Philip Coventry. The same company that Anthony had met before. As previously, Anthony apologized for what he termed an inconvenient intrusion. Susanna Coventry seemed very sure of herself. Anthony, for a time, finessed as to the real reason for his latest visit. Much general conversation ensued. Philip Coventry was as disgruntled as ever. His criticisms of Scotland Yard, and of the police generally, were even more trenchant than they had been on the previous occasion Anthony had met him. Every other remark he made was tinged with cynicism and salted with satire. Anthony treated him patiently and refused steadfastly to be baited by anything he said. He had met people of this type before and was experienced in the handling of them. Crayle was much as usual. Cheerfulness and a kind of semi-depression alternated with him almost regularly. Anthony judged that he was still chafing under Valerie Moffatt's stern decree with regard to their postponed marriage. Palmer was frank and open—as seemed to be his wont. At his ease and always the complete master of himself and his surroundings. Anthony deliberately touched on various points connected with the murder. As though he were making additional inquiries, and never suggesting that he was in any way nearing a solution. The field of suspects was in his opinion still too large for him to force successfully the hand of the guilty party. There was ample time for that, he considered, when two or three people had been eliminated. Slowly and by very gradual steps, Anthony came to his ultimate point.

"And now before I go, Mrs. Coventry, would it be convenient for me to have another look at Mr. Coventry's room? I've been having a special talk with Inspector MacMorran on the general situation, and there's one point upon which I'd like to refresh my mind."

"Certainly, Mr. Bathurst. I'll take you in myself." Susanna Coventry rose. Palmer, always the gentleman, went to the door of the library and opened it for his hostess. Mrs. Coventry took precedence, as was natural. "There you are, Mr. Bathurst—just as it was when you were here before. Not a speck of it's been touched. I've been careful to see to that. Inspector MacMorran's been down again once or twice and another man called here and took some photographs. I've given orders to the maids that they're not even to dust the room. In all the circumstances, I think that's just as well, don't you, Mr. Bathurst?"

"Oh—undoubtedly. Where there's dust there's danger."

Susanna Coventry looked at him sharply, but Anthony's face was passive and unruffled. "Shall I stay in here with you?" she contented herself with saying.

"With pleasure, Mrs. Coventry. That is, of course, if you care to. Now I just want to satisfy myself on one or two points in respect of this room. Some little time has elapsed since I was in here, you know."

"Do you mind if I ask you rather a pertinent question, Mr. Bathurst?"

"Not in the least, Mrs. Coventry. What's your question?"

"Do you think . . . do you believe . . . right down in your heart . . . that the police will ever find the murderer of my husband?"

"Frankly, Mrs. Coventry?"

"Frankly, Mr. Bathurst. I want you to answer my question in all sincerity. To the best of your own knowledge and belief."

"Well, then, I am certain that your husband's murderer *will* be found, arrested and punished. If not by the police . . . by somebody acting for them. Why—I might even catch him myself! You never know. There are more unlikely things." Anthony smiled at her.

"That gives me heart," she said, with a sigh of relief. "But tell me, Mr. Bathurst, have you managed to establish anything like a motive yet for my husband's murder? I know that that was the point which was troubling you when you were here last."

Anthony temporized with her. "Not exactly—but I can truthfully say that we are well on the way." He fed her astutely. "I can assert with confidence that we shall have most of the threads in our hands before the week's out. You can be assured of that, Mrs. Coventry."

She nodded as though the news he had given her had comforted her. Anthony made a tour of the room in which Coventry had died. Mrs. Coventry went back to the others and spoke to Hubert Palmer. Anthony was making an attempt to memorize everything in the room. He had attempted something of the kind when he had visited it before. This time, the mental inventory was to be much more comprehensive. Anthony's mind went back to an evening in his life when he had been but eight years old. At a Christmas party he had carried off first prize (a box of inferior chocolates) for remembering more than any other competitor the names of various small articles which had been scattered on a tray. If he could do it then, he surely ought to do it now. The note-books, the different furniture pieces, the position of the telephone, the books in Coventry's library, the superb carpet, the few ornaments, the pictures, the book-case itself, the rather cunningly-wrought ink-stand, fine ash-trays of a massive type, a sort of beaten metal, and then finally the *portière*. Anthony's eyes again ravaged the room. Yes—he had missed something! There was a carved model of a sampan hanging on the side wall. Anthony went close and inspected it. He certainly hadn't seen the like of it before. He felt it was somewhat out of place in a room of the character of a library. But it showed no signs of having been tampered with. Anthony had no doubt of that. Annoyance grew in Mr. Bathurst's mind. There seemed to be nothing in the room, after all, to excite the slightest comment. The sampan model, perhaps, but beyond the fact that it was unusual, there was nothing else about it to cause him the most trifling misgiving. And yet he must obey the promptings of his intelligence. Anthony took one last glance round the room. He endeavoured to take a complete mental photograph of it. Out of this exercise, every corner and every significant feature of it, would be impressed, as it were, on the retina of his mind. This was the best and the only other thing that he *could* do before he left to rejoin Mrs. Coventry and the others.

"Any luck?" asked Palmer cordially, as he met him on the threshold.

"Don't know. Afraid not. Don't seem any nearer than I was before. Inspiration hides from me. Eternally fugitive. Hangs her head almost in sheer silence."

Crayle smiled. "Perhaps she wants you to go after her. Have you thought of that? That's conceivable, you know, if she's a woman, as you suggest."

"Pursuit on my part—uncontrolled—might drive her farther away," Anthony answered him, in the same mood.

Palmer entered the lists of argument. "Suppose the pursuit's controlled, might that make a difference?"

"It will still remain pursuit," riposted Anthony.

"Then you must play her at her own game," put in Peter Crayle. "As Valerie isn't here, it doesn't matter so much what I say about her sex. When the cat's away—"

"Peter," cried Palmer, with banter in his voice, "surely that's going a bit too far. Concerning the lady of your heart, too—I should advise you to watch your step, my lad."

Anthony said good-bye to Mrs. Coventry. He thanked her for her courtesy. She looked up at him as he held her hand. "I'll remember what you said a few moments ago, Mr. Bathurst. In view of that, I shall expect to hear important news at any moment. Besides my own anxiety—there are Valerie and Peter to be considered. I must think of their happiness. Don't forget that."

"I don't and I won't, Mrs. Coventry. You may rely on that." Mr. Bathurst paid his respects to the others and took his departure.

Philip Coventry, when he had gone, tossed his head. "No nearer than he was before," he quoted. "Nothing like facing up to failure—I must say. Well—I didn't expect any more, so I shan't be disappointed. Nobody's life is safe these days. If you ask me, the whole of our police force requires reorganizing. Too much la-di-da college stuff. And the sooner it's reorganized the better."

There was an awkward silence. After all, Coventry had lost a father and his mother a husband. There were perhaps both reason and excuse for personal bitterness. Palmer endeavoured to adjust the awkwardness of the situation. "Well—you never know—even now the police may have something up their sleeve. They often pounce when least expected. Let's hope it will be like that in this case."

"You don't get very fat on hope," countered Philip Coventry.

Crayle ranged himself with Palmer. "Hang it all—you must give them a little more time, Phil. Like me—possess your soul in patience."

"I know," growled Coventry, "jam—but always jam to-morrow! Sorry and all that—but those sentiments of yours cut no ice with me. They leave me stone cold. I stand on results—not empty promises."

Crayle grinned. "Hope, my dear boy—may be emptied in delight."

But Phil Coventry turned away—he would have none of him!

CHAPTER XIX
MR. BATHURST STARTS AGAIN

ANTHONY lolled his length in an easy chair and smoked tobacco. Good strong satisfying stuff. The smoke clouds made a wispy halo round his head. His best brains were being brought to bear upon the problem of the association of the dead Aubrey Coventry with the living firm of Gaunt, Marston and Co., of Brunskill Corner, Southwick in Sussex. He was determined before he went to bed to discover the common factor between Coventry and these dealers in antiques. For that there was a common factor, he felt positive. At some time in his life Coventry must have made contact with the firm in some way. It was Anthony's task to discover what this contact had been. He deliberately retraced his steps. The fake Silas Montgomery had nominated Coventry's library as the venue for their sensational appointment. This was not only according to Rayner,

Coventry's secretary, but had also been corroborated by that shadowy figure in the background—Austin.

It was reasonable, therefore, to regard the room as highly important. As he had argued to himself yesterday. That was the point, as far as he could remember, where he had stuck. At that and the parcel which the murderer had brought to the room with him. Anthony conjured back the details of the room. Where, in the equation, did Coventry's room where he was murdered, equal the firm of antique dealers? That exactly was the problem which he had to solve before he could really begin to move. He went through the various details of the room again with the utmost care. As he was remembering them out of his latest visit to Danvers Gate. The note-books . . . the telephone . . . the table . . . the chairs . . . . Suddenly Anthony sat up and gripped the sides of his chair. What a blind fool he had been to be sure! The pictures! He recalled a phrase that Alec Marston had used. "No, sir, that picture is not a genuine Rubens—it's only a copy." Why—Coventry had had two pictures in his room. They were still there! Anthony knew them only too well. They were copies of Rembrandt's 'Saskia at her Toilet,' and of what Anthony imagined to be originally a Holbein. A red-haired girl wearing a dress of the Tudor period. He remembered that the pictures faced each other. One on each wall. They were hung almost directly opposite to each other. Anthony stopped again. Another idea had flashed into his brain. . . . His fingers quivered with nervous excitement. Good Lord! . . . why hadn't he thought of it before? Zylphara's words . . . words that had come to him out of her trance. What were they now? He tried to recall them. Anthony flogged his brain for an exactitude of remembrance. 'Two women.' . . . That would be Saskia and the other . . . whoever she was . . . 'not friendly' . . . 'they oppose each other' . . . 'it is because of these women'—that had been the precise moment when the clairvoyante's voice had trailed away into nothingness. 'They oppose each other.' They did! Of course. Wall facing wall. . . . How doubly, even trebly blind he had been! Holmes's words to Watson came to him. 'Lecoq! Lecoq was a miserable bungler.' He had been worse than even Lecoq himself had ever been. Mr. Bathurst could think of no more damning censure. Then something else came to him which fitted beautifully into the new scheme of things.

The parcel which the blue-overalled man had brought with him in the taxi . . . just about the size of the pictures on Coventry's wall. But he had brought it *to* the house in Danvers Gate . . . surely if it were theft . . . he would have carried the parcel out of the house when he went away! Something wrong there! What was the real meaning of the parcel? There must be something else about it. . . . Anthony cudgelled his brains for the answer to the question. Almost immediately he began to castigate himself again. Why in the name of conscience hadn't he asked Marston if any man in blue overalls had recently done business with him? Better than to have plied him with that string of wearisome surnames. That particular question would have probed right to the marrow of the matter. Yes—he had missed a golden opportunity there. Sheer neglect! He had done no more than chance his arm in the manner of the most clumsy amateur. He had already made so many mistakes—since he started on the case—he surely couldn't make another. For one thing it would be against the law of average—and he believed in the law of average. Thus Anthony flagellated himself. He knocked the burnt tobacco from his pipe. The white flaky ash left the bowl easily. He filled the pipe again. He was contemplating his next move. Which should it be? There were several that promised well. Anthony thought them over carefully one by one. In the order of their present attractiveness. He weighed the pros and cons of each. With quick confidence he made his decision. He would communicate at once with young Marston. For the moment, at least, Marston was the king-pin. . . . Anthony pulled a piece of writing-paper towards him and produced his fountain-pen. This job he was about to do wanted thinking over. A careless phrase, or an ill-chosen one, might put Marston off and thus militate against the smooth working of his plan. Anthony deliberated. First his address and the date. Then he began to write:

'DEAR MR. MARSTON,

'You will remember my call yesterday at your place and the reason which brought me there. Since that visit I have made a most interesting and important discovery.'

Anthony carefully underlined two words.

'In view of this development I feel that I must consult you again with regard to a matter concerning which your advice as an expert will be invaluable to me. Indeed, I am quite sincere when I say. that you are probably the only man in the country who can supply me with this particular advice. Will you, therefore, meet me at Victoria the day after to-morrow at about half-past eleven in the morning? If so, I shall be eternally grateful. Select the train which suits both you and the time nominated. I shall wait until you come. I hate to mention it, but I shall be happy, of course, to defray all expenses. After all—business is business.

'Sincerely yours,

'ANTHONY L. BATHURST.'

He re-read what he had written. It would do for his purpose, he considered. It was just enough. Neither too much nor too little. That letter should be dispatched to young Marston at once. The natural alternative, to send a telegram, would gain but little time and might put him off. There was just the chance of it. Some people reacted unfavourably to telegrams. They regarded them, Anthony thought, as bordering on the peremptory. Marston would get his letter early on the morrow. That would give him ample time to come up. Mr. Bathurst slipped out and caught the last post. As he went to bed that night he felt more satisfied with his progress than for many days. He was on the right track at last. He would take old Andrew MacMorran to Victoria to meet young Marston. From there they would go 'to the pictures' . . . in the house at Danvers Gate.

CHAPTER XX
THE PROFESSIONAL TOUCH

WHEN Alec Marston came through the barrier at Victoria at 11.28 on the following morning but one he found Anthony Bathurst, whom he knew, and Chief-Inspector Andrew MacMorran, whom he did not know, waiting for him. He walked straight up to Anthony, smiling all over his face and cordially shook hands. Anthony produced the Inspector. "Glad you've come, Mr. Marston."

"Only too pleased. Bit of an adventure for me, you know. Life is pretty humdrum down in Sussex for most months of the year. We chaps just jump at a bit of variety. Well, where do we go to from here?"

"First of all," replied Anthony, "we will drink. I can think of no more attractive exercise. What do you say, Andrew?"

"If that means you're payin'—yes." He winked at Marston.

"Andrew," said Anthony severely, "is it recorded in quires and places where they sing that the last time you stood a round, Sir Walter Raleigh knocked over your tankard of mead . . . or was it Simon de Montfort that was the culprit? . . . Here we are."

He led the way through the doors to the buffet. "Find a table, Andrew, and make Mr. Marston comfortable, will you? What shall it be? Three beers?" Anthony went to the counter and asked for supplies, He joined the others with the drinks. He looked whimsically towards the Inspector. "Shall I start, Andrew?"

"Probably," returned MacMorran drily, "I'd lay a tenner on it."

"Good. Now, Mr. Marston, I told you in my letter I wanted your expert advice. Without any hesitation you have come to give it. Very sporting of you. The Inspector and I appreciate it. In that letter also I suggested that you were probably the only man in the country who could give me the particular expert advice that I needed. That was by no means a *façon de parler*. I meant every word that I wrote."

Marston nodded, and flushed at the compliment. "You can count on me, gentlemen, I'll give you my word on that. Now tell me what it is you want."

"I want to talk to you about pictures. I believe that the conversation is going to prove highly interesting."

"It should be," Marston smiled.

"First of all, I'll talk about a picture which I'll describe to you to the best of my memory and ability."

"Go on," said Marston, with a grin. "I'll listen and try to help you."

Anthony took a long drink. He began to speak. "The picture is of a young woman in Tudor dress. Call her a girl. To be nearer the mark. She is red-haired. As far as I can remember, she is wearing a necklace with a pendant attachment. It struck me when I saw it for the first time that it was a copy of one of Holbein's pictures. I think I can recall having seen one at Hampton Court when I was in my teens." Anthony noticed that Marston was smiling with excitement. "Well, Mr. Marston," he said, "does it happen that you have something to tell me?"

"I should think I have—and no error. I am able to solve your first difficulty." Marston leant forward and placed a hand on Anthony's arm. "Listen to this. Within the last month we executed a commission to supply a copy of Holbein's 'Princess Elizabeth.' That's the name of the picture you remember seeing at Hampton Court. You were quite right. I told you when you called at our place the other day that we supplied copies of well-known pictures to order, didn't I?"

Anthony rubbed his hands and nodded. Even MacMorran felt a touch of excitement when he heard Marston's statement.

"You did, did you?" said Mr. Bathurst to Alec Marston. "A commission—eh? Whom for?"

"Oh—let me see—what was the name now? I expect I shall be able to remember if you give me long enough. It was a young fellow who gave me the order. Horn-rimmed glasses and toothbrush moustache. I dealt with him myself. Chap about two or three and twenty."

"What address did he give?"

"None at all. He called and collected the copies when we had them ready for him."

"Naturally," exclaimed Anthony ruefully. "Not so good. He would! And would give a false name as well."

"You luck's still out," grinned Marston who, it must be admitted, was thoroughly enjoying what was for him an entirely novel situation.

"I haven't finished yet," retorted Anthony, "by a long chalk. You wait. Prepare yourself for yet another question. This rime I happen to know more about the particular picture. Thanks to Charles Laughton and Elsa Lanchester. To say nothing of Gertrude Lawrence."

Marston could scarcely restrain himself. Words trembled on his lips.

Anthony temporarily ignored him, however, and went on with the utmost nonchalance. "When you executed your commission for a copy of Holbein's 'Princess Elizabeth,' did you by any chance do one also of Rembrandt's 'Saskia at her Toilet'? Because, before you answer me, Mr. Marston, I'd like to place a nice little bet that you did."

Marston was in like a flash. "You win, Mr. Bathurst. All the way. It was a double order, and the two pictures were the two that you have named. Now you must let me buy some beer. You deserve it!"

"D'ye hear that, Andrew?" cried Anthony, prodding MacMorran in the ribs.

"Which?" said the Inspector. "About the pictures or concerning the beer?"

"We are now," exclaimed Anthony triumphantly, "arriving at something which has so far eluded us. The question of motive, Andrew. Before the morning has entirely gone, you will see better what I mean. At least, I hope so." Marston returned with the beer. Anthony taxed him again. "Tell me, Mr. Marston, what would be the value of the two originals?"

Marston's eyes fairly goggled at the idea. He made rapid calculations. On the back of an envelope. "Put it at £120,000 and you won't be a long way out."

"What?" cried MacMorran. His movement caused him to spill beer. Mr. Bathurst raised his eyebrows reprovingly at him. "Hear what comfortable words Mr. Marston says, Andrew! Extraordinarily comfortable. Over a hundred thousand Jimmy O' Goblins! Much more appetisin' than a kick on the knee-cap or a sock on the jaw."

MacMorran admitted: "That explains a lot."

"It certainly does, Andrew."

Marston interrupted. He was still in a state of eager excitement. "But just a minute, gentlemen. I'm not sure that you aren't jumping to conclusions. I don't want you to start building up too much on wrong premises. These pictures were only copies of no real value. You aren't overlooking that fact, are you?"

"*Your* pictures were copies, Marston," returned Anthony drily. "I'm wondering concerning the use to which they were to be put. As a matter of fact, I have a question for you on the tip of my tongue with regard to that point."

"And that question is?"

"Tell me all you know of the two originals. Can you do much for me in that direction? If you can, it will be a tremendous help."

Marston nodded, as eagerly as ever. "Oh, yes . . . I can tell you quite a lot."

"Take the Rembrandt picture first, then—do you mind: What do you know about that?"

"'Saskia at her Toilet'? Well—I can tell you something with regard to that which you'll find very interesting. You've made me think twice—I can tell you. If my memory serves me correctly, it was the property of a South African mining magnate who died suddenly a few years ago. I believe that it was his original intention that the picture should be sold by his trustees to pay the extremely heavy death duties on his estate. But his plans went awry. For this reason. As luck would have it, thieves broke into his house—it was somewhere in Kent, I fancy—and stole the Rembrandt together with several other old masters that he had owned."

Anthony nodded. "This is good. Just what I wanted to hear. Go on, Marston."

Marston obliged. "This robbery was perhaps one of the greatest art robberies of the century. The total value of the pictures stolen was in the neighbourhood of £100,000. But I haven't finished yet. Now listen to the sequel. Because you can almost call it that. A big reward was offered by the trustees. Some of the pictures were recovered but—mark my words, gentlemen—*not* the Rembrandt. I *think* there was an arrest."

"I remember the case," contributed MacMorran. "You're right. There *was* an arrest. It was the belief of my people at the Yard that the pictures which weren't recovered were burned by the thieves. A yarn went the rounds that they made a bonfire of them. Personally—I didn't take it in. Bit too tall for my way of thinking."

"It looks to me as though you were right, Andrew. Was anything more ever heard of the 'Saskia,' Marston?"

"As far as I know, Mr. Bathurst, nothing. That's why I'm beginning to think that you may be on to something. I told you just now that you'd made me think twice." Marston nodded his head confirmingly.

Anthony came in again. "Now tell me about the presumed Holbein. What was the title you gave it? 'Princess Elizabeth'?"

"Well, here in this case—the going isn't quite so good. For this reason. It will take some explaining, I'm afraid." Marston hesitated. Anthony waited for him. He appeared to be thinking hard. "It's like this. Let me put it to you in this way. Holbein is believed to have come to England in the year 1536. He is supposed to have come to this country on a two years' commission to paint portraits for Henry VIII. At this time, I should say that Elizabeth the Princess was about three. I fancy—speaking without the book—that she was born in 1533. Yes—she was three. Now Holbein is known to have painted her several times. The most famous picture of her is, of course, the one known as the 'Hampton Court Holbein.' In this, Elizabeth seems to be about nine or ten. Which means to say that the portrait must have been painted not long before Holbein died. That was in 1543. He died of the plague—Henry VIII had been so pleased with him that he had doubled his salary to keep him in England. But—and here comes the exciting part of the story—from your point of view that is, he is *supposed* to have painted another portrait of Elizabeth just about the same time as he painted the Hampton Court picture. Elizabeth, according to history, gave the picture to her brother, the then King Edward VI, when she was about eighteen years of age. But the most exhaustive inquiries by generations of art experts and historians generally, have failed to discover what eventually did become of this picture. Notice the similarity of conditions *now* between this Holbein and the Rembrandt."

"Just a minute, Marston. Something else I want to know." The interruption came from Anthony. "Was the Holbein at Hampton Court very much like this other picture that's missing? Can you tell me that?"

"Well—here's the rub. They are *believed* to be almost exactly alike, Mr. Bathurst. Elizabeth is a young girl in each of the pictures and is about the same age. She wore a head-dress in the missing picture almost identical with the one she wears in the Hampton Court one. The costume worn, too, is very similar in both cut and style. In size as well, it would appear that the two pictures correspond—according to all the reports that we have about them. Have I made myself clear to you, Mr. Bathurst?"

"Quite clear, Mr. Marston. I think that the Inspector here would agree with me that you have given us some very valuable information."

"I do—most definitely," said MacMorran. "All the same, I don't quite see where we are. To tell the truth I haven't been able to sort things out properly yet—and am still a bit hazy. After all, they were only copies that you made, Mr. Marston, as you said yourself. And there's no value in copies."

Anthony smiled. "That's where Mr. Marston comes in, Andrew. You listen carefully and you'll see what I mean in a minute or so. Because you and I are going to take him along to see Mrs. Coventry at Danvers Gate."

Marston seemed in no way disconcerted by the proposition. On the other hand, he showed that he found it rather attractive. "How far is it to go—this Danvers Gate, Mr. Bathurst?"

"Not far. A quarter of an hour in a taxi will see us there. I'm looking forward to a highly interesting five minutes with you, Marston. Unless I'm greatly mistaken you'll find it so as well. *Allons.*"

Mrs. Coventry, for once in a way, was somewhat flustered when she saw Inspector MacMorran on her doorstep. When she saw that he was accompanied by Anthony Bathurst and another whom she did not know, she appeared to regain her natural poise and confidence. MacMorran gave her but little indication of the real reason behind their visit. He allowed her to think that Marston was sailing under the flag of the Yard. On the way to the house, Anthony had arranged with MacMorran certain ways of approach and campaign. MacMorran, be it noted, had quickly and with but little argument, fallen into line with Anthony's suggestions. After a few moments' conversation with Susanna and Philip Coventry and a few reasonably innocuous questions from both MacMorran and Anthony, they wandered more or less aimlessly (or so it would have appeared to the superficial observer) into the room where Aubrey Coventry had encountered the fake Silas Montgomery and had met his death. Here MacMorran made a surprising request to the two Coventrys. Request, let it be said, is a euphemism. "My colleagues and I will be alone in here for some little time, Mrs. Coventry. If you and Philip Coventry will be good enough to excuse us—"

The words were polite enough, but the tone of MacMorran's voice conveyed to his hearers with no possible doubt the significant nature of his authentic intention. MacMorran made a quick sign to Anthony when the two Coventrys had withdrawn.

Anthony locked the door at once behind them. "Now, Mr. Marston," said the latter, "there's your meat. Take a look at 'em." He pointed dramatically to the two oil paintings on the opposite walls.

Marston shook his head with an easy smile. "No need for me to look at those, Mr. Bathurst. I can tell 'em at once. They're both ours. Gaunt, Marston and Co., all over 'em. From canvas to frame. I spotted 'em directly I came into the room. They comprise the order about which I spoke to you earlier. They are the two pictures for which we were commissioned. Not bad for copies, are they? Notice their suggestion of age. Nice work if you can get it."

Anthony nodded. "Do me a favour, Marston. Take them down, will you, please?"

Marston took a chair to the side of the room and lifted down the 'Saskia.' He turned it over and placed it on the desk table. "Look," he said, "clean as a whistle. As it should be—seeing it's only a month old. Now glance at the wall, gentlemen, and you'll see what I mean."

Anthony and the Inspector saw that there were marks on the wall which it was impossible for this particular picture to have made. Anthony nodded. "Take down the 'Elizabeth,' will you? I'll call it that and chance it." He smiled at Marston.

"No chance about it—on that point. That's a portrait of Elizabeth of England all right," returned Marston, "you needn't harbour any doubts, believe me." He carried the chair upon which he had stood, to the other side of the room, placed it again as previously, and took down the copy of the Holbein. Again he turned it over before putting it on the table. "There you are, you see—in just the same condition as the Rembrandt. Clean as a baby's—er—reputation. Look up at that wall and you can see for yourselves that it hasn't been there for many days. There you are, gentlemen, scenery by Harker, dresses by Paquin, costumes by Fox, pictures by Gaunt, Marston and Co. And that's the bundle."

MacMorran grinned at the young fellow's exuberance. This fellow that Bathurst had enlisted was a good scout and a worthy ally.

"Well, Andrew," said Anthony, "what's our next move from here? I confess I am a little doubtful."

"And I'm no different from you, Mr. Bathurst. I'll not be denying it." Marston rubbed the end of his nose.

Anthony motioned the two men towards him. "We know now, Andrew, that these two Gaunt Marston pictures were in the parcel which was brought here by the man in the blue overalls. Or, at any rate, we're as certain as we can be on the point. The shape and the size and everything. But what's worrying me now, is what the same gentleman took away with him. Which I presume, Andrew, is a matter that's also worrying you."

MacMorran nodded.

"May I make a suggestion?"—this from Marston.

"Naturally we should welcome it," returned Anthony.

"Find out all that you can concerning the pictures which the late Mr. Coventry had in here at the time of the murder."

"Exactly," replied Anthony. "I was on the point of putting forward an identical suggestion. Are you with us, Andrew?"

"Ay. As I see it, the course is inevitable. Line of inquiry is through Mrs. Coventry, I take it?"

"Think so. Ask her to come in now, Andrew."

MacMorran went to the door, opened it and called to Mrs. Coventry. Surprise and anxiety were on her face when she entered.

"Sit down, Mrs. Coventry, will you, please? We want a word with you."

She looked rather pathetically from one to the other of them.

"We want a little information from you, Mrs. Coventry, information which, we may as well tell you at once, we regard as extremely important. I hope that we shan't have to keep you more than a few moments. Your late husband possessed two pictures which were hung in this room. You know them well, naturally."

"Marston—do you mind, for Mrs. Coventry?"

Anthony indicated the two pictures that were lying face downward as he had placed them on the table. Marston stepped forward smartly and brought them over to Mrs. Coventry. "Are these they?" Anthony asked her. "Please look at them carefully."

She glanced at them. "Of course they are. You've just taken them down from the wall, haven't you?"

"You are quite sure of what you say, Mrs. Coventry? There's no doubt in your mind at all?"

"Certainly I am. All the same, I don't understand. Why are you—"

Anthony turned the portraits over so that she could see the backs of them. He observed that she gave a start of surprise.

"Wonderfully clean, aren't they, Mrs. Coventry? Scarcely a speck of dust on them. Too clean for a term of years, don't you consider, if you come to think things over? You've had yours for more than a few days, I take it?"

Mrs. Coventry knitted her brows. "I am a trifle bewildered. Would you mind if I consulted with Philip—my son?"

"With pleasure, Mrs. Coventry. Will you ask him to come in?"

Mrs. Coventry went to the door and called Philip Coventry. Philip Coventry came in. He looked stubborn and determined. As he entered, he flashed a look of askance at his mother. "Come here to me, Philip, will you, please." She beckoned him to where Anthony had left the pictures. His surprise increased. Anthony watched both the Coventrys as carefully as he knew how. The pictures were now lying face upward. "These portraits, Phil," said Mrs. Coventry, "do you recognize them?"

He glanced at them. "Of course I do. They were the Guv'nor's. Very keen on them he was. Been in here for three or four years or so. Why the inquisition, though? What's the point? More Scotland Yard scintillating brilliancy?"

Susanna Coventry made a gesture of dissent. "Never mind about that, and please be calm. Turn them over, Phil."

Her son obeyed her and saw at once what she meant. Anthony was still watching. A puzzled frown came on Coventry's face. He took the Rembrandt copy and turned it over each way once or twice. Then he shook his head as though the problem which he had been suddenly called upon to face was too big for him. He put the 'Saskia' down and turned his attention to the copy of the Holbein. Anthony saw him bend down and look closely into the oil painting. He shook his head again before raising it. "This is not my father's picture. It is very like it, and while it was hanging on the wall above the eye-level the differences wouldn't be noticed. Certainly I should never have spotted them. But there *are* differences when you look at them closely, which I have just detected. For example, there was a tiny parting down the middle of my father's picture. It looked to my eye as though in the original instance two pieces of wood had been joined together. That's one difference. In addition to that, there were certain faint scratches discernible on my father's copy. Some were in the top right-hand corner, and also there were a few quite distinguishable across the girl's face. They looked, to my eye, to be as much like cuts—diagonal cuts—as anything else. My father, I may say, was of the same opinion. He bought both of them at a sale. They came from a private house in Ilford, Essex. Rayner will give you the full address if you ask him. My father pointed the scratches out to me when he first had the picture."

Marston went across and whispered in MacMorran's ear. "May I butt in and ask him a question?"

"Certainly. Go ahead."

Marston took advantage of his opportunity. "Mr. Coventry—was your father's picture—the picture of the Tudor girl—signed at all, to your knowledge?"

Coventry emphatically shook his head. "No. It had no signature at all. Or date either. My father looked for both when he first purchased it. It was quite valueless, of course. Only a copy. Even though it may have been of an old master. So I don't see what all the fuss is about. Let alone this absurd substitution which seems to have taken place."

Marston eyed him queerly and spoke to him again—quietly. "How do you know that they were valueless, Mr. Coventry?"

Coventry gave a light easy laugh. "My dear zealous young fellow, by the price my father paid for them, of course. If you know of a better guide than that, I'd be delighted to hear of it."

The normal cynicism of the man was returning.

"Money doesn't always talk, Mr. Coventry," replied Marston, with quiet emphasis. "I'll explain myself. Sometimes a valuable article changes hands—and the vendor is blissfully ignorant of the treasure that he is disposing of. It's happened before in business—many times. There's no reason why it shouldn't happen again. History, so we're told, is credited with the quality of repetition."

Phil Coventry shrugged his shoulders. The gesture said eloquently: "Very well, have it your way and I'll have it mine."

Marston nodded to the Inspector. MacMorran understood from the nod that he had asked all that he desired to ask. Susanna Coventry was staring at her son as though she had been totally unable to comprehend anything of what he had said. MacMorran made a sign to Anthony and Marston. They rose from where they had been sitting. "Bring those pictures along," ordered the Inspector. He went to the table and gave Mrs. Coventry a receipt for them. She took it from him almost mechanically. Phil Coventry watched the proceedings with a certain obvious disfavour. As MacMorran and the others left the library he shrugged his shoulders again. There were still criticism and censure in the movement. On the way to the Yard, Marston had much to say—a good deal of it distinctly relevant.

"Did you hear me ask him about the signature on the 'Holbein'?"

"I did. I confess I wondered what your real point was with regard to that?"

"Why this—and it's important. You can judge for yourself. The fact that the portrait was both unsigned and undated helps your case. It does, I assure you. Because it was a known peculiarity of Holbein's that he seldom signed or dated any of his pictures. Indeed, he only did so in the most exceptional cases. Another point, Mr. Bathurst, which should make you sit up and take notice more than ever is this. Do you recall what young Coventry said about the parting down the middle of his father's portrait? He said that it looked to him as though the painter had originally joined together two pieces of wood."

"I do, Marston, very well."

MacMorran was listening intently to the conversation.

"Well, note what I'm going to tell you. Holbein's panels were often *two* pieces of wood fastened together. The National Portrait Gallery pictures of Anne Boleyn, Edward the Sixth, and Mary Tudor, all known to have been painted by him, are, each one of them, split in an exactly similar manner. What do you say to that?"

Anthony whistled softly. "So Coventry had a Holbein and a Rembrandt, had he? That's what it looks like, doesn't it? The pair of 'em worth six figures—eh? Well—well—well! And if we want to find out where he got them from we must ask Rayner! The Rayner who meets clandestinely the wife of Morris Sere! Things are beginning to hum! Do you hear all this, Andrew?"

"Ay. I hear it, Mr. Bathurst. Those portraits make a rare difference."

"They were rare pictures, Andrew, which is even more to the point. Well, Mr. Marston, you've been a treasure to us. It was a red letter day for me when I got into touch with Gaunt, Marston and Co."

"It wasn't altogether a bad day for me," returned Marston, with a sigh that proved the sincerity of his words. Anthony and the Inspector shook hands with him.

Chapter XXI
RAYNER TALKS

WHEN the telephone rang in the Coventry house at Danvers Gate it was Susanna Coventry who answered it. Phil Coventry happened to be with her at the time. "Who is it?" he asked curtly.

She shook her head at him enjoining silence. Conventional words followed, then certain information. She put her hand on the mouthpiece. "It's that Inspector of Police, MacMorran."

"Curse the man! What's he want now?"

"Where he can find Rayner. I told him that he had left here for the time being. I haven't said yet that I know where he is. Should I, do you think?"

Coventry frowned as he considered the question. "Suppose you'll have to. There's nothing much in it, really. Even if you don't let on—they'll find him without any difficulty. So what's the odds?"

Mrs. Coventry nodded. She spoke again on the telephone. "As far as I know, Inspector, Rayner is staying temporarily in North London. I'll let you have the address. Twenty-two Mountfall Crescent, Tufnell Park. It's close to the Tube station. Will that do for you?"

Phil Coventry watched her. She replaced the receiver. "He seems satisfied. So it's all right. What do they want Rayner for?"

Coventry was impatient. "The picture matter, of course. I told them when they were here that Rayner could find them the details as to how the Guv'nor acquired the pictures in the first place. So I'm not surprised. I wasn't in his confidence at the time and Rayner was. Don't you worry about it. There's one thing—they seem to be on the right road at last." Susanna Coventry sighed and returned to the work she had been doing when the telephone call had come through. Had Phil Coventry been with MacMorran and Anthony Bathurst when they arrived at 22 Mountfall Crescent, he would have felt even more convinced as to the soundness of this, his most reverently expressed, opinion. They called early by deliberate intention, and found Rayner at home. MacMorran and Anthony Bathurst had arranged, on their journey down, that all references to Sere should be avoided by them until the concluding stages of the interview. The last condition they desired was the interviewing of a Rayner who had been placed upon his guard. Actually, it must be admitted, Rayner was comfortably cool and self-possessed when they were shown in to him. He had accommodated himself in a house which, in appearance and design, was typically 'North London.' As MacMorran had remarked to Anthony when they first saw it: "Just the same sort of place where Crippen did in Belle Elmore. It reminded me of his house directly I saw it." The Inspector quickly got to grips with the gist of the matter. Rayner nodded confidently.

"Any information concerning the late Mr. Coventry and all matters concerning him—well, you've only got to come to me, gentlemen. Nobody can serve you as well as I can in this respect. I was at his side, his right-hand man all the time I was in his employment. When he was taken, it was a bad day for me, I can tell you. I'm afraid I shall not see his like again."

MacMorran at once got down to details. "There were two pictures in Mr. Coventry's room, Rayner. On opposite walls—one faced the other. You know them well, of course."

Rayner looked up at him sharply. "*Were* two pictures in his room? Why the past tense? They're still there, surely? I know for a fact that they were when I was last in the room."

"For certain reasons—which I cannot discuss at the moment—they are not there now. Those that you saw recently have been removed—by my orders, let me say."

Rayner shook his head. "I'm sorry—but I don't think I understand."

"Don't let that worry you—skip it. But listen to this. Do you remember your late employer buying the pictures?"

Rayner nodded acquiescence. "Yes, very well. He picked 'em up at a sale. Don't know what he actually gave for 'em, but you could find that out easily enough if you wanted the information."

"Where did they come from—can you remember?"

"Wait a minute—let me think. It's on the tip of my tongue. . . . I know. . . . Ilford. In Essex. That's where they had been. A private house and its effects were sold up. The late Mr. Coventry was always interested in old pictures and he secured this pair when he had the chance. These weren't anything to speak of . . . the frames were the best part about them, in my opinion."

"Where did he purchase them? Any idea?"

"Almost certainly at one of Thorogood's sales. That's the only place he ever attended to my knowledge for anything of that kind. I expect he went down there one day, spotted the pictures and decided to buy them."

MacMorran made a note of the name. Anthony came into the conversation. "Had your late employer any expert knowledge of pictures . . . would you say?"

Rayner twisted his face. "No-o, I don't think so. No-o, I should say not. He admired a fine piece of painting—I've often heard him say that—but I don't think he had anything like special knowledge with regard to pictures."

"Did he often transact picture deals?"

"Oh, no. And this was the only occasion I can remember him buying any, although he was so keen on them. You aren't trying to tell me they were valuable by any chance—are you?"

"We regard it as extremely likely," replied Anthony.

Rayner's eyes evidenced his astonishment. "Is that a fact? Well, I must say that I'm surprised. I was with Mr. Coventry for a considerable time, but I never suspected that, and I don't think the Guv'nor knew it himself. Well, well, surprises do come one's way and no mistake."

MacMorran intervened with a further question. "You mentioned Thorogood's sales just now. Can you give me further details of these people?"

"I can, Inspector. I've seen their invoices. The full name of the firm is Thorogood, Chalk, and Coverley. Their address is somewhere in Gloucester Road."

Again MacMorran jotted down the information. "Thank you, Mr. Rayner." He gave a slight nod towards Anthony Bathurst.

Mr. Bathurst understood and took the cue. "Before we go, one more question, Mr. Rayner. The late Mr. Coventry had an unusually close business associate. Not exactly a partner in the accepted sense, but a man in conjunction with whom he did a great deal of business. I refer to a man named Sere. Morris Sere, to be exact. Can you tell me whether this man Sere was at all interested in pictures?"

Rayner flicked a thread from his coat before answering.

"I really couldn't say, Mr. Bathurst. All I can tell you is that I have never heard my employer discuss pictures with him. If that's any guide to you." He shrugged his shoulders.

"You know Sere, I take it, pretty well, Mr. Rayner?"

"Oh, so-so. Not what I'd call well. I met him upon occasion. I was bound to, of course, seeing that I was at Mr. Coventry's elbow, as you might say."

MacMorran cut in curtly. "Perhaps you could tell us something about this man Sere's wife. Again—I have much more than an idle reason for asking."

Rayner rubbed his top lip. "What should I know about her? Beyond what is the common knowledge of everybody. She's Vere Valentine, the film star. I take it you know that yourself, Inspector?"

"I do. And that's all you know about her? You're quite sure of that?"

"Of course. I'm not much of a lady's man, Inspector. They're not in my line. Getting on in years, you know."

"You're not the only one. We all are," commented MacMorran harshly. "Did the late Mr. Coventry know her pretty well? I suppose they were bound to meet . . . socially . . . at times, weren't they?"

"No-o, Inspector. As far as I know, Mr. Coventry and Mr. Sere had business associations only. Nothing beyond that. To the best of my memory the two families didn't make a practice of visiting each other."

"Would you know Mrs. Sere if you met her in the street?"

"Oh, yes, of course. Just as most people would. I've seen her on the pictures several times."

"Scarcely a real test that, is it?"

"Well, it's a help. Besides, you run across her photographs in the newspapers quite a lot. Oh, yes, I should say, with every confidence, that her face is a familiar one to most people." Anthony detected an unusual tone in Rayner's voice as he spoke the last sentence.

Rayner went on: "Without presuming, gentlemen, may I ask you a question? Do you suspect anybody of Mr. Coventry's murder?"

"Anybody and everybody," growled MacMorran. "That's the reason why we're taking the trouble to ask you these questions."

Rayner looked scared at the Inspector's reply. The composure with which he had commenced the interview had obviously been gradually diminishing. Anthony smiled encouragingly. "What the Inspector really means is that we haven't come to see you for the sake of your *beaux yeux*."

Rayner smiled back at him. But the smile was both forced and feeble. "Well," he said nervously, "come to that—I didn't suppose that you had. I'm not exactly a f-fool, you know."

Anthony put a further question to him.

"While you were acting as secretary for Mr. Coventry, can you remember if he ever had an offer from anybody to purchase one or both of the two pictures?"

"If he did, he didn't t-tell me about it. I never heard of it."

"You think you would have?"

"I'm certain I should. Seeing the position I held with Mr. Coventry. As certain as any man can be of matters like that."

"Tell me this, then. Can you recall any conversation you heard about the pictures or any inquiry from anybody concerning them?"

Again Rayner shook his head. "No. None at all. Mr. Coventry bought them from Thorogoods at the yard in Gloucester Road, had them sent home to his house in D-Danvers Gate, and then had them hung up. That was the b-beginning and the end of them as far as I'm aware. Until to-day."

Anthony turned to MacMorran. "I've asked Mr. Rayner all that I want to ask him, Inspector. I don't know whether you've any new points to—"

MacMorran walked towards the door. "No, I'm through. Good morning."

Round the corner of Mountfall Crescent, Mr. Bathurst grimaced at the Inspector. "So he didn't come clean, our Mr. Rayner! Now—I wonder why?"

MacMorran looked steadily ahead of him. "I wonder why he told lies, Andrew," went on Anthony, "and why falsehood was upon his tongue. If you ask me, Andrew, you'll have to make him talk some more."

"Yes, I think I shall. I'm putting a man on to our Mr. Rayner as you call him . . . pronto."

MacMorran stopped and entered a telephone kiosk. "Chatterton?" asked Anthony, when MacMorran rejoined him.

"No," replied the Inspector savagely—"not Chatterton!"

CHAPTER XXII
THE YARD AT GLOUCESTER ROAD

"HERE we are, Andrew," declared Anthony Bathurst. MacMorran gave orders for the car to be stopped. "There are the names we are seeking. Thorogood, Chalk, and Coverley. A comforting sound to my ear, Andrew. Like Abana and Pharpar—rivers of Damascus. Remember 'em, you old ruffian? Or have they slipped away from you?"

"Before my time," replied the Inspector, "come along and I'm after you."

Anthony alighted from the car and the Inspector followed him. They entered the premises of 'Thorogood, Chalk, and Coverley—Auctioneers.' A man with a bristling moustache and a large-brimmed bowler hat approached them. MacMorran made himself known. The man patted his pockets with a strange tenderness as though they were in pain. MacMorran began to explain the nature of his inquiry.

"Hoomph," returned the bowler-hatted one. He took the rim of his hat and pushed the hat to the back of his head. Then he remarked brightly and with surprising intelligence: "You'd better come into the office."

MacMorran gave instant agreement.

"Hoomph," said the man, for the second time. "Now you say you can't be sure of your dates. Not even certain of the year, are you? Not such bright boys, to my mind."

MacMorran apologized for the nebulous nature of his inquiry.

"Coventry," repeated the representative of Thorogood, Chalk, and Coverley. "Danvers Gate! Now, dash me if I don't remember reading something about that in the old 'linen' the other day. It's familiar to me somehow. Oh, yes, I know. The murder. Wonder it didn't strike me when I read of the murder first of all. Now, you gentlemen, just give me a minute or so, and my old brain may get to work and deliver the goods." He thrust out his moustache and blew vigorously. To MacMorran he looked like a walrus. To Anthony he suggested 'Old Bill.' "Just half a cock linnet," he went on to say. "I was living down at Orpin'ton at the time. Because I was on Charing Cross platform. Yes, that's right. Say 1934. About February, it was. Wait a minute. Rather fancy myself at dates. You know, 'Mr. Memory.' 'What are the Thirty-nine steps?' 'The Thirty-nine steps are . . .' Bang. Right in the guts. That's got 'im. Good picture that. I enjoyed it." He crossed to the shelf and took down a book. "Think a lot of old Robert Doughnut. That's what I call 'im. You know—my fun! Makes my missus wild when I say that. You ought to see her. Don't half get her rag out." He turned the pages of the book. "She foams at the mouth every time she 'ears me say it—proper one for a bit of 'ero worship. Ah well—it don't hurt me, and if it pleases 'er, what's the odds?" He continued to turn the pages of the book. "It was after Christmas, I feel certain—and before Easter. That makes me almost sure it was Feb. I usually get away sharp on time in Feb. There's not a lot doing you see, about that time. And I was on Charing Cross platform, goin' home to Orpin'ton. Didn't 'ave a bad little place down there. Yes . . . that's about it. Feb. Round about Pancake Day. And the name was Coventry. Of Danvers Gate. West." More flicking of many pages. Then suddenly his face wreathed in smiles. "Here we are, Meredith. We're in. What did I tell you? Feb. 12! Here you are. You can see the entry for yourself." He turned the book round and held it out to the Inspector. "See the date? Didn't I tell you I was 'ot stuff at rememberin'? Right month and right year first pop. Where my finger is—see it?"

MacMorran bent forward and read the entry before holding it for Anthony to see. The latter read: 'Two oil paintings in gilt frames—Mr. Coventry—Danvers Gate, W. Sale of household effects, No. 19 Dines Road, Ilford. Price £20 the pair. To be delivered by our van before Saturday next.' "There's the entry," continued the bowler-hatted person. "Sold by Mr. Chalk—the paintings were. Our Mr. Chalk, that is. I can tell that by the handwriting. This entry's been made by Mr. Charles Chalk."

Anthony intervened. "Would it be possible for you to give us one more item of information?"

"I'll do my best, sir—if you'll tell me what it is you want."

"Could you tell me the name of the previous owner of these two oil paintings which Mr. Coventry bought from you?"

"Yes, I can do that for you. As easy as kiss your—hand. Thanks to the excellence of my filing system. You want the name of the owner of 19 Dines Road, Ilford. It'll take me a moment or two—if you don't object to waiting."

Anthony smiled. "After all it's what I must expect."

The bowler-hatted individual took down a dusty file of what looked like correspondence. "'Struth," he muttered jocularly, "where there's dirt there's danger. 'Ighly perilous 'ere I should say." He knocked the edges of the file. "'Ere we are again, 1934. Important year that. Let's see—we want February, don't we? Somewhere about the beginning of the month it would be. About a week I should think before the sale. I'll try about the 4th or 5th." Punctuated by many and varied imprecations, Bowler Hat's task was commenced and carried on. His curses, however, were comfortably benevolent. They carried no violent vindictiveness with them. On the contrary, they were smooth and sociable spitfires. Anthony watched him curiously. He felt that there was a certain rough efficiency about the fellow. He was of the type of which people say 'he knew his job.' Even though he might well be of the baser sort. The man stuck to his monotonous work of separating the orders. MacMorran said nothing. Like Anthony, he watched the proceedings and waited patiently for results. They were rewarded. The man stopped suddenly in his task with a bulky finger holding the place between two sheets of paper. "Got it!" he exclaimed triumphantly. "'Struth—I don't know what failure means. The word ain't in my dictionary." He rolled one of the pages back with his bulky finger. "No luck for you, I'm afraid," he announced disconsolately. "The bloke at 19 Dines Road, Ilford, was a 'stiff.' The property of the *late* Mr. Edward Izzard. He croaked some time before the sale."

"I take it that means we learn no more," said MacMorran.

"Sweet Fanny Adams," supplemented the man in the bowler hat, "and that's a solemn fact."

"You mentioned the name just now of one of your partners," interposed Mr. Bathurst, "Mr. Chalk, I think it was?"

"Quite right, sir, Mr. Chalk. That was the one. What about him?"

"Is he by any chance on the premises?"

"Oh, yes. He would be. He's the one partner that usually is. It's his job to be. Would you like to have a word with him?"

"That's just what I would like." Anthony transferred a currency note to the custody of the bowler hat.

"Thank you, sir. Very nice of you. I'll see what I can do for you. Come along with me, gentlemen, will you?"

MacMorran and Anthony accompanied him into the office of Messrs. Thorogood, Chalk, and Coverley. "Sit down," said Bowler Hat, "you'll find chairs. I'll send round and see what I can do for you."

MacMorran and Anthony found the chairs he had mentioned, and suitably seated themselves. Within a few minutes their friend of the yard returned. "I told Mr. Chalk who you were and what you wanted from him. Thanks to me, everything's O.K." He put his forefinger to the side of his nose and winked prodigiously, before showing them into Chalk's private apartment.

"Thank you, Jackson. Now what can I do for you?" said Chalk. He was tall, spare, and thin-faced. His eyes were of watery pale blue colour, and a huge pipe dangled rather incongruously from his lips.

The jovial Jackson explained what Anthony wanted in particular, and the object of the visit generally. Chalk listened to him patiently. Then, to Anthony's surprise, he ventured a remark.

"Although it's some time ago I remember Coventry coming here very well indeed. As a matter of fact, round about that time he was a fairly frequent visitor to our sales. I think that they interested him. I myself have knocked down several articles to his bidding. I remember those two oil paintings that Jackson here's been talking about very well indeed. Coventry offered twenty quid for the two of 'em and got them for that figure. You may find it difficult to believe, but I can see his face now when I knocked 'em down to him. He was sitting in a corner of my auction room. I was used to seeing him there because he always sat in the same place. I am glad to have been able to assist you."

Jackson puffed out his cheeks. These were his thoughts: 'Good job Mr. Chalk was on and not that pompous old fool Thorogood with his absurd "pop, pop, pop" method of asking and answering questions! Besides, Chalk had a good memory, whereas old Thorogood couldn't remember the date of his own birthday.'

Anthony leaned forward towards the second partner of the firm.

"I wonder if it's taxing your memory too highly to ask you this, Mr. Chalk?"

Chalk looked at him in invitation. "Ask on! There's nothing like eating the pudding to prove its goodness."

"You claim to be able to remember some of the circumstances under which Coventry bought the two oil paintings."

"I do. Distinctly."

"Good. You raise my hopes considerably. I wonder if you can remember this. Did he seem at all anxious to purchase them?"

"Anxious?" Chalk seemed a little doubtful with regard to Anthony's point. He began to shake his head. Anthony amplified it.

"Yes, did he give you the impression that he would be prepared to go to a heavy price to get them?"

Chalk shook his head. He lifted the big pipe that dangled from his mouth and knocked away some of the burnt ash. "You know," he remarked slowly, "you're asking me rather a lot—still I'll do my best for you. Let me see if I can revisualize the scene of the sale . . . remember it more accurately."

Anthony was interested to see Chalk shut his eyes in an attempt at increased concentration. After a short interval he opened them. "No, I've tried to piece things up as well as I can, and I wouldn't say with any confidence that Coventry showed anxiety to get those two oil paintings. Of course—when you're selling things by auction, and I've had twenty-five years' experience at the game, you're inclined to treat the circle of people round you as one entity. I'll try to explain what I mean."

Anthony broke in. "Don't trouble to, Mr. Chalk. I know what you mean perfectly. You mean in the same way as an experienced actor treats an audience. Through one focal-point."

"That's exactly what I mean. And it's because of that fact that the task you've given me isn't as easy or so simple as it might appear to be at first blush. Although to tell the truth, I'm getting half an idea that something's coming back to me. It's just floating about in my brain at the present moment."

Anthony and MacMorran stayed silent. If Chalk were really on to something, any interruption, no matter how trivial, might well break his train of thought. Anthony could hear deep breathing sounds. They were emitted from the bowler-hatted Jackson. Suddenly Chalk came away from his mental tension. His face cleared and he smiled. "It's come to me," he declared simply. "Just a mere fragment of reminiscence. Nothing more than that. But when Coventry bought those pictures in my rooms he had a companion. And if I'm any judge the companion was keener to get them than Coventry himself was."

Anthony smiled back at Chalk. He spoke very quietly.

"And that companion, Mr. Chalk—I'm extremely interested—could you describe him at all—have you the vaguest memory?"

"Very little, I'm afraid. The merest trifles. Perhaps just—an impression. Made up of a detail or so."

"And they are, Mr. Chalk?"

"A big bulky man. Wore a heavy overcoat. Moustache. Ends very pointed—you know—spiky. Oh—and one more thing—a flower in his coat."

MacMorran rose. Anthony glanced up at him. "I've heard enough," said the Inspector, "because I know who that man is. Without a doubt."

"Who?" enquired Anthony.

"Sere," returned MacMorran. "Morris Sere."

"Who," said Anthony softly, "according to the excellent Rayner has never evinced the slightest interest in pictures . . . valuable or otherwise. Rather extraordinary that."

Chalk leant forward towards him. "You know, gentlemen, I've given you a fair amount of information . . . suppose we reverse the position and you return the compliment? What's the real business behind this visit of yours concerning twenty quid's worth of oil and canvas?"

MacMorran smiled a dry smile. "Make your twenty a hundred and twenty thousand . . . and we've an idea that you'll be pretty near the mark."

Chalk opened his mouth in amazement. "What!" he yelled, "and I had 'em in my yard here . . . well . . . I'm *damned*!"

"There's many a true word," said Mr. Bathurst, grinning at him, "but I expect you know the rest."

The big pipe was trembling in Chalk's mouth. Even the irrepressible Jackson could find no coherent words with which to describe the situation. "Hoomph," came once again from his parted lips.

Chapter XXIII
DIRECT ATTACK

Anthony Lotherington Bathurst frowned, wondered, and then frowned again. Matters which had been mere suspicions in his mind were becoming now much more like certainties. As he stood outside the door of his flat in the prevailing conditions of spitting rain and darkness, that telephone message which he had recently received and which had purported to come from Inspector MacMorran, seemed more shadowy and more unsatisfying than ever. Luckily, however, when he had journeyed half-way to the Yard, he had given way to a sudden inspiration and had decided to test its authenticity.

The test had sent him hurrying back to the flat as fast as his legs would carry him. Somebody evidently had wanted him completely out of the way, for a period of an hour or so. That hour or so had been cut down now to a mere forty minutes, thanks to the wave of sense that had come to him. His ringing of the bell met with no response, so Mr. Bathurst stretched out his finger and rang again. This time he kept his finger on the bell and pressed it hard. Where the blazes was Emily? Anthony fumbled for his key. As he did so, the rain which had been more threatening than actually active, took it into its head to descend upon him relentlessly. The suddenness of the downpour equalled its strength. Cursing softly to himself, Anthony found his wayward key in an unaccustomed pocket and opened the door. He stood in the hall. The hall, for some obscure reason, was damnably dark. Where in hell was Emily? Anthony stood in the hall and listened. There wasn't a sound. He reached out a hand and switched on the light. But that action belonged to his imagination. For no light came in response to his effort. Mr. Bathurst cursed again and struck a match. Looking towards the ceiling he observed that the light bulb had been removed. Mr. Bathurst now began to think more seriously. He had no desire for a scrap in conditions of utter darkness. With no weapon beyond his fists, he would almost certainly be at a decided disadvantage. The uncanny silence hurt his ears. Also his heart had begun to pace up a bit. The match flame licked his fingers. He dropped it and trampled it out for safety's sake. To his infinite surprise, he could now hear the ticking of his watch. Then, as his entire nervous system tensed, a door creaked up above and there came to his ears the sound of a light footfall. Anthony stood there just inside the door—listening hard. He called loudly to the woman above. "Is that you, Emily?"

But no feminine voice replied to him. Only another faint creak and the light shuffle of feet crossing a floor somewhere. There was no doubt about it now. Somebody was upstairs in his apartments. Anthony felt distinctly uncomfortable as he stood in the hall and waited. Whoever the intruder was he knew that Mr. Bathurst was downstairs. Anthony bent down, put his hands in front of him, found the flight of stairs and commenced to crawl up them. His progress was slow, but almost noiseless. Step by step he made his way up the flight of stairs. He prayed that the enemy (for ten to one it was a hostile visit) would neither see nor hear him for some little time. When his fingers came to the top steps of the first straight flight and the subsequent turn towards the landing, Anthony stopped. He must endeavour, in some way, to mitigate his strategical disadvantage. While he was deliberating thus concerning his plan of campaign, he heard another faint move that could be, at the most liberal estimate, only a few feet above him. He held himself tense and taut. Now he could hear something more! Breathing! Steady controlled breathing that was almost horribly intimate with him. Anthony clenched his fists. The breathing seemed closer. Anthony tried hard to pierce the darkness. His eyes were helpless. His ears had become by far his most useful sense-assets. He heard a door flung wide and pushed hard against a wall. Instinctively, and almost entirely unconsciously, he partly rose from his crouching posture, and turned his head in the direction from which had come the sound. At that psychological second, the enemy struck! There came a swift padding rush of light footsteps from somewhere above and a body, strong and hard, hurled itself upon his. Anthony was borne backward and half fell, half rolled across the stairs. He grabbed at an invisible face as he fell, but could feel only cloth and hair. A buffet on the mouth smashed back his head causing him intense pain, and in a desperate attempt at retaliation, he lashed out viciously with his left leg. His assailant was violently vicious, and the force of his assault needed all Anthony's powers of resistance to stem it. Anthony's foot caught the man in the side. At least, he judged it to be the side because the man gasped at the blow. Anthony swung over again and dived up and across the stairs for knees that he could see but dimly. The knees avoided the intended tackle. Anthony was now at least a couple of stairs beneath his opponent. That is to say, the opponent was in a position of undoubted strategic superiority. More so even than he had been when he launched the first attack. But he had fallen as Anthony had, and their two bodies wrestled desperately against each other. Their breathing came in hard, sharp gasps. Anthony shot out a hand in an endeavour to grip his assailant by the ankles. But the man squirmed, and then by a quick movement of the body shot his full weight against Anthony's face and throat.

Anthony crashed down the stairs with the weight of the man's body on top of him. He landed at the foot of the stairs on his back and, as he fell, his opponent's heel caught him a nasty blow at the side of the head. Suddenly Anthony felt insufferably sick, and a strange blackness enveloped him. He seemed to feel the man with whom he had been fighting roll away from him in the direction of the front door. He thought he heard the door being opened, and the very faintest idea came to him that it had been shut again. That was the moment when a comforting oblivion came on him, and Life, temporarily, to an end. When light came again and took the place of the cloud of darkness, Anthony propped himself on his elbow, rubbed his mouth and jaw with an unusual tenderness, and then laughed to himself. The laugh, it should be said, held other qualities than mere mirth and homely humour. He felt in his pockets, found his matches and struck one. So far as he could tell, beyond a badly cut lip and an egg-like bruise on the side of the head, he was comparatively undamaged. Then his mind began to function normally again. Who was it he had been trying to find. Emily? Where could the girl be? He called her name loudly three times. Then he ran headlong upstairs with a chill, nameless fear plucking at his heart. His hand found a switch that gave him light. Soon after that he came upon Emily herself. She lay full length by the dirty-clothes basket in the bathroom. Anthony cursed under his breath. Her wrists and ankles had been tightly bound by cord. They had been lashed cruelly by a master hand. A handkerchief had been stuffed into her mouth and her mouth tied by a towel. Anthony went on his knees and untied her. For a time Emily lay there motionless. Anthony found brandy and poured a few drops down her throat. She shook her head at him—both blankly and weakly. "What, Emily," asked Mr. Bathurst, "in the name of hell has been happening to you?"

She shook her head helplessly and asked for water. He gave her water. Then he lifted her bodily and carried her into his own room. He laid her on the settee. Gradually a semblance of colour came back into her cheeks. She began to talk. Anthony heard all she had to say. Grim and hard faced. This was her story. She had been reading in her own room. A ring came at the bell, about five minutes after Anthony had gone out. Of course she had answered it. She really thought that Mr. Bathurst had returned for something he had forgotten. As she opened the door, it was pushed against her violently, and she had been smashed against the wall. Only semi-conscious, a hand had seized her, another hand had been placed over her mouth and she had fainted. When she had come to, it was Mr. Bathurst himself who was kneeling at her side. She was so sorry to have been silly, but she had had no choice from the first. She hadn't the slightest idea as to who her assailant had been. She hadn't seen him. Anthony cut her short with an expression of complete and sympathetic understanding, and told her of his own experience. Emily now was concerned over his cut lip. He must bathe it. He certainly would! Emily herself must get to bed at once. Emily made for bed with lagging footsteps. Anthony looked ruefully at his clothes. He was dirty, dusty, and dishevelled. The best thing he could do at the moment would be to pour himself out a drink. That best thing he did. Without a second's delay, he mixed himself a stiff one and drank more than half of it at a gulp. The second half followed its predecessor almost immediately. Anthony then sat down and thought seriously over this latest development. Things were moving! There were points about this latest business which he considered distinctly attractive. Mr. Bathurst grinned to himself as he wiped his lips with his handkerchief. He would try to get MacMorran on the telephone. He was lucky. MacMorran was at the Yard. "Did you send for me about an hour ago, Andrew?"

"I did not. Should I have done?"

"Don't know about that. Anyhow, I've been thinking things over. Listen to a recital of dark deeds." Anthony told MacMorran of the incidents of his evening. He heard the Inspector whistle at the other end. "What have you got?"

"Nothing to worry me. A biff in the east and south that cut my lip, a bruise on the conk, as your Aldgate friends would say, and clothes that have been generally man-handled. You'll have to include the cost of repairs in the Yard's next expenditure account. I shall insist on my rights."

"Some hopes," commented MacMorran laconically. "You don't know the old man. All the same though—you've made me think."

"Nice work," chuckled Anthony. "Who's that I can hear talking in your room?"

"Hemingway. I've just told him that some nasty, big rough man has been knocking you about. The noise you heard was Hemingway laughing."

"You tell him he's completely devoid of feeling."

"He says it's better than a talkie. Bathurst of the Lone Patrol." MacMorran dropped his voice. "Think it's the Coventry case?"

"Oh Lord, Andrew—have a heart. What's come over you? Is there a glimmer of doubt on the point? In bookie's mathematics I'd lay a hundred to one on its being pure, unadulterated, undiluted Coventry!"

"I suppose you're right. Someone knows about you and Coventry."

Anthony laughed softly as he spoke into the mouthpiece. "Someone knows more than that, Andrew. Someone knows that we're a damn' sight nearer than we were a day or two ago. That's the point and it's sticking out a mile. In fact I *might* say that someone knows a great deal more than is good for him, or that he bloomin' well ought to know! Agree, my avuncular Andrew?"

"Afraid I must, Mr. Bathurst—now you put it like that. Might be a help, you know."

"You can go further than that. *Must* be a help. Limits the arena, Andrew. Who knows what we know? Answer is a lemon. Don't tell me that you've been talking."

"No fear of that. You're alluding, of course, to—pictures."

"Absolutely, Andrew. Liz and Saskia. Two smart girls that grew up. It resolves itself into this. The headway we've made in the picture direction, has made somebody feel desperately uncomfortable. Result—a gentleman we're after has decided to strike back. More than that—*has* struck back."

MacMorran grunted. "That's why you rang me, I suppose?"

"That's why, Andrew. For no other reason. Well, I won't disturb your rest any longer. You can start snoring again. But I thought you would like to know the half-time score. Cheero, Andrew."

"Cheero, Mr. Bathurst. Take care of yourself." MacMorran replaced the receiver and turned to Hemingway, his subordinate.

"This oughtn't to be, you know, Hemingway. It's no laughing matter. They nearly got Mr. Bathurst. Won't do. Don't know what the old man will say about it."

"Sir Austin?"

"Ay, Hemingway. He won't be at all pleased, you know, when he hears about it."

"Can't be helped," contributed Hemingway. "No use crying over spilt milk."

"That's all very well," said MacMorran, wagging his head sagely, "but it mustn't occur again."

"It wouldn't have done—if they'd got him," observed Hemingway darkly,

MacMorran stuck to his guns. "Seriously, Hemingway, we can't have it. The old man won't have it. Not at any price. If it does, we shall be for it. Besides, I've a soft corner in my heart for Mr. Bathurst. I wouldn't have him hurt for the world. He's one of the best."

"Don't take it to heart, Inspector. The Yard can't be held responsible for everything. It can't do impossibilities."

"That's where you make a big mistake, Hemingway. The Yard has got to do impossibilities. That's what the Yard's for." Hemingway snorted critically.

"See what I mean," continued Inspector MacMorran.

"I do—and I don't," replied Hemingway.

"Good," said MacMorran, "that's all right then—you must get a clear view of these things."

<h1 style="text-align:center">Chapter XXIV
THE NEAREST OF NEAR THINGS</h1>

IT WAS, however, the next incident of importance that made Anthony sit up straighter and take more notice. During the days that followed the affair that had taken place in his flat, he had an uncanny presentiment that there was enmity intimate nearly all the time. When he went out, he had that strange chill feeling that he was being shadowed by somebody whose emotions towards him were by no means indicative of even a benevolent neutrality. On one occasion indeed when passing down the Strand hard by Bedford Street, he was on the point of interviewing a man who had stuck persistently to his heels for some considerable time when his better judgment asserted itself and he abandoned the idea. The fellow who had shadowed him was about forty-five. Middle height, lumpish build, dark hair greying round the edges and, on the whole, quite decently turned out sartorially. Anthony was annoyed with himself when the man passed on. He himself had stopped and turned round with a violent urge to knock the bloke down and jump on his face. This would never do, he told himself. He was getting rattled. Events were getting on his nerves. That same evening, too, as he was on the point of entering his flat he heard the sound of running footsteps. There was something about the sound that was sinister—also the steps were coming towards him—an idea which he found distasteful. It was very dark and as he turned in the direction of the flying feet a shape came hurtling out of the darkness. Somebody was evidently in a most tremendous hurry. Anthony braced himself to what he thought was the inevitable shock. The flying shape, however, turned suddenly and swerved away from him at what seemed like the very last possible second. And Anthony stood there, a little unnerved and cursing himself roundly for allowing an incident of that kind and simplicity to poke the gust up him. Things were getting worse! Was he getting too old to take it? Mr. Bathurst went in that evening, thoughtful and determined. Also he slept by no means as soundly as was his habit. In the morning he again took himself to task. He had begun to toy with certain definite ideas, now, with regard to the Coventry murder. Once again he was basing these ideas on the decisive factor of imparted knowledge. Only those who knew certain details could possibly take certain action. The latter was the complement and the corollary of the former. Anthony spent a quiet day designedly, and in the late afternoon strolled along to the Illyrian Super-Cinema, Leicester Square. Since that memorable evening when he had seen the *première* of *The Painter of Ferrara*, in the company of MacMorran and Police Constable Pike Holloway during the investigation of the sensational Merivale murder, he had visited this particular cinema fairly frequently. He liked the atmosphere of it and also the size of the seats in the circle. This evening the attraction was *Time and Time Again,* a picture which had been almost universally heralded by the more competent critics as another *On the Spot.* He entered the theatre just after five o'clock. He nearly always chose this time for visiting for more than one reason. There was little congestion and therefore plenty of comfortable seating to be had and also he was out again in the region of eight o'clock. A time which was not unduly late for dinner. Both of these mentioned conditions suited him. On this occasion the attendance at the time of his entrance was rather larger than the normal, but he managed to find his usual seat unoccupied. The left-hand end-seat of the fourth row of the centre-formation of the circle. Anthony settled down and stretched his legs into the gangway in the hope of entertainment and what was even more to the point—relaxation. *Time and Time Again* was certainly good. There were no two opinions about that. It was an American production with punch, drive, and artistry. Anthony stretched his legs still farther. In this seat he always had bags of room. Here indeed was comfort, entertainment, and a temporary cessation at least from the faiths, hopes, and fears of this transitory life. Anthony was beginning to feel good for the first time for many days. To feel, too, that the perils and dangers of existence were more than comfortably distant. The picture came to the stage when it was about two-thirds of its length through and instead of ending conventionally as it had more than once looked like doing, now gave abundant promise of added strength in its final settings. Anthony felt more than satisfied. More than pleased that he had surrendered to the impulse to come. This picture he was watching had nothing of the tiresome complications according to the usual formula. At the precise moment the picture reached its dramatic climax, Anthony half-turned in his seat to light a cigarette. This was the movement which in all probability saved his life. The sound of a revolver shot was scarcely heard throughout the cinema for a reason. It synchronized perfectly with the shots on the screen at the picture's dramatic high-spot. But Anthony was suddenly conscious of a burning, searing pain in his left arm just below the shoulder. His right arm went to his left in a first instinctive attempt to discover the extent of the damage. What his hand felt as it crossed over to its fellow-arm told him for certain that he had been shot. He felt a little faint and decidedly sick. He rose unsteadily to his feet. Things were getting just a little too hot to be pleasant. Anthony made his way slowly up the circle to the back. Two attendants were on duty. One man and one girl. Anthony spoke to the man, "Would it be possible for me to have a word with the manager? At once, please," he said quietly.

"Certainly, sir. Come this way, will you, sir?" Then, looking at him a little curiously, the attendant said anxiously: "Aren't you feeling too well, sir?"

"I'm well enough," replied Anthony, holding his left arm with his right hand, "my trouble is rather different. Difficult though it may be for you to believe—I've just been shot at. I presume that we go down this way?"

They went to the manager's private room. The manager, in immaculate evening dress, was short, round, and darkly hirsute. But he had an eye that twinkled. He listened to Anthony's story. Happily he was, first of all, severely practical. "Come with me to the lavatory. I've some 'first-aid' stuff tucked away in there. Keep it for sudden emergencies."

Anthony followed him. The manager locked the door and took off his coat. Quickly and deftly, with rolled-up sleeves, he cut away the sodden shirt-sleeve and bared Anthony's left arm. "Flesh wound," he said tersely. "Just above the biceps. I'll bathe it."

He took Anthony to a basin, and ran the water for him, to which he added a touch of antiseptic. "Bullet gone clean through," he said between his teeth. "Luckily for you it's missed the bone. Don't understand it a little bit—but we'll talk of that side of it later on. In the meantime—" He found a roll of bandage and unpinned it. Equally deftly, as he had performed previously, he bound the wound in Anthony's arm. "There you are! Not a bad job of work that, though I says it myself. What about a 'spot' of 'Scotch' to finish things off?"

"It would place me even more deeply in your debt," returned Anthony.

"Toddle along this way then and the 'Scotch' shall be yours. I mean ours. But first of all let me help you into your coat."

Anthony again accompanied him to his room. Inside the room once more he went to a tray and poured out a couple of drinks. "Say when." Anthony obliged with the time limit.

"Now tell me all about it. Because I'll say, quite frankly, that this occurrence writes a new chapter in the history and record of the Illyrian, Leicester Square. At least—since it's been under my management."

Anthony looked at him over the rim of his glass. "Once again—my best thanks. You're very kind. May I sit down?"

"Sure. Why make hard labour of anything? Park yourself just wherever you choose."

Anthony found a chair and made himself as comfortable as he could in the circumstances. From his wallet he took a card and handed it to the Good Samaritan. The latter read it.

"Good Lord," said that worthy. "So you're Bathurst! Delighted to meet you. I remember the Merivale murder only too well. I suppose I had better introduce myself. My name's Sanders. Lacey Sanders."

Anthony returned the compliment.

"Now just spin the yarn in the way you want to," said Lacey Sanders.

"I'm on the Coventry case. The recent murder in Danvers Gate. That fact will do better than anything else as a preamble. You know what I mean—it may explain certain whys and wherefores which in the ordinary way would take a hell of a lot of explaining. Get me?"

"Absolutely. Go on from there. I'm beginning to see a fair amount of daylight already."

"But all the same I don't want you to get me wrong. Don't imagine that I was trailing anybody in here. I wasn't. I came here purely for entertainment."

Sanders frowned. "And got it!"

Anthony smiled back at him. "I suppose that's one way of putting it. Anyhow I'll tell you exactly what happened to me after I got in here. I was sitting in the circle. Centre block. Fourth row. Left-hand end-seat."

Sanders nodded an intelligent appreciation. "That's the first thing I wanted to know. If you hadn't told me soon I should have asked you. Ten to one you were fired at from the left hand side of the theatre."

Anthony nodded. "I agree with you. And there's this point also to be considered. I can remember moving just before I was hit, you know—a generous movement. I turned to light a cigarette. That sudden movement I made was instrumental, in my opinion, in saving my life. Instead of getting what was coming to me amidships I got it, as you know, in the arm."

Sanders was all vibrant eagerness. "But wait a minute. There's just this. It's chiefly what's puzzling me." He stopped for a second. But before Anthony could speak he was in again. "It's the sound question. How it is that you didn't hear the report of the gun? Of the shot being fired? More than that even—how is it that nobody else in the theatre appears to have heard it either?"

Anthony nodded at his questions. "Good questions, each one of them, but I think that I can explain them all with one answer. The same answer will suffice each time."

Lacey Sanders beamed with approval. "Oh, good man! If you do you'll take a load off my mind. How's the arm now?" He had been quick to see that Anthony was fidgeting with the bandage.

"Giving me hell rather. Still, never mind about that, can't be helped. What can't be cured must be endured. But back to your questions. I said I could explain them with one answer. Your picture, *Time and Time Again*—I take it you know it inside out?"

"And backwards and forwards and up and down and side-ways," quoted Sanders cheerfully. "But what's your point about it?"

"How long is it timed to run? According to the official schedule?"

"One hour, fifty minutes. Ten minutes under the two hours."

Anthony made a calculation. "One hundred and ten minutes. Yes—that would be about it." He looked at his watch. "Suppose we say one hour, forty minutes—that is to say ten minutes from the finish?"

Sanders understood that he was working something out. Another question was put to Sanders. "What's the position of the picture at a hundred minutes' run? What's the situation?"

This time it was Sanders's turn to calculate. "Wait half a sec., and I'll tell you. I should say the attack on the gangsters in the cabaret. Domingo Vorzani is cornered behind the line of fruit-machines. The

G. men close in on him. As they are doing that, Helena comes along the floor with the knife that killed her lover, Giuseppe, between her teeth. Domingo thrusts out his arm—"

Anthony interrupted him. "Any shooting about then?"

"Any shooting? I'll say there is. Hell's delight for some seconds."

"Exactly," returned Mr. Bathurst—"and there you have the answer to all your recent questions."

Sanders's eyes flashed in understanding. "Of course, of course! What an idiot I was not to have thought of that before. Synchronization. Synchronization of sound. That point eluded me—and I manage a modern cinema. Well, well, well! What an idiot I was to be sure."

Anthony grinned at him. "That's my story, Mr. Sanders. Anyhow, it's the only one I can put up. A poor thing possibly, but mine own." His right hand went across to his left arm as his face twisted with pain.

Sanders was anxious. "Is that bandage too tight? Shall I readjust it for you? Do let me!"

Anthony shook his head. "No. It's all right. I'm a damn' fidget—make a bad patient—that's all."

Sanders frowned. "Another 'Scotch'? Don't say no. Jove, a top-hole excuse. I don't drink with the distinguished every evening, you know." He poured out more drink. Anthony again imposed the necessary time limit. To tell the truth he was by no means ungrateful for the spirit.

"I'll tell you what," announced the irrepressible Sanders. "I'll get a sling fixed up for that arm of yours. I know where I've got some stuff. That's a much better idea. You'll want it well as soon as possible, I don't doubt. Don't worry about me. I'll be back in half a jiffy." He dashed out of the room, the same bundle of energy now that he had been at the commencement of the contact. Back within the space of a few minutes, he fixed Anthony's arm in a sling of black silk which afforded a condition of greater comfort than Anthony had so far known. "How's that, old son?" asked Sanders, surveying his handiwork with pride. "Nice and comfy?"

"As I said—you're the top. Now—if I extend you a nice sweet invitation—will you accept it?"

"Depends," Sanders laughed and showed white even teeth. "Where do you want to take me? Scotland Yard or somewhere? Because I don't know that I particularly—"

"Nothing like that. Dinna fash yersel! I feel that I'd like to take you for a little stroll round the inner precincts of your own theatre. I seem to have heard somewhere that charity begins at home. Not that that's the only reason I'm asking you."

"I can see you've a weird notion of charity. Still—I'll come with you. I can guess where you're taking me. Though I doubt very much if it will teach us anything."

"You never know." They began to ascend the stairs down which the attendant had conducted Anthony about half an hour previously. "From this wound which you dressed in my arm just now—you will agree that I was shot at from my left? Yes?"

"Oh, every time. No doubt about it. The bullet had entered on the outside and come out on the inside. Direction of flight—from the left."

"Good. Now if my memory serves me correctly, there's a curtained entrance to the circle on the left-hand side of it. It's level with the front row—or about level. I ought to have told you before, Sanders, that I'm a fairly regular patron of yours and know the topography of the place pretty well."

"Didn't know we had been so honoured. Still—go on."

"Do you agree with my point about that curtained entrance?"

"Oh—yes, of course. I know where you mean. So you think that—"

"I do. That's why I want you to come with me and have a look at it. Not very far away now, are we?"

"Next opening," replied Sanders laconically. "Follow me."

Anthony did as instructed. "Here we are," said Lacey Sanders. "Here's your curtained entrance."

"Get rid of that attendant," whispered Anthony. "We don't want to publish too much at this stage. Not a good policy."

Sanders nodded and spoke to the man who was standing by the curtains. The man received his orders and drifted off. As soon as he was out of sight Anthony and Sanders approached the hanging curtains at the entrance. "Best quality velvet," remarked the latter. "I chose it myself and there's none better in London."

"Got a torch?" said Anthony. "We may want it for close inspection." Sanders nodded. "O.K." They went close to the hanging velvet.

"Get a line from here on where you were sitting," remarked Sanders. Anthony pulled the folds a little to one side and looked into the circle. Sanders ranged himself with him. "Fourth row—centre—left extreme. Just there—see?"

Again Sanders nodded. "I see."

"Now," whispered Anthony to his companion, "if I wanted to shoot anybody sitting there—where I was sitting—I should require my gun to be . . . somewhere about here. Agree with me?" He crooked a finger round an imaginary trigger and pushed it into the velvet softness of the hanging curtain. Sanders brought his torch close to where Anthony's finger was pressing. He whispered back. "What the man would do, I think, is this. At least this is how it appears to me. It's what I should have done in like circumstances. He wouldn't be wise to poke the gun through because it might have been seen by somebody. Either in the sitting audience out there or by those passing in and out. He would therefore take a sight, as it were, and then deliberately pull the curtain across the muzzle of the gun to shield it from being seen. One thing is pretty obvious—say what you like—that, sitting in that seat you were a first-class target for a rod. The bloke would take aim, as I said, and then use the curtain."

"If your idea's right, then we ought to find some evidence somewhere about here." Anthony indicated a portion of the curtain.

Sanders at once brought his torch into play. This time he hadn't long to wait for results. An exclamation from Anthony was enough to convince him. "There you are, Sanders," he cried, "just to the right there. Look! There's a nice clean-looking hole through which I was potted at. Talk about a sitting pheasant! I'm inclined to think that I'm more than lucky to be alive. More even than I thought just now. Not that one expects treatment of that kind in a cinema of the quality of the 'Illyrian.'"

Sanders looked graver now than he had looked all the time. "I don't like it," he said quietly but ominously. "I don't like it one little bit. Seeing this hole drilled in my velvet has sort of brought things home to me. Previously, when you told me that yarn it seemed more like an adventure, something with a thrill in it. Now I know it's pure dirt."

Anthony smiled at him whimsically. "Pure dirt and no deception—eh?"

"As you say. Well—now that we've run this to earth what's the next thing to do?"

Anthony brought him away from the curtains and they stood against the wall. "Where can we go to? I wish that I knew. Absolutely nowhere. I may think a hell of a lot, but I can prove nothing. For the time being."

"Well—you know more or less where you are. There's that can be said about it."

"I fancy I did before I visited the 'Illyrian.' I knew most of the words of the chorus—believe me! What it really means is this. The signal's set dead against me. I must be even more careful than I have been. Still—I haven't finished here yet awhile."

Sanders appeared to be thinking deeply. "Do you know, Mr. Bathurst," he said carefully, "I'm just a little at sea. Floundering a bit. Something else has occurred to me. How the devil did your marksman manage to pick you out as you sat there in the dark? When I looked in just now I couldn't distinguish anybody in any of the seats. Dashed if I know how he could possibly—"

Anthony checked him by a touch on the arm. "Don't worry about that. I thought along the same lines. First of all. But the solution came to me quickly. It's preposterously simple directly you look at it. My gentle friend with the gun must have been seated close to me in the audience. He followed me in here in all probability, marked me down and the exact spot where I was sitting. After he had the place well fixed in his mind's eye it was a comparatively easy matter to slip out of his own seat and stand in the curtains and shoot. What do you say to that?"

Sanders nodded. "Yes, I think you're right. Working it like that would have meant all the difference to him."

"Now do something for me. Something else, I ought to say. I told you just now that I hadn't finished here yet. Go round and have a word with your various attendants—do you mind? Try to find out for me if any of them noticed anybody hanging round that curtain we've just left? It's possible that he may have dallied there for a moment or so and been spotted. In the ordinary course of events people either go in quickly or come out quickly . . . and don't attract particular notice."

"That's a bright idea," concurred Sanders. "I'll scout round for you. In the meantime you will walk slowly back to my room and keep your eyes skinned."

Anthony shook his head. "No danger now. It's all over—for to-day."

Sanders turned on his heel. "I hope you're right. Wait for me in my room till I come back."

Anthony returned to Lacey Sanders's room. His arm was beginning to feel more stiff and more painful. He sat and traced a pattern on the manager's desk with his forefinger. He was thus employed at the moment of Sanders's return.

"Nothing doing," said the last-named with curt directness. "Not a hope! Not a squeak or a smell of anything. I've tackled every man and girl who's been on the job, or near the job. Not one of them saw a thing. Sorry—but there it is!"

"Ah well. Can't be helped. Even if it didn't come off that doesn't say it wasn't worth trying."

"What do we do now?"

Anthony shrugged his shoulders. "I thank you for all that you have done for me and you can go to bed to-night serenely conscious that you have done your good turn both for to-day and many days to come."

"Nice of you—only too pleased. Well—here's to our next meeting. And may it be soon and under happier circumstances. Come along next week and see Freddie Dean in *My Little Bus*. It's supposed to be the funniest picture since *It's Wanted Immediately*."

"Right. That's on then. I'll make the date now. Goodbye."

Anthony sat with Andrew MacMorran and Sir Austin Kemble in the Commissioner's room. Sir Austin looked at the black silk sling with open disfavour. "Been making yourself a nuisance to somebody or merely speaking out of your turn?"

Anthony frowned at the sally. "Afraid you've got it wrong. Nothing active on my part, sir. Very distinctly passive in fact."

"Eh? How do you mean? I don't know that I—"

Anthony leant back in his chair and contributed a statement of hard facts. MacMorran, as he listened, showed signs of a similar anxiety to that which he had communicated to Hemingway. Sir Austin was both astounded and shocked. "Dashed hard to believe, Bathurst."

"No, sir. On the contrary I was convinced directly I felt the pain in my arm. Not much more than an hour ago. There's a spent bullet somewhere in the Illyrian Super-Cinema that will bear out my story when we find it. There are a lot of people in there now whose presence made that job a little difficult."

Sir Austin ignored the sarcasm. He nodded heavily. "Of course. Of course." He accosted the Inspector. "You know, MacMorran, I don't like this."

"I agree," murmured Mr. Bathurst—"in fact I am with you, sir, *in toto*."

"However cavalierly we may be inclined to regard it, the feet remains that it oughtn't to have occurred," continued the Commissioner to MacMorran. "I suppose it's the Coventry business all right?"

"Or all wrong, sir."

"Well, you know what I mean. What do you say yourself, Bathurst?"

"Not a doubt of it, sir. If only I knew just the little more I should feel confident—as it is I'm still groping rather. Which leaves me more or less on tenterhooks!"

MacMorran leant forward towards him. "But we're warmer, Mr. Bathurst. Much warmer than we were. We agree that we're making somebody feel decisively uncomfortable."

"And he's passing that feeling on to you—eh, MacMorran?"

Anthony's eyes twinkled. He forgot his arm, turned quickly in his seat and winced at the pain of the sudden movement. Sir Austin noticed it. It made him more concerned than he had been before. "I don't like it," he repeated.

Anthony rose. "Another week, sir—and things may look better. At any rate we'll hope so. I think there's every chance of it."

Sir Austin grunted. "Look after that arm of yours, Bathurst. It's a bit on my conscience, you know."

"Now I shall worry," replied Mr. Bathurst.

MacMorran walked with him to the door. Anthony turned and spoke in his ear. "Be ready to move, Andrew," he said, "at any given moment."

"Rely on me," replied Inspector MacMorran.

"If only for one thing," continued Anthony.

"What's that?"

Anthony bent down and whispered: "The old man's conscience!"

CHAPTER XXV
SERE AND YELLOW

As LUCK would have it, the wound on Anthony's arm made excellent progress. Daily dressings and Emily's unremitting care and attention reduced the inflammation and after some little time the arm began to heal nicely. The stiffness decreased and gradually the pain diminished. During the whole of this waiting period, Anthony kept a watchful eye on everybody strange or unfamiliar with whom he happened to come in contact. After another chat with MacMorran with regard to the Marston end of the case, he decided that the time was ripe for him to call upon the person who so far had managed to keep in the shadowy background of the case, although his presence, most of the time indeed, had been well advertised.

"I'm inclined to think, Andrew," Anthony remarked to the Inspector, "that you've let Morris Sere run loose for too long a time."

"No. Not at all. Don't you believe it. Mr. Morris Sere hasn't done much or gone very far away from Home Sweet Home without the Yard knowing all about it. Remember—I can't do as I like with him. I haven't unlimited powers. I'm not the Gestapo. Incidentally, too, there's nothing whatever which really connects him with the case. It wasn't his fault he went with Coventry when the pictures were for sale. If you're so concerned with him, why don't you pop along and see him yourself? Or his missus? I reckon she'd be more your handwriting if the truth's known."

Anthony's eyes mocked him. "Come, Andrew, come off it. That's not worthy of you. My monomark's 'Galahad.' And every suggestion to the contrary is a base libel." He flicked the ash from his cigarette. "All the same, you old ruffian, I'm tempted to take your advice."

"Yes," said MacMorran drily. "And I'll bet it's on all fours with your inclinations. That's the main reason why you find it so attractive. The address is Patmos Gardens, Number 22, I fancy."

"Good. I'll let you know how I get on."

When Anthony arrived at the address in Patmos Gardens which MacMorran had given him, he found that his quarry, Mr. Morris Sere, was out. But Mrs. Morris Sere was at home and Anthony informed the maid that he would be charmed if Mrs. Sere would favour him with a few minutes' interview. Mrs. Sere, who this afternoon was much more Vere Valentine than Gladys Sere, consented to the suggestion. When Mr. Bathurst was shown into her presence, he gathered the impression that the lady had just returned from an outing of some kind. She seemed to have but recently shed her hat and coat. Anthony, at his first sight of her, thought of her as a rather adorable person, curiously magnetic, who was pre-eminently just the size that a woman should be. For Mr. Bathurst had strong ideas on this point. But her eyes were her chief attraction. Great wide blue lakes set in a face in which were beauty, personality, and . . . yes . . . character. Her body was slim and straight and Anthony knew at once that this was a woman who counted, in no matter what circles she found herself. At the moment, as she stood facing him, he thought that she was very slightly, perhaps, on the defensive.

"Mr. Bathurst, I believe. Won't you please sit down?"

As she spoke she looked at a tiny watch she carried on one of the fingers of her left hand. "My husband's late. But you may expect him at any moment. Is there anything that I can do for you, do you think, while you're waiting?"

"Thanks. It's good of you. Do you mind if I smoke?"

She smiled at him bewitchingly. "Not at all. I was going to tell you to. If you want to know, you really took the words from my lips."

Anthony held out his case to her. She chose a cigarette with dainty precision and stood slenderly erect. Anthony lit the cigarette for her. Her feet were close together and her nose just a trifle uplifted. Anthony was quick to notice that she wore no jewels at all. He could see no rings beyond her wedding ring—a small thin band—and neither bracelet nor pendant. But she looked hard-polished from tip to toe and all personal radiance. She smiled at him again.

"Now what is all this about? A council of war?"

"Why war?" he returned in the same tone. "I should hate to think that you regarded me as an enemy."

"Scotland Yard," she replied archly, "hardly suggests . . . how shall I put it . . . utter friendliness. Correct me, of course, if I'm wrong."

"Doesn't that depend on how we ourselves individually stand with regard to it?"

She smiled. "I'm perfectly certain that you have no wish to discredit me."

"You are right. My visit has a much more ordinary reason behind it. All I desire is a few minutes' conversation with your husband."

"Can I have three guesses as to what you want to talk about?"

"Would that be necessary? I doubt it."

Anthony's smile should have been completely disarming. She laughed naturally. "Perhaps you are right, Mr. Bathurst. I may need only one. Shall we see if I'm right? Yes? Then here goes. The Coventry murder case! Well?"

"I won't contradict you for a moment. One was all that you needed. I'm delighted to think that my judgment of you and your powers was so accurate."

"Why?" she inquired, ignoring Anthony's last remark. "Why do you want to see my husband about Aubrey Coventry's death? I can assure you that he knows nothing about it."

Anthony felt certain now that she sounded a little anxious. He finessed with her. "But he may be able to help me in one or two other directions. He knew Coventry so well. Did business with him. Was his partner in a good many business deals. From that standpoint alone he seems to have known Coventry as well as anybody—with the possible exception of Rayner—the man who acted as Coventry's confidential secretary. So you see he *may* be able to give me a line on one or two things. At any rate—we're hoping so."

She was about to reply again when Anthony observed that she appeared to be listening. "I think he has just come in," she said.

"My husband, I mean. I heard the door. You need not move—he will come straight in here." She laughed again. "I mean it. Such devotion you never did see. David and Jonathan were as daggers drawn—compared with us. You are surprised to hear me say that? I suppose it *is* unusual these days—to say the least."

She had certainly taken his Rayner thrust well, but, thought Anthony, the woman is a professional actress. That makes a difference. Ordinary weapons can't be expected to bring the success that they normally do.

"No," he said, in answer to her with a shrug of the shoulders, "it may interest you to know that I have trained myself to show no surprise at anything that any woman may say to me."

This pleased her, for she laughed again just as Morris Sere entered the room. Anthony remembered what MacMorran had said about him. He took a good look at Morris Sere. He saw a man with a massive frame and a big face at the top of it. Sere was not handsome—few real men are—but he had fearless level blue eyes, rather small and deep-set, and a jaw that in Anthony's opinion was the most noteworthy feature about him. It would certainly make people think twice, if not three times, before they angered him or even crossed his will. Then there was his voice to be considered. He spoke to his wife, and Anthony, when he heard its rumbling bass note, was reminded of the noise one hears at the edge of a spring freshet when the boulders are shifting. "I was held up," he explained. "That's why I'm a trifle late. Abnormal amount of traffic on the road this afternoon."

Vere Valentine's eyes had smiled at him. "I'll bet you passed more than passed you. Let me introduce you, though. As you see— we have a visitor. I might almost say a distinguished visitor. This is Mr. Anthony Bathurst. My husband."

"Pleased to meet you," said Sere simply. "But what's the idea? Or are you just another friend of my wife's? Ought I to know you?"

His wife was sweetness itself as she explained matters to him. Sere laughed at the explanation. "Now—isn't that too bad? I didn't think I should be visited because Aubrey Coventry got himself bumped off. Ah, well, we live and learn. Get me a whisky and soda, will you, my dear. Perhaps this gentleman friend of yours would care to join us?"

Vere Valentine moved and swiftly arranged the needful. Morris Sere appreciated his drink. He put down his glass. "That's great. First real stuff I've tasted to-day. I don't keep the ordinary muck here, Mr. Bathurst. Can't stomach it!"

"So I've already appreciated, Mr. Sere."

Sere picked up his glass. His wife took it from him.

"I think I'll draw my chair up and talk to you, if you don't mind. In a way, I shall welcome the opportunity. I'd sooner meet my worries in the open than have them skulking behind my back. Sit over there, Mr. Bathurst."

"You don't mind if I stop, do you, dear?"

Sere looked at his wife. His eyes seemed to be searching her face as though he were puzzled at her question. "It doesn't matter to me, my dear. Please yourself. I don't suppose you'll hear anything to your disadvantage. I may have grown in girth these latter years, but I don't think I've increased in conceit of myself. Still—I ought to leave that for others to say, I suppose. Now what's your business, sir?" He heaved his bulk in Anthony's direction.

"You need tell me no more than you please—you know that, Mr. Sere, I don't doubt. But we are puzzled and have been puzzled for some time now with regard to the death of the man whose name you mentioned just now. Aubrey Coventry of Danvers Gate."

Anthony noticed that Sere was staring at him with hard inquiry. "You been hurt in the arm?"

"Yes. Some few days ago now. Nothing to worry about. Healing nicely."

"I thought you had been, from the way you were moving it just now. What happened?"

"Somebody who imagined he had a grievance, took a pot-shot at me and missed, which was just as well from my point of view."

"You don't say! Well, you surprise me." Sere's voice held a kindled note of enthusiastic admiration.

Anthony persisted. "To get back then. To Coventry. I am right in stating that you knew him extremely well?"

"You are. None better. I've known Aubrey Coventry for many years. A decent chap at times, and at others a cunning old twister."

His answer was so direct that Anthony decided at once to short-circuit the inquiry. To come, as it were, to the vital points at issue immediately. "Have you any idea then, Mr. Sere, as to any reason why Coventry may have been murdered? For murdered he most certainly was."

Sere took his time over replying. "Well," he said eventually, "when you ask me that, you ask a big question. Any idea—you said—as to why somebody—some person or persons unknown—got Aubrey Coventry? In the prime of his existence. That takes a good deal of thinking about."

"That's what I want. I want you to think about it."

Sere looked up and his eyes met Anthony's eyes. "Doesn't it come to this? Why *do* people get themselves killed? I figure things out in this way. Either somebody wants to rub off an old score or because they've got something that somebody else wants. I'm not so far out, am I, if I put it like that? You ought to know. You've had experience."

He gave his heavy body another heave. Anthony deliberately avoided a direct reply. He desired that Morris Sere should continue with his exercise in audible thinking. It might be well worth listening to. Sere noticed this. "You're not talking—eh? Going to button up on me and want me to go solo, I suppose? And Vere here, too. What's amiss with her? Not saying a word. Well I'm blessed—how circumstances do alter cases, to be sure. I'd never have believed it. Never mind. Let's get down to our little problem again. Which of my two suggestions fitted my old pal, Aubrey Coventry?"

"In that, I'd like your opinion, Mr. Sere."

"You would! Well, then, I'll ask you something as a bit of make-weight. What does that little rat of a secretary of Coventry's say about it? That scallywag Rayner? Have you been round and asked his opinion?"

Before replying, Anthony turned his head almost idly and glanced towards Vere Valentine. She cleverly evaded his direct gaze. For the time being her eyes seemed demurely centred upon the thin band of her wedding ring. "We have interviewed Rayner, certainly,"

Anthony answered, "but unfortunately it appears that he can help us but little. Beyond making the appointment for the man who called himself Silas Montgomery with Coventry, he seems to have taken no further part in the matter. Oh, yes, Rayner's been very much in the background. That's really one of the reasons that has brought me to see you."

Sere growled. "Well then—I know nothing. All I can do is to use my loaf. You, as an amateur 'busy,' should know very well what I mean by that. Find out who hated Coventry, or, as an alternative, find out somebody who wanted something from him. So much—that murder wasn't too big a price to pay for it. Then you'll be getting somewhere."

Anthony smiled at him, but the effort was more conventional than sincere. "I agree with you, Mr. Sere. But I want you to direct me if you can."

"Direct you? I don't understand."

"Towards the person you outline . . . or, alternatively, towards the possessions of Coventry that were thus coveted."

"Search me," said Sere coolly. . . . "I'm not doing your work. No bon. That's your job, not mine."

Anthony tried again. "Well . . . since you force me, and you have, somehow . . . I'll make a direct attack. Do you know of any possession of Coventry's that was immensely valuable?"

"My dear fellow," returned Morris Sere. "You get this straight. I was connected with Coventry on an occasional business matter. I wasn't his keeper or his father confessor. I know absolutely nothing of his personal possessions. Why the hell should I? He kept them to himself. As I keep mine to myself. Including my dear old Dutch."

He lurched over on his chair towards his wife. "That's true, isn't it, my dear? Add your sweet voice to mine."

"Of course," she answered . . . "any other point of view would be unthinkable."

Anthony wondered if the claws were sheathed and whether a secret duel was being waged between them—under his very eyes. He made a swift mental review of the situation as it had developed during the interview. It was neither his desire nor his intention to force the issue with regard to the sale of the pictures on the premises in Gloucester Road. If Sere kept off it, he would keep away likewise. He determined therefore to lead from another suit.

"A somewhat peculiar complication in the case," he said slowly, "is this. I mention the circumstances because, naturally, they are not generally known. A few hours before his death Coventry visited a clairvoyante."

Vere Valentine dropped something which she stooped and picked up quickly from the carpet. Anthony continued. "The name of this clairvoyante was Madame Zylphara. At least that's the name under which she practises her calling. I mention this fact because it almost suggests that Coventry had something on his mind at the time, and went to this woman for advice. Some people, you know, have a vague faith in the fortune-telling fraternity, whereas these same people would scorn to take counsel or advice from eminently sounder sources." Anthony stopped to see the effect of his words. To his utter surprise, however, Sere calmly placed the ace on his king. "You needn't worry yourself about that. There was nothing whatever in that incident. Nothing at all. I knew of it. I learned of it from Mrs. Coventry soon after Coventry's death. I'll tell you what actually occurred and how it occurred. Coventry came across the woman quite by accident. Down in the country somewhere. He had nothing on his mind as you suggest. Not a bit of it. And it may interest you to know I called upon her myself. Not long afterwards. I don't really know *why* I went to her. Put it down to sudden impulse on my part. I was just interested—that's all."

Anthony looked at him shrewdly. This man was an unusual combination. It was extraordinary, he thought, also, how quiet Vere Valentine was. He would be prepared to bet that it was far from her normal condition. But Morris Sere was speaking again. "I think Coventry's sudden death—and a murder at that—upset me much more than you would imagine. It takes a lot to upset me in the ordinary way of things. I can assure you, though, that it fairly shook me up. I've recovered now, of course, but I felt at the time that I simply must go to this Zylphara woman and find out if she had anything of importance to tell me."

Anthony was in like a flash. "And had she?"

Sere shrugged his heavy shoulders. Vere Valentine was watching her husband with the closest of attention. Some seconds elapsed before he replied. "In answer to your question—no! Nothing that is of the slightest importance to anybody but myself."

There was a note of finality in his voice. It was not possible for Anthony to have anything but one mind with regard to this. He determined, therefore, to accept the inevitable and to bring the interview to an end. No matter how near he might bring Mr. Sere to the water he felt convinced that he would not be able to make him drink. "Before I go, I should like to ask you one more question, Mr. Sere," he said quietly.

"What's that?"

"A few moments ago you mentioned the name of Coventry's private secretary, Rayner. And you went on to refer to him in rather uncomplimentary terms. May I inquire if you had any reason for that?"

"You may—but there's this to it. I'm not bound to answer."

"I'm aware of that, of course."

"No. I called Rayner a rat. I still call him a rat, and if you came here to-morrow and every day for a year—I'd call him a rat three hundred and sixty-five times. As to why I call him a rat—well, that's my business and my business it's going to remain. Got all that?"

"Yes," said Mr. Bathurst in resignation. "I gather that you and he are not what are commonly called 'old chinas.' Though I can't tell which of you feels it the more."

"That makes no difference to me," returned Sere with dogged emphasis. He turned to his wife. "You heard that, my dear?"

"I heard what you said quite plainly," responded Vere Valentine.

Mr. Bathurst made his exit.

There was a smile on Sere's face as he went out.

Chapter XXVI
EXPERT

"I have seen Morris Sere. I have also at the same time seen Mrs. Morris Sere." Anthony Bathurst announced these facts to Inspector MacMorran.

"Go on," said the latter. "I'm more than interested in what you have to tell me."

"The gentleman in the case postulates two causes of murder. We will call them, for the sake of brevity, revenge and cupidity. Note that carefully, Andrew. Now why do *you* think people commit crime? Your opinion should count for something."

MacMorran looked out of the window. It was some appreciable time before he answered. "I have often asked myself that question. One's bound to, in my game. What's *your* answer?"

"In my humble opinion, Andrew—Vanity. Let me recall to you, in that connection, the words of the preacher. Vanity, you see, parents so many other conditions. It's the grandparent of self-consciousness. Fear's the parent. There you have the three generations."

"I don't know that I really follow you," said the Inspector.

"I'll explain, then. To my attentive class. I expect you've noticed that I adore being didactic. On my hind legs. You've probably noticed that too. Take our murderer. Any murderer will do. For example, our friends of that diabolical strappado when you and I looked into that sinister little problem of The Purple Calf. The murderer begins by being full of his own importance. Puffed with pride. Covets his neighbour's ox or his ass. Or anything that is his. Thinks that the particular possession is all wrong. Absurd error of distribution and so forth. This condition of covetousness disturbs his moral balance. So he takes the law into his own hands and adjusts the differences. That covers the cupidity class."

MacMorran remonstrated with him. "I was going to say . . . that doesn't explain all the murders by a long chalk."

"The other class is just as easily explained, my dear Andrew. Again—another projecting vanity. Our murderer, in this instance, gives way to his lust for power. Desire for spotlight and notoriety. Must be the big shot. The Triton among the minnows. *Aut Caesar aut nullus.*" MacMorran nodded. "Quite right there. I fully agree. Old Kaiser Bill was outed all right when the time came."

Anthony frowned. "Dear old Andrew!" He went on again at once. "So, as in the previous instance, our friend attempts this exercise in readjustment, and removes one or two people whom he chooses as the instrument of the theory that *he* counts much more than *they* do."

More remonstrance from MacMorran. "How does this affect Sere . . . and Mrs. Sere? By the way, I can inform you that she hasn't seen Rayner again according to the reports that have come through to me."

"In that connection I can tell you something. Sere doesn't like Rayner. Placed him in the rodent class. Utterly and totally, entirely and definitely. By no means a blood-brother. In fact, beyond a trenchant criticism of Rayner, Sere didn't tell me very much." Anthony leant back in his chair. "I don't know what to make of Sere. I had a nasty feeling all the time I was with him that I should have done better to have stayed at home. If he does know anything, he's a thundering good actor, Andrew."

"Perhaps he has to be—in order to be a match for his wife." MacMorran's comment was dry and caustic. Anthony was impressed by it. The Inspector took a letter from his desk and tossed it across to Anthony. "Cast your eye over that, Mr. Bathurst. I fancy it will interest you."

Anthony read the letter. It was from Alec Marston, had been written on the previous day and was worded as follows:

"Dear Inspector MacMorran,

"I have been able to pick up an item of news in connection with our mutual and recent interest. I think that it is both important and significant. I am calling to see you at noon to-morrow, as I think you should be informed of it at once. Please ask Mr. Bathurst to be present."

"If you hadn't come round I was going to send for you. Shouldn't like to disappoint the lad. Even though he may have peculiar tastes."

Anthony looked at his watch. "We haven't long to wait before he arrives."

"Don't worry. I've arranged it. Hemingway has had orders to bring him straight up."

"Good. Then we'll possess our souls in patience and wait for the pair of them."

Marston, actually, wasn't a matter of two minutes late. A temporarily solemn Hemingway ushered him in and was ordered by MacMorran to hold himself in readiness—whatever that may mean.

Marston, when he entered, wore his usual smiling face. "You're in a good humour this morning," remarked Anthony after they had shaken hands.

Marston beamed. "I suppose I am. And why shouldn't I be? I've picked up a valuable piece of information."

Anthony interposed a hand. "Just a minute. Before you go any farther. You say 'picked up.' Let me know what you mean by that exactly. Did the information you refer to fall into your lap or did you go after it? I'd like to know about that before you tell me another word."

Marston flushed a little and hesitated for a second.

"Well, Mr. Bathurst, I may as well confess without any beating about the bush that I went after it—to use your own phrase."

"Thanks. That clears the air. Go on."

Marston made a fresh start. "Well—how shall I put it? I'm in on most of the trade workings and I've met, in my time, a number of highly influential people. I've even been at times in a position to help one or two. Done them little favours occasionally. So I have an 'approach,' as you might say. Well—I placed a judicious inquiry in the right quarter. Based, of course, on the two pictures of our mutual interest and what we think we know concerning them. And I've learned this. But first of all I must ask you a question. Does the name 'Van Hoyt' suggest anything to you?" He paused.

MacMorran decisively shook his head. "No. Not to me. Never heard the name."

Anthony, however, received the mention of the name very differently. "Yes. It does. You refer to the millionaire family of Van Hoyt. Hang on a second and I'll tell you quite a lot about them. One of them has been settled in England for many years now. That's Cornelius. He lives in Shropshire. I had occasion to visit him some years ago when I was looking into that bizarre mystery of The Chosroes Cross. The other brothers are, I think, Wallis Van Hoyt and Bronson Van Hoyt. Bronson is the eldest and the richest. They've stayed in the States. The father was Sylvanus Van Hoyt. He was a 'railroad King' who augmented an already large fortune by marrying Anna Delaney, the only daughter and also only child of old Julius Delaney. The famous Chicago wheat operator. The Van Hoyts now are perhaps the richest family in the world. So you see, Marston, I do know something of the name 'Van Hoyt.' Now you're in play again."

Marston regarded him with open admiration. "I should say you do—and no mistake. You know a great deal more about the family than I do myself. F or one thing my knowledge is confined to only one of the three brothers you mentioned. That's Bronson Van Hoyt, the eldest. Now Bronson Van Hoyt is reputed to possess the finest collection of old masters in the whole of the U.S.A. He has spent lavishly to obtain this collection, and, with the huge resources of wealth that he has at his disposal, you can readily see how he has managed to acquire his collection. You are following me closely, gentlemen, aren't you?" Anthony and MacMorran assented. Marston, more gratified than ever, warmed to his task. "Well, gentlemen, I'd like you to listen to this. Very recently and not over long after the murder of Aubrey Coventry, Bronson Van Hoyt came to this country on the *Mauretania* and stayed for a week in London. Note that."

Anthony rubbed his hands. "Go on, Marston—this is getting highly interesting."

"I thought you would appreciate it. Nice and warm, isn't it?" Marston gave a quick glance towards MacMorran as though he were inviting that gentleman's approbation also. But the Inspector's face was impassive. He was waiting for additional developments before he was prepared to wave his personal flags. Marston continued: "I can also tell you that during his brief stay in London, Bronson Van Hoyt called once, and perhaps even twice, on a man named Carlton Sands. When I tell you that this Carlton Sands is regarded as an art expert—perhaps one of our greatest experts—particularly on Holbein—you will see better what I'm really getting at. In other words my question to you, Mr. Bathurst, and to you, Inspector MacMorran—is *what* brought Bronson Van Hoyt from Brooklyn to little old London town just after the murder of Aubrey Coventry?"

Anthony had immediate questions for Marston.

"Where does this man, Carlton Sands, live?"

"Not far away. Somewhere near Chelsea, I believe."

"What sort of reputation has he?"

Marston was guarded in his answer. "Well, with regard to that I don't really know. I'm bound, though, in fairness, to say I've never heard anything against him. But a big parcel of commission is a temptation, when it's as safe as houses, and almost anybody who's human can fall for it. Especially in these days when, for the majority of us, living's so precarious. You see what I mean, don't you?"

"H'm." Anthony turned to the Inspector. "Ever heard of Carlton Sands, Andrew?"

"Can't say that I have. But if he's always kept the right side of the law—I shouldn't do. Once upon a time I hadn't heard of you. So there's nothing much in that, is there?"

Marston impetuously cut in. "I'm going to finish up by saying this. In my humble opinion Bronson Van Hoyt came over for the Holbein and the Rembrandt. They were offered to him through the medium of Sands, and on Sands's own expert valuation, and if we call on Sands we must be on the heels of Coventry's murderer. To you that may sound ultra-confident, but I'm pretty sure of my ground."

MacMorran frowned. Anthony looked at the backs of his nails. "Do you know, Marston, another question comes to my lips. I can't avoid it. You must attribute it to my curious nature. You said a little while ago that you placed an inquiry in the right quarter. Could you enlighten us just a little further with regard to that?"

Marston was frankness itself. "I was prepared for you to ask me that. I referred, I think, to a *judicious* inquiry. I placed my investigation through a man named Abraham Marassky. He is the biggest art dealer in Europe. He operates from all the capitals of Europe. His London offices are in Oxford Street. I have a line of approach to him through a Mr. Lodge of Crowborough for whom I have transacted several pieces of business."

"I see. Turn Sands up for me in the telephone directory—do you mind, Andrew?"

MacMorran reached for the book and turned the pages. "Stanford 822," he remarked laconically. "Shall I get him?" MacMorran moved to grasp the receiver.

"No. Just a minute, Andrew. Let Marston get him. It's his bundle. Play the game and let him see it through."

Marston coloured. "That's O.K. with me." He asked for the connection. Anthony and MacMorran watched him. Some minutes passed. Then Marston replaced the receiver. "No answer," he announced. "Number engaged?" queried Anthony.

Marston shook his head. "No. The girl said she could get no reply."

Anthony remained in thought for some few moments. "Tell me," he said eventually, "would a man of the status of Bronson Van Hoyt buy pictures of that kind—as we think—two of the most valuable old masters—without making too many inquiries? Is it a likely proposition? You see what I'm getting at?"

MacMorran shook his head. "Doubtful, if you ask me."

Marston burst in with the expression of a different opinion.

"Oh, but he would—believe me! I know so much about the game. Collectors—and with regard to pictures he's no more than that—have no scruples at all. I almost said they had no morals. They are almost always obsessed with the sole idea of getting hold of the prize. That's the only thing that counts with them. Ordinary considerations don't weigh with them at all. In every other respect they would probably behave with the utmost decency, just like ordinary civilized people, but when it comes to adding to their collection something they've been after, perhaps, for years—oh, boy!"

Anthony gave confirmation. "I think Marston is right, Andrew. The more I think the more I find myself in agreement with him. In fact I'm very much afraid that the Saskia and the Elizabeth are in the same positions as 'my Bonny'—and you know where he is."

MacMorran nodded. "Ay. It's feasible. I've met some of these so-called collectors in my time. Down their one line of thought—which is very often their only one—they're fair scatty."

Anthony turned to Marston again. "You said that Carlton Sands was a Holbein expert specially, didn't you?"

"Yes. He's one of the last words on the Holbein pictures. You see—if Bronson Van Hoyt *were* after those pictures—he ceases to be a millionaire when the scent is running high—he becomes a collector—nothing more and nothing less. And that's what I'm afraid of."

"Andrew," said Anthony Bathurst with sudden decision, "tell Hemingway to have your car ready in ten minutes. Marston and I are coming with you."

"Where?" inquired MacMorran.

"To the residence of Carlton Sands—that eminent authority on Holbein. Five Ascot Walk, Chelsea. Telephone number, Stanford 822."

"You certainly know your own mind," said the Inspector as he rose from his chair.

"How right you always are," returned Mr. Bathurst.

Chapter XXVII
THE LOSER PAYS

MacMorran's car drew up outside the residence of Carlton Sands. The sky was overcast and a drizzling rain was falling which made the entire surroundings seem as thoroughly unattractive as could possibly be imagined. The Inspector alighted, followed by Marston and Anthony. "What is this fellow, Marston?" inquired MacMorran. "Is he married or a bachelor?"

"Not certain about that, Inspector. But I rather fancy he's a bachelor. I think, too, that his age is somewhere in the late forties."

"I see. Well, come on—we'll rout him out and find out what he has to say for himself. We may pick up something." The trio made their way to the front door. MacMorran rang the bell. They waited in the porch. There was no reply. "Ring again, Andrew," prompted Anthony. MacMorran rang the bell for the second time. Again there was no reply. The Inspector looked at Anthony interrogatively, but he said curtly: "We might have known, bearing in mind what happened to Marston when he telephoned just now."

"I wonder," said Anthony quietly.

MacMorran went on from where he had just stopped. "I wonder, too," he said equally quietly, "as to whether it's a case of the bird has flown. I shouldn't be surprised. To tell the truth the idea came to me when we were on our way here. I'm rather surprised in a way that you didn't think of it."

Marston's face showed unmistakable signs of disappointment. Anthony shook his head gravely. "How do you know I didn't, Andrew?"

"Well, I'm assuming you didn't, otherwise you wouldn't have brought us on this wild-goose chase."

Anthony frowned. "Don't you scream before you're hit, Andrew. It's a mistaken policy, that. It's not the best MacMorran by any means. Now listen to me carefully. I want you to open that door."

"Why?"

"Call it one of my awkward hunches if you like. I've had 'em before, as you know, and you haven't done too badly out of 'em, now have you?" he asked.

Marston bent down and inspected the lock. "It's a Yale," he remarked.

MacMorran looked at Anthony doubtfully. "You know I don't like doing this. If I make a mistake and there's a moan—"

"*Can* you open it?"

"I've something here that will open most of its kind. You've seen me use it before."

"Don't argue, Andrew. Let me see you use it now." Anthony was seemingly determined. MacMorran thought for a moment before he inserted his master key. The lock yielded easily to the pressure. The three men slipped into the hall. "Very quiet," muttered MacMorran.

"Too quiet," supplemented Anthony. Marston looked round curiously. "Nice place."

Anthony pointed to the floor. "If he went, he went in a hurry. Four days' morning papers there. Didn't acquaint his long-suffering newsagent of his wanderlust. I like my hunch even better than I liked it before. Come with me and have a look round, Andrew."

They went quietly along the length of the hall until they came to the first room. Anthony opened the door. It was obviously the lounge. 'And empty at that.' The emptiness of it was rather over-whelming. Even MacMorran, whose reactions to most conditions were by no means rapid, sensed it immediately. He turned. "Seems a bit god-forsaken, if you ask me."

Anthony nodded. "I agree, Andrew. Lead on, though. Humanity must lie ahead." The three pairs of feet moved farther along the hall.

The house was dead in a flat, dark way. Another door was on their right. Anthony stopped suddenly in front of it. His hand stayed the others. A new expression came on his face, and he put a finger to his lips. MacMorran and Marston halted at his side. Anthony thrust his head forward. His attitude was that of one who listens for the slightest sound. The Inspector and Marston not only waited, but listened with him. There was no sound that came from this dead house. Anthony took the handle of the door and turned it. He and his companions entered the living-room of Carlton Sands, the man who knew a lot about pictures and almost all about Holbein.

"My God!" said Anthony. He spoke in a whisper, but Marston in the rear caught the words, and at once felt horribly sick.

Chapter XXVIII
THE NEAREST PART

Carlton Sands sat at his table. Or rather the body of Carlton Sands. His left arm was flung outstretched across the table. His head was sunk on his breast. Towards his left. Much of his blood had left him, and could be seen in an ugly stain across the blue of the table-cover. Marston trembled as he looked. Ho had not realized before that a sight of this kind could shock him so; MacMorran went to the body. "Mind your sleeve, Andrew," said Anthony, with quiet and curt significance. MacMorran said nothing. He just shook his head. He moved the dead head more to one side, where it lolled like a broken-necked doll. From where he was standing, Anthony saw that the dead face was twisted and contorted. He spoke to MacMorran. There was authority in what he said.

"Just above the collar-bone, Andrew. Notice that? The place where a wavering hand should strike. A wavering hand, shall we say, that, although it wavered, wanted to make sure."

MacMorran rubbed the ridge of his jaw. "There's one thing—you do think of things, sir." He caught sight of Marston's white face. "And you stand back out of it, d'ye hear? I don't like it myself—and I know how you're feeling."

"It's the blood—and his face," muttered Marston, as he drew away towards the door. There came a silence. The only sound in the room that came to their ears was that of the clock ticking on the mantelpiece.

MacMorran's was the voice which broke the silence. He gestured towards the body. "How long, would you say, Mr. Bathurst?"

Anthony rubbed his cheek. "I'm a layman, Andrew. So my opinion's worth little or nothing. Probably rather less than your own. If I must have a shot at an answer . . . say last evening some time. He may have been away and come back. Judging by the papers. How about making certain?"

"Yes, of course. You're right." He called to Marston, who came a shade closer. Marston listened attentively, and Anthony heard occasional words. "Divisional surgeon . . . Dr. Pryde." Anthony remembered him . . . "and the photographers, Merritt and Finney, say you're speaking for Chief-Inspector MacMorran . . . you know this address where you are . . . and tell them as sharp as they like."

Marston slipped seemingly gratefully out of the room.

Anthony moved up to the table and began to make critical contribution. "Nothing on the table, Andrew. No notebooks this time. Nothing in the room at all except just ordinariness. Ordinariness and death. Notice what I mean? Everything is normal except that a man is dead who should be living. If it *were* a party before the blow was struck, everything that was 'party' has been cleared up. Very tidy. *Too* tidy, I must say."

"No weapon," grunted MacMorran.

"Part of the tidiness. Our murderer murders with due care and attention. I'm sorry, but I'm insisting on that, Andrew. It's important."

MacMorran cocked an eyebrow in his direction. "Blue Overalls?"

"Not this time. Same person, of course. But attired differently. Sartorial distinctions. Safe bet that. Sands knew too much: in case we found him, put a few awkward questions to him and he decided to talk. Here we have one more striking testimony, Andrew, to the attractive reticence of men who have given up the ghost."

"Yes. Yes. It fits—I agree."

"What puzzles me," went on Anthony, "is that Marston . . ." he stopped suddenly as though a vital thought had presented itself to him.

MacMorran seemed not to notice it. His thoughts evidently were elsewhere. "Time Marston was back," he said, as though he had grit between his teeth. "Telephone can't be far away in a district like this."

Anthony listened to sounds of weather. "It's raining like hell. And he's got no coat."

MacMorran's serious tension asserted itself. "Don't be damned silly. He's all wet—er—and chilled to the bone, I suppose! There's a dead man here . . . and you talk like . . ."

"Like a clown—er? Perhaps we're both of us clowns, Andrew. Oh, curse it . . . why can't I think?" As he spoke the bell rang—shrill and insistent.

"Marston," snapped MacMorran.

Anthony let him in. Marston walked to the foot of the stairs.

"O.K.," inquired Anthony, "at 1212 Whitehall?"

Marston nodded. "Ten minutes. At the most. So they say. What have you done?"

"Done? Tried to think. And made a feeble business of it."

Marston's breath was coming quickly. "Why was he"—he jerked his head towards the farther room—"killed like that?"

Anthony smiled bitterly. "Because he knew so much about 'Holbein' and too much about somebody else."

Marston shivered at the implication. "That's a horrible thought. That because you had knowledge which other people hadn't—you're murdered like that, struck down from behind in cold blood."

Anthony nodded and looked at him gravely. "It seems that more than one kind of knowledge is a dangerous thing. But you'd better tell the Inspector about his messages. He's been getting a bit impatient."

"I suppose I had."

"Come with me, then. For all we know he may be feeling lonely. He's a quaint old bird, MacMorran."

Marston hadn't seen Anthony in this mood before. Behind the touch of flippancy his ear could detect a note of hard purpose. He began to wonder what it was exactly that had wrought this change in him. They went back to MacMorran and the body of Carlton Sands. Before the Inspector could speak, there came the sound of car wheels and the bell rang again. Anthony gestured to Marston and returned to the front door. To admit two men in plain clothes who touched their hats to him and entered without a sound. One was the photographer, who carried the tripod apparatus. MacMorran received them and gave them their orders. The men began their work quietly. Again the bell rang. Again Anthony played the part of janitor. This time it was Pryde, the divisional surgeon. He grinned at Anthony as he entered—pink and tubby as ever. They shook hands. Anthony followed him into the room wherein lay the work he had to do. Doctor Pryde opened his bag and went to the body.

"H'm. Very nasty. Stabbed in the back." He busied himself with certain movements. "Sticky job—eh? Knife or dagger with longish blade. Penetrated to the base of the right lung. Lot of haemorrhage naturally." Pryde's deft hands removed clothes. Clothes that had been worn by Carlton Sands.

"Blood everywhere. Shirt and vest pretty well saturated. Nasty business. Didn't live long after the blow was struck. Barely a minute."

Anthony nodded towards the corpse. "When would you say it happened, Doctor?"

"When? H'm. Blood's all dried up." He felt the dead man's arms, tested muscles, and peered into his eyes. "Let's see. Some time between seven o'clock last night and midnight. Near enough."

MacMorran came in. "That definite?"

Pryde nodded. "Pretty well. You can take it as not being much out."

Anthony took advantage of the conversation to slip from the room. He went upstairs. The journey was fruitless. He encountered nothing which gave him pause to think. He called to MacMorran from the landing above. The Inspector came up and went round with him. "Any luck for prints downstairs, Andrew?"

"From what my chaps say, I doubt it. Plenty of prints all over the place, but nothing very good they tell me. All of Sands himself."

"How long will Pryde be?"

"Not long now. He reckons he'll be away in less than a quarter of an hour. When he's finished, I must see about getting that body away."

"Where's Marston?" asked Anthony.

"Downstairs somewhere. Bit green round the gills. This job's upset his tummy. He's gone all queasy. Funny how it takes 'em when they're not used to it."

Anthony nodded. "Andrew," he said solemnly, "I want to tell you this—we're very near our murderer. Don't misunderstand me, though. I don't mean that he's in our hands and that we only have to close them to get him. But he's *watching* us whereas we can't watch *him*! I mean that he's *near*. Just that and nothing else. So we must keep cool and our heads till the crucial moment comes. I've had a brain wave. I want that black cloth cap that was picked up in the parcel of clothes from the railway carriage. Get it for me as soon as you can, will you?"

"I'll send it round later on in the day. Suppose we get back to Pryde." Anthony followed him down the stairs. MacMorran went on ahead to join the others.

"Doctor Pryde's going now, Mr. Bathurst," he announced a little later over his shoulder.

"Not before a fall, I trust," returned Anthony, as he shook hands with the divisional surgeon.

Pryde crossed the room and shut his bag. "There's one thing," he said jocularly, "it's an ill wind you know—these little matters do mean that we bump into each other occasionally—don't they? Cheerio!"

"That's nice of you, Doctor," responded Anthony.

CHAPTER XXIX
LET GO THE PAINTER

ANTHONY Lotheringon Bathurst talked with Langley Seabrooke Escreet. Escreet was perhaps one of the six leading analytical chemists of the day. Anthony knew a girl who knew Escreet well, and had been able to make a special contact with him by reason of her good offices. Anthony's present conversation with Escreet concerned a black cloth cap. Escreet, in fact, had a good deal to say about it. This condition was unusual for Langley Escreet, because as a rule he said little about most things, which again was in indirect proportion to his thoughts.

Anthony said: "So I take it from what you say you've come to certain conclusions."

Escreet's eyes twinkled responsively. "You may. As a matter of fact, I've formed some very definite conclusions."

"Now hold on a second. You are absolutely positive of what you're going to say?"

"Absolutely. You needn't harbour the slightest shadow of doubt about it."

"Good. That's how I like a man to talk. Now shoot!"

"We have made several tests in the lab. with regard to your cap. On the lines which you suggested in your letter when you sent it to me. Investigations have been made from time to time for the differential halogen absorptions of some of the more common oils and fats. They have an analytical value with regard to the unsaturated linkings in the various fatty acid molecules contained therein." Escreet looked up. "You are following me, of course, Bathurst?"

"Well—near enough. Go on."

"There are iodine, homine, and chlorine values which may be determined. The iodine by the usual WIJS method. It is known that there may be hydroxyl grouping in the molecules. From a compound mixture so treated, the resultant ester maybe hydrolysed with excess of potassium hydroxide in alcohol, and the fatty acid liberated in the usual manner. Get me?"

"Er—perhaps I see your drift. But don't mind me—go on."

Escreet continued for a time in the same vein. After some moments, Anthony came in again. "If I may short-circuit you and remain courteous at the same time, what did you get?"

"This. The man who wore this cap habitually was a painter. We have established that for a certainty. The absorptions of paint have been found there by five entirely different scientific processes. Whereas the cap externally neither shows paint nor smells of paint."

Anthony whistled between his teeth. "A painter—eh? Could you go any farther than that? A painter of what kind, would you say? Pictures or just a bloke that has a slap at the bathroom?"

Escreet grinned infectiously. "A brush bloke who paints from a pot. A real white-coated genuine member of the Painters' Union! You know the kind—blimey Bill—but you ain't 'arf shovin' it on thick round the edges. Go easy—chum."

Anthony whistled again. "Buildings—eh? And big ones at that, I suppose. Who'd have thought it?"

Escreet nodded and relapsed into his former matter-of-fact manner.

"Well, Bathurst, is the information of any value to you now that you have it? If it is, you're welcome to it such as it is, and I'm pleased to have been able to supply it."

"My dear fellow, all information that's sound and accurate and touches my problem must be, *per se*, of value. It can never be in the way as it were, or superfluous. It's the *useless* knowledge that comes to one that isn't needed. In that reference, I always think that we may remember the words of the immortal Holmes. Do you mind if I recall them to you?"

Escreet smiled. "Not a bit of it. Carry on."

"It happens early in the recorded history of the master's career. When Watson made his first acquaintance with Sherlock Holmes, the latter said something like this: 'A man's brain in its original state may be likened to an empty attic. He has to stock it with the furniture of his choice. The fool on one hand crowds it with useless lumber of all kinds. But on the other the skilful workman exercises care with regard to the stock that he takes in. He chooses with discrimination the particular tools that will help him to do his work. Of these, he collects a large assortment which he keeps in the most perfect order. And it must be remembered, too, whilst on the subject of furnishing that the attic cannot be distended to any extent. Its walls are not elastic. For,' says Holmes, 'you can always rely upon this fact. There comes a time when, for every additional piece of knowledge that is taken in, something goes out which was there before. So it is of the highest importance that useful facts are not elbowed out by utterly useless ones.' You may recall that Watson was amazed at Holmes's profound ignorance of the Copernican theory and of the composition of the Solar System. He was equally astounded, too, at Holmes's reception of his amazement. 'What do I care, my dear Watson, if we go round the sun? If we went round the moon it wouldn't make one atom of difference either to me or to my work.'"

Escreet acknowledged the argument with a quick movement of the head. "To an extent, I agree with him. I can see what he meant and I think he was right."

"I'm glad of that. It makes me feel that I haven't been wasting my time."

"Well, you know what's in front of you. Your job is to find a painter."

"No, I don't think so."

"The painter, then, who wore this cap." Langley Escreet as he made his amendment pointed to the article which had been under discussion. "No, I don't think that even." Escreet corrugated his brow. "No? What then? I'm sorry—but where was I missing the point?"

"You're not exactly missing the point, Escreet. It's just that you haven't the details of the problem at your finger-ends as I have them. My job is to find *the man who wore the painter's cap*—in addition to a suit of blue overalls. Which is by way of being a somewhat different proposition, you will admit."

"I see. I suppose I was jumping to conclusions rather. How did he get hold of it? Did he borrow it, do you think?" Anthony Bathurst smiled. "As the divine William puts it: 'Convey the wise it call.' Consider it confusion of *meum* and *tuum*. In other words, Escreet, I think he stole it."

Again Escreet's eyebrows went up. "Strange thing to steal, Bathurst. A painter's cap!"

Anthony shrugged his shoulders. "Values are always relative. A cap of this kind was needed; when one came to hand it was appropriated. Suppose we describe the misdemeanour as 'stealing by finding.' Our murderer wanted a cap, he saw one lying handy somewhere . . . and . . . *carpe diem*. It's a convenient and utilitarian philosophy and one of the oldest known to mankind."

Escreet nodded. "What's your next step, then?"

Anthony considered the question. "I'm inclined to think that I shall review the whole case." He stopped abruptly. Langley Escreet noticed a strange look come into his eyes. He continued: "And then, my dear Escreet, when I have done that thoroughly, I shall make discreet inquiries as to certain large buildings and institutions that are situated in the City of London. Some of them, you know, may have been recently painted. Don't you think it's extremely likely?" His grey eyes twinkled as he spoke.

"One never knows. At any rate, I'm with you so far. I shall be interested as to how you get on."

"I'll make a point of letting you know."

"Thank you," said Langley Escreet.

"On the contrary," said Mr. Bathurst, "thank you."

Chapter XXX
VALERIE PLAYS THE GAME

ANTHONY moved the morning page from its propped position against the matutinal coffee-pot, and put in its place the letter which Emily had just handed to him. For some few seconds he studied the handwriting on the envelope. It was bold and well formed and entirely unfamiliar to him. "If I had to bet," murmured Mr. Bathurst to himself, as he removed the top of an egg, "I'd put just a modest stake on a woman, but a woman educated above ordinary standards." Before opening the envelope, he carefully prepared his toast. When that was ready he opened the envelope. He was at once glad that he had done so and not waited until after he had finished his breakfast. For what he read most certainly pleased him. It shall be recapitulated here.

'DEAR MR. BATHURST,

'I haven't the slightest doubt that you will be completely surprised when you open and read this. Almost as surprised, in fact, as I am to find myself writing it. That sounds so very feminine, doesn't it? Also—another funny thing—Peter—you remember Peter, don't you?—has almost dared me to write it—and so I'm taking up the dare and have literally chanced it. But I must tell you this. You may or may not remember—personally, I think it's a sure thing that you do—but I swore to Peter that I wouldn't marry him until the mystery of my uncle's death had been cleared up. When I said it I meant it. No girl could possibly have meant anything more. Peter—he's a dear boy—but like all you men, terribly obstinate—was frightfully upset at my decision. And that's putting it mildly. He simply refuses to accept the situation. He points out that it may never be solved, the murder, I mean—and in that case I shall never be able to marry him. Which thought, the dear boy *will* keep on saying, makes him too miserable for words. "Never," he points out to me, "is such a dreadfully long time." And, of course, in a way he's right. Well, to cut a long story short—for the last week or so he's been positively hammering away at me in the hope of breaking down my resolution and making me reverse my decision. So far I've resisted him. Been absolutely adamant. When I make up my mind on anything it's usually made up for good! But—and this is in the strictest confidence, Mr. Bathurst—my will-power is beginning to waver. It's the look on his face. So pained and reproachful. I really believe that he's suffering untold agonies—all on account of poor insignificant me. Poor old Peter! And this is where I want your help, dear kind sir. Will you please let me know as soon as you possibly can whether you think that there's the slightest chance of the police solving the mystery of Uncle Aubrey's death? Because if there's not, I feel that I shall just have to give way. But if there is, I could still hold out for a time and then, when it is all cleared up, marry my Peter boy, and feel that I'm not just an ordinary weak-willed woman whose determination and resolution can always be broken down by a mere male! All frightfully feminine, isn't it? I feel that by writing to you like this, I shall achieve more than if I wrote to that hard-headed Inspector of Police. You will understand my motives so much better, I am sure. So, Mr. Bathurst, be an absolute angel and let me know the position as soon as you possibly can. I'm not asking too much, am I? You can give me a kind reply without giving away any official secrets. With sincere apologies for bothering you on what, after all, I suppose, is a purely private matter,

'I remain,

'Yours sincerely,

'VALERIE MOFFATT.

'P.S.—Please regard this as absolutely confidential.'

Anthony read the letter carefully and smiled all over his face. "'The ways that lovers use,'" he quoted. "Now what can I reasonably say to a loving lady anxious to get her man, and at the same time maintain her supposedly superiority complex?" Mr. Bathurst buttered more cold toast. He chuckled to himself as he surveyed the image of himself as fairy godmother. 'Each man in his time plays many parts.' For the time being, he placed Miss Moffatt's letter on one side, and devoted his attention to finishing his breakfast. This accomplished, he meditated for a few moments before commencing his reply.

'DEAR MISS MOFFATT,

'Many thanks for your most interesting letter which I received this morning. First of all, with regard to your postscript, please rest assured that I shall respect your confidences most implicitly. Have no fears on that account. As to your request, I am delighted to be in a position to furnish you with the following information. For a week or two at the most, stick to your resolution. You will lose nothing by it, and will be able to hold your head up as the girl who kept her word, and at the same time fulfilled her promises! From that last statement of mine you will be able to deduce that I have every hope that the mystery of your uncle's murder will be solved within the period of time that I have mentioned. If I didn't think so, I should have no hesitation in telling you. This is the broad reply for which you have asked me. And believe me, I was never an incorrigible optimist. Beyond that, of course, you will realize I am unable to go. So that's that. And in addition to all this, there's my personal point of view, which I beg of you not to disregard. For, in the words of Oscar Wilde: "It is sweet to dance to violins when Love and Life are fair. To dance to flutes, to dance to lutes, is delicate and rare." Which, being interpreted, my dear Miss Moffatt, means that I should love to dance at your wedding. Don't disappoint me.

Sincerely yours,
'ANTHONY L. BATHURST.'

He carefully directed the envelope and then handed it to Emily for the channel of the post. "After all," he said to himself, "I've told her nothing that can do any harm, and if she wants to have her own way as badly as she indicates in her letter, well then, she can as far as I'm concerned."

The letter out of the way, Mr. Bathurst sought the comfort of his arm-chair. He still had to perform that exercise of reviewing once again the whole problem as he had promised himself, and as he had stated to Langley Escreet. He felt confident that given one more link he would be able to assemble the entire chain and grasp the truth. He felt equally confident that this all-important link *was* there, close at hand and ready for the taking—the link which all the time, so far, had eluded him. Anthony packed his pipe with a plentiful supply of Balkan Sobrani and lit it. For a long time he sat there and smoked—the tobacco clouds around and about his head. His mind was uneasy. He seemed to be faced always, when he analysed the particular problem, with a barrier which was insurmountable. *If*, he argued to himself, Aubrey Coventry had been inveigled by the fake Montgomery into granting that last interview, why, if the possession of two old masters had been the criminal's objective, as now appeared to be moderately certain, had the technique been so clumsy? Why *murder* the man? Why not steal the pictures by the methods of ordinary housebreaking or burglary? Even if the interview had been necessary for the murderer as a preliminary, for a purpose which at the moment wasn't clear, why conclude it with murder when the pictures could have been so easily stolen? There was no struggle! At least, there was no visible evidence that Coventry had put up a fight in defence of his belongings! There were the chairs at the table, it is true—and the notebooks—at that precise moment the light flooded Anthony's brain . . . and he knew why Coventry had been murdered! As his excitement grew, he rose from his chair. He must contact MacMorran at once. As he took hold of the 'phone, he realized, too, the meaning and the methods of the snarling man. The two matters were of a perfect pattern. Each fell into place with swift precision, and both he and MacMorran had missed the sheer significance from the start. He asked for Whitehall 1212, and within a matter of seconds was talking to the Inspector. MacMorran listened for some considerable time.

"It may take some time, Andrew," said Mr. Bathurst at length, "but I'm dead certain that I'm right."

MacMorran made further contribution and as he did so an idea came to Anthony. "Leave it to me, Andrew," he said. "I'll work the oracle with the Commissioner. He usually lets me have my own way when I want it badly. I'll tackle Sir Austin myself. That O.K. your end?"

"As far as the old man goes, you're welcome. I'll hang on till I hear from you again."

"Won't that arm of yours ache?" grinned Anthony.

"You know verra well what I mean," returned the Inspector.

"How you do flatter yourself, Andrew."

Chapter XXXI
REACTIONS (SABBATH)

IT IS to be recorded that Anthony was having his second 'Clover Club' before MacMorran arrived. "Really, Andrew, you and I are full of differences. I am never late for dinner. There is an old saying indeed, extant in the Bathurst family, coined, I believe, by an historic Bathurst, known as 'Great Aunt Susan,' to the effect that the Bathursts will never be rich because they have wolves in their bellies."

MacMorran snorted. "Wolves! She must have used a microscope."

"Emily," said Mr. Bathurst, "serve dinner, please. The Inspector has a warped outlook."

The dinner was good, and when Emily produced the port MacMorran began to talk the business of the evening.

"Sir Austin tells me that I'm to act on your instructions. You've seen him, I take it?"

"Seen him, talked to him, and agreed with him as to a course of action. This last was suggested by me."

"There's no need to tell me that." MacMorran took the decanter and filled up his glass again. He pushed the decanter over to his host. "You see, sir, I've grown accustomed to your little ways. Now listen to me for a while. You've worked the Commissioner and I *think*—mind I only say I think—that I've pulled the strings with the B.B.C. There's nothing like publicity for real value . . . as you yourself will agree."

"Tell me what you've done, Andrew."

MacMorran beamed. "I had a brain-wave the day after you rang me up. I was thinking over your suggestions, and it entered my head that Findlay Neilson is by way of being a second cousin of mine. My father's mother and Findlay Neilson's grandmother were sisters."

"Findlay Neilson? . . ."

"Look in your *Radio Times*, Mr. Bathurst, and you'll see where I'm getting to."

"This week's copy?"

"Any week," retorted the Inspector. "Findlay's a regular, not an occasional. The family as a whole feels right proud of him."

Anthony routed out his current number of the *Radio Times*. "Which day, Andrew, and when and where?"

"Look at the normal programme for Sunday afternoon. It's usually somewhere about four o'clock. You can't miss it." Anthony turned the pages as the Inspector directed. Suddenly he nodded. "O.K., Andrew, I've got it."

"Read out what it says—do you mind, Mr. Bathurst?" Again Anthony obeyed instructions. MacMorran listened with feelings of warm pleasure and eyes that sparkled. Family pride and vintage port make an almost irresistible combination. "Here you are, Andrew. I'll give you the full force of it. 'Ghosts. A new word game for listeners. Actors versus a B.B.C. staff team. Val Gielgud, etc., etc., etc. Master of Ceremonies and referee—H.F. Woodgrist. The game presented by Findlay Neilson.'"

MacMorran took up the parable the moment Anthony put down the paper. "Now Findlay, as I said to you just now, puts on a show of that kind regularly. I won't say every week, but as good as every other week. They've been wonderfully successful, too, let me tell you. Well, Mr. Bathurst, are you travelling in my direction yet?"

Anthony nodded. "I think so, Andrew. You think you could influence this twenty-second cousin of yours to do something for us. There's Crayle, too. Neilson might induce him to help as well. Another string to our bow is not to be despised."

MacMorran grinned and helped himself to yet another glass of port. "I'll say it isn't. Now the point is, shall I see Findlay on my own or shall we go along there together? If you ask me, Findlay will jump at the chance. It'll be a great advertisement for him."

"You go, Andrew. Official Scotland Yard will be more impressive than anything I could put up. In case the idea's accepted, leave the arrangements to your cousin."

"What shall I suggest particularly? Have you anything in mind?"

Anthony reflected. "Would it have to be on these lines?" He indicated the *Radio Times*. "I suppose it would, wouldn't it, Andrew?"

"This sort of thing is Findlay's speciality. It's what he's made his name at. So it looks like it. What's your best parlour game? Postman's Knock or Here's a pretty thing—a very pretty thing."

"Curb your sarcasm, Andrew. If that's the best mood my port can give you, I'll get Emily to make you a nice hot cup of cocoa."

MacMorran bridled at the threat. "Not that, Mr. Bathurst. Anything but that."

"I used to be pretty good in my salad party days at an indoor game which was called 'Reactions.' I'll give you a rough idea of the game as we played it." The Inspector listened to Anthony's explanation.

"Sounds pretty good to me," he volunteered. "I'll give young Findlay a rough idea of it, as you have given it to me, and see what he makes of it. You'll work it in teams, I suppose, the same as they've got in the paper there for this 'Ghosts' joke? It ought to mean splendid publicity—which is just what you want, you say. I can't think of any better method, I admit."

"When can you see Findlay Neilson?"

"I could pop along to Broadcasting House to-morrow evening."

"Good. And get Neilson to rope in Crayle as well. I'll meet you in the 'Bolivar,' say, at half-past eight. That suit you?"

MacMorran made a note of the appointment. "That'll suit me down to the ground. The 'Bolivar' at 8.30 to-morrow evening."

Anthony passed the decanter to him. "One more glass, Andrew. One for the road."

"Thank you, Mr. Bathurst. I don't mind if I do. Just one." Five minutes after the Inspector's departure Mr. Bathurst sat down to write two letters. The first of these was addressed to Sir Austin Mostyn Kemble, K.C.V.O., D.S.O., Commissioner of Police, New Scotland Yard, and the other to Findlay Neilson, Esq., Broadcasting House, London, W.1. Mr. Bathurst took great care in the wording of the letter to the Commissioner, but with regard to the communication addressed to Findlay Neilson it may be recorded that it was penned with infinite exactitude.

The Radio programme for the Sunday afternoon of a fortnight hence contained the following announcement: 'Reactions. A new parlour game for listeners. "Sleuths" versus a B.B.C. staff team. "Sleuths"—Anthony Lotherington Bathurst, Reginald Fortune, Colonel Anthony Ruthven Gethryn, Philip Trent. B.B.C. staff team—Peter Crayle, Productions Manager and Radio Adapters Lionel Gamlin, Variety Compere; Val Gielgud, Director of Features and Drama; and Vernon Harris, writer and part creator of "Band Waggon." Master of Ceremonies and Referee, Harvey F. Wood-grist. Presented by Findlay Neilson. Now here is a new kind of parlour game for you and one in which the wit and wisdom of the players will be strained to the utmost. Reactions, after this, it is safe to say, will become the pastime of the many. The B.B.C. has gathered together for the entertainment of the listeners, two teams of talent and a galaxy of stars. Gethryn, Fortune, Trent, Gielgud, and Gamlin. What names are these to conjure with! These are the rules of Reactions. Each player in turn will be required to guess by means of clues given him by the other side the famous person he is representing. That is to say the person whose identity has been placed upon him by the members of the opposing side. He will be given a maximum of eight clues which will be offered to him in what may be described as three waves—a first group of four clues, a second of two, and the third and final group of two more. If he deduces his identity from four clues (that is to say from the first wave) he will score the maximum of three marks. If he requires two more clues to guess successfully, he will score two marks, if he still requires the last two clues for a successful answer, he will score one mark. If he fails altogether, having been offered the entire eight clues, he will obviously score nothing at all. The team of "Sleuths" will be captained by Colonel Gethryn and the B.B.C. staff team by Val Gielgud. So draw up your chairs to your radio sets on Sunday afternoon next and listen to your fill. It should be mentioned, *en passant*, that the various clues will take the form of poetic quotations, apt allusions, or may even be presented to the player as the short snatches of a song.'

The studio was completely full on the actual Sabbath afternoon when the game of wit and wisdom took place. MacMorran had noted from his place near the control-room that Hubert Palmer, Phil Coventry, Rayner, and even Vere Valentine accompanied by her husband had all found sufficient interest in the affair to arrange to appear in person. And, just before zero hour, a man sidled by the Inspector with a smile on his face and MacMorran realized as. the man brushed past him that Alec Marston had come all the way from the shores of the Adur in the county of Sussex. At four o'clock exactly the red light showed and 'Reactions' was on the air. Harvey Woodgrist was in his stride at once. With his usual charm and facility, he told the audience and the players the rules of the game. "Any questions from either of the teams before we start?" Lionel Gamlin was in immediately. "Just one preliminary question, Harvey, if you don't mind—are the people we are supposed to represent, living or dead?"

"Both—I mean either, Lionel."

"Thank you, Harvey—that's worth knowing, my lad."

"Now, Colonel Gethryn," said Woodgrist, "will you toss with Val Gielgud here for choice of innings?"

"Certainly, Harvey." Anthony Gethryn rose—a smile in his green eyes. "I'll spin the coin, Val. Will you call?"

"Of course. Woman."

"It's heads. You bat."

"Trust a woman," murmured Val Gielgud.

"Now, Colonel Gethryn," directed Woodgrist, "will you open to Val, please. Four clues. The first from you, the second from Bathurst, the third from Fortune, and the last from Trent."

Colonel Gethryn grinned. The clues were rained at Val Gielgud thick and fast. "Test-tubes are his triumph." "Often disposes of a final ticket." "A knight in the morgue." "Hanging by a single hair."

"Oh, lord," returned Val Gielgud, "I assure you I haven't the foggiest. Sounds pretty ghastly to me. I should think the chap's dead—whoever he is. If he isn't, he ought to be. May I have two more clues, please?"

The two Anthonys obliged. "Remains to be seen." "Detection by dissection." Their opponent continued to shake his head. "I'm most solidly sunk. And two more, please? My last faint hope of success?"

Fortune replied with gusto. "Scientific Resurrectionist." Trent whipped in. "Always has it in the bag."

"My mind's a complete blank. I'm sorry, you chaps, I'm letting you down badly, I'm afraid. I feel that I ought to know it. I'll have a shot. Sweeney Todd, the demon barber of Fleet Street. How do I go?"

"You don't! No marks, Val," returned Woodgrist with cheerful derision. "The correct answer is 'Sir Bernard Spilsbury.' Now will you and your team bowl to Colonel Gethryn?"

"Here's a snorter, one right on the wicket, Colonel Gethryn. 'A leather-beater by trade.'" "His theme song came from the *Mikado*." "Under the fender and amongst the ashes." "One of our opening pair and yet only a knave." The words had scarcely left the last speaker's lips when Anthony Gethryn's answer came short and swift. "Jack Hobbs."

"Three points to the 'Sleuths'," murmured Harvey Woodgrist, "and congratulations, Colonel Gethryn, on first blood."

A burst of spontaneous clapping came from the audience in the studio. "Now, Bathurst. It's your move. Will you start against Gamlin, please?"

Anthony Bathurst responded quickly. "His not the place whereon the wild thyme blows." "1066 and all that." "A great deal to his credit." "Full of strange oaths and . . ." Gethryn spoke the fourth clue with relish. Val Gielgud, he thought, looked a little self-conscious. But Lionel Gamlin assessed the clues with quick appreciation. "Montague Norman." "Three points, Lionel. Well done."

Another flash of clapping. "The scores are equal," called Woodgrist, "but the 'Sleuths' have a wicket in hand. You, Lionel—again to Bathurst."

"His bark (Bach) is better than his bite." "Swaying multitudes with a fragment of himself." "Strange to relate—'Trees' is not his favourite song." "Flourishes all the year round."

Bathurst was almost as quick as Gethryn had been. "Sir Henry Wood," he flashed back. The audience had now taken hold well. They clapped furiously. Woodgrist called the scores. "'Sleuths' lead—six points to three. I must call Mr. Fortune. Against Crayle, please."

Reggie Fortune huddled himself together in his chair. "Gave me the pip," he murmured, with a fortunate chuckle. Trent went on. "Struck lucky with a safety match."

The others followed quickly. "An iron ration for the cavalry." "Inventor of nocturnal mechanization." Peter Crayle was cool and collected. "H'm," he said quietly, "not so bad perhaps. Certainly might have been worse. I'll have a smack at it. Ian Hay."

"Six points all," announced Woodgrist. "Crayle to Fortune now. Right away, Peter."

"They gave him the air." "Gave Britons the Cain." "Used to be such a healthy man." "Timber from a Royal meadow."

"My hat," said Mr. Fortune, "that's where I feel I ought to say 'quite, quite.'" He blinked at the four members of the B.B.C. team round-eyed. "Oh, my aunt—I'm stuck. I should have stayed at home with Joan and consumed many muffins. Soaked in butter. May I have two more? Two more of your wretched clues, I mean."

"Used to stamp about a lot." "Suggests a water-baby."

Reggie Fortune's face cleared. He wiped his forehead with a handkerchief. He looked across the studio with reproachful eyes. "Oh lord—yes. My dear chaps, I really thought I was scuppered. You mean that Johnnie who's been put in charge of the thingimmy jig . . . what's his name? Er—Sir Kingsley Wood. Yes, that's it."

"Two points, Mr. Fortune. 'Sleuths' lead, eight points to six." Clapping again from the audience in the studio. Harvey Woodgrist went on. "We are nearly half-way through. Mr. Trent, please, to Vernon Harris."

"No need for him to try slimming." "Of course he can." "Often said nay (ney) when he meant yes." "A close affinity with the Southern Railway."

Vernon Harris shook his head. "I'm in the same boat as Fortune just now. Two more clues, please."

"An isolated instance." "Needed a little corporal punishment."

Vernon Harris beamed when he heard the last statement. "Le petit caporal—eh? That's right down my throat. Napoleon Bonaparte."

"The scores are level," declared Harvey Woodgrist, "but Mr. Trent has still to bat for the 'Sleuths.' Vernon—will you kindly oblige?"

"Certainly, Harvey. Been waiting for my chance all the afternoon. Thirsting for it! Only wish I had 'Big' and 'Stinker' here to hold my hand. Here you are, Trent. 'Brief life is here his Portion.'" "His name is very much in evidence." "A dockside labourer." "Possesses a natural instinct for Boxing people."

Philip Trent smiled. "The good wine is reserved for the final stages. My deduction from those four clues is 'Sir Patrick Hastings.' Am I right, Mr. Woodgrist?"

"Quite right, Mr. Trent. And the half-time score is eleven points to eight in the 'Sleuths" favour. There will be a wait of two minutes before we commence the second half of the proceedings." The red light went out. The audience in the studio relaxed. For them, perhaps, more than for the contestants, the tension and the hilarity subsided. Suddenly and acutely, as a balloon will collapse when pricked. Bursts of interested conversation could he heard from various kinds of people. The stamping and shuffling of feet. MacMorran, from his coign of vantage, watched the people keenly. Anthony twice caught the Inspector's eye. He himself deliberately refrained from looking in the direction of the audience. Almost at once the red light showed again and the second half of 'Reactions' was on the air. "Colonel Gethryn batting," declared Harvey Woodgrist. "This time I shall not keep to the previous order of going in, so will the various players be on the *qui vive*, please, to hear their names called. Val, will you open fire, please?"

"By Jove, I will, like a shot. Something's got to be done about this. 'A feature of the Mediterranean—but that's only half of it.'" "Has raised many a laugh by her own." "She married the right man—but she might have got clawed." "Might well be taken for a County Councillor."

Anthony Gethryn grinned joyfully. "Thank you very much, Val. I can't help feeling that you've been very lenient with me. Take Cicely Courtneidge."

The audience signified their approval. "Fourteen to eight," cried Woodgrist. "Lionel Gamlin—will you follow?"

"Have a heart, Harvey. I've hardly got over my previous ordeal." The referee continued. "Mr. Bathurst, will you oblige our Lionel?"

"Only too pleased."

"His wife had a way with her." "Suggests a Zulu warrior." "Probably preferred eggs for his breakfast." "Had small Latin and less Greek."

"A-ha! I seem to recognize that last bit. I thought I was sunk for good until I heard that. Like a breath of summer that was. Now let me see if I can call upon the magic sea of memory that we hear so much about?" Lionel Gamlin put his hand across his eyes. "Something's coming home. At eventide. Ben Jonson said that last bit. It was shoved into me in the fourth form or thereabouts. Now what book were we doing at the time? I've got it. The Bard of Avon, gentlemen. Otherwise the divine William Shakespeare."

This occasioned a terrific burst of applause. The master of ceremonies again called the scores. "Fourteen to eleven. A close game—but the B.B.C. staff side will have to make a big effort very soon if they want to level up. Mr. Fortune, next. Now, Lionel, it's your turn to attack."

Lionel Gamlin groaned. "No rest for the super-wicked! Now, Reginald! Here goes and listen carefully—because these clues are mustard. 'What a relief!' 'Sinister greeting.' 'Be prepared.' 'The minor's hero.'"

"I am a simple soul and have a modest heart," returned Mr. Fortune pleadingly, "and this effort of mine, O my Gamlin, will be ranked by me as one of my best pieces of work. You see how it was—there were so few words. Yes, it would be like that. Of course! Charming—quite charming. Baden-Powell, of Gilwell in Essex. Am I right, Mr. Referee?"

"You are. And smart, too, Reggie. 'Sleuths' lead by seventeen to eleven."

"Oh, my aunt," murmured Mr. Fortune, "as Gamlin said: 'What a relief!' Now I can maffick."

"Vernon Harris," called the referee, "will you take what Fortune has in store for you?"

"Sounds like a page from *Old Moore*," said Harris. "Carry on, Reggie."

Fortune blinked. "Get ready, Harris. This is straight for your castle." "Close to the cook." "He wanted such a lot." "Irish—and proud of it, too." "Found Hampshire fatal."

Harris pulled at his top lip. "Doesn't sound too good to me! Wait a minute, though. I must adopt Mr. Chamberlain's motto. Try—try—try again. Perseverance wins the day. Even if it means begging for two more snorting clues. Wait half a second, though. 'Close to the cook' and 'Hampshire fatal.' I've got it. Kitchener of Khartoum! How's that, umpire?"

"Seventeen-fourteen," declared the popular Harvey—"and Mr. Trent to bat. Will you bowl, Vernon, please?"

"Only too delighted, Harvey. And it's going to be a nasty dirty messy ball, at that. 'There's one thing that's certain, Begging his pardon, He brought down the curtain, Upon a fine garden.' 'A nice blending of spirit and stone.' 'One more River to cross.' 'The theatrical Wooderson!'"

Trent, at this last allusion, looked puzzled. Then he slowly shook his head. "I'm sorry, but may I have two more clues, please? Do you mind, Vernon?"

"Not a bit of it, old chap. Only too pleased. Seems to me there's life in the old B.B.C. yet. You want the best clues. We have them. 'Dear old Pals.' 'Thin Ice—S Bend.'"

Still Philip Trent shook his head. "I'm afraid it's all mud to me. I'm still floundering." He thought hard for some few minutes. "And I'm afraid, too, that I must ask for the remaining two."

"Stole and vestment."

Trent held up his hand with a smile of triumph. "No more. Shan't want the other. J.B. Priestley."

"One point—by the skin of his teeth—'Sleuths' lead—eighteen to fourteen. Now, Val, old man, it's up to you."

"I'm ready, Harvey. Do your worst, Trent. Imagine I'm the ghost of Sigsbee Manderson."

"This is a full toss on the leg-side, Val. 'Another darling of Justice.' 'A poppy plus an Indian Love lyric.' 'A very up-to-date Twentieth-Century Maid.' 'Thousands of fans to keep her cool.'"

"Aha! That's right down my street, my dear Philip. Most welcome, too. I am about to retrieve my severely damaged reputation. 'Shirley Temple.' Am I right, gentlemen?"

The studio audience signified in the approved manner. The referee called the reckoning. "Eighteen to seventeen in favour of our masters of detection. By Jove—what a battle! Now, Bathurst, let's see what Peter, here, can serve up to you."

"I don't pay the singer." "Man and Superman." "Love's Labour Lost." "O mistress mine . . . but not in spies."

Anthony shook his head. "Two more clues, Crayle, please? At the moment, I haven't a glimmer."

"An eye for beauty." "Oranges—six a penny."

Mr. Bathurst looked across at the master of ceremonies. "With some diffidence, I'll take a crack at Nell Gwynne."

This time Harvey Woodgrist shook his head. "Nothing doing, Bathurst. Bad luck. You lose your last two chances. The correct solution was 'Don Juan.' Now you're up against Peter here and the score is still one point in favour of the 'Sleuths'—eighteen to seventeen. What a finish! Ready, Bathurst?"

A shrewd observer might have noted that at this moment MacMorran, in Sunday suit, and looking strangely unlike his official self, began to mingle with the audience in the studio. Marston seemed to be looking for a signal of some sort. They heard Anthony Bathurst's voice come across the studio and they knew that Crayle had fallen in with his plan and was going to play the part that Anthony had assigned to him.

"A Brush with the Sixteenth Century." "Spreading Canvas." "Duchess of Milan." "This way to Hampton Court."

Crayle shook his head. "I'm not at home to any of that."

The referee intervened. "One point will put you level. Two points will win the game for your side, Peter."

"Give me two more clues, please," said Crayle.

"The Carlton Club." "The Sands of Time."

Crayle's face was a complete blank. "Two more, please."

"He died of the Plague." "It wasn't this one who swam the Channel."

Peter Crayle shook his head for the second time. "It's worse and worse as far as I am concerned. I can fit several of the clues, but then one or two of the others scupper me completely. May I ask a question?"

"Certainly," returned the master of ceremonies. "But of course I can't absolutely promise to answer it. I reserve the right to refuse."

"Naturally," said Peter. "I understand your position perfectly, but I'm keen to win."

There was a silence for some seconds. "I'll take a chance, Harvey. It's win or bust—I know full well. Henry the Eighth."

Harvey Woodgrist shook his head regretfully. "The correct answer is Holbein the painter. The score remains the same. Eighteen points to seventeen. The 'Sleuths' win by one point. My congratulations to them and to Colonel Gethryn, in particular, as their skipper."

Most of the audience stood and clapped their approbation of the show in general. Inspector Andrew MacMorran stood and watched them. He was carrying out a programme of duties exactly as he had been instructed by Anthony Bathurst. So was Crayle. So was Neilson. MacMorran watched Rayner speak some words in an undertone to Vere Valentine before the latter slipped away quickly with Sere. He saw Palmer shake his head at Philip Coventry. And then, as Marston approached him with a smile upon his face, he heard Hubert Palmer say to Coventry quietly but distinctly: "Holbein stuck out a mile. I had it on the third clue. When the fourth came, I was absolutely certain of it. Peter should have picked it up. He disappointed me."

But Phil Coventry showed disagreement and MacMorran heard pregnant words. "That's all very well, but don't forget that Holbein was right down your street. Just your handwriting. Meat and drink to *you*. But one man's meat may be another man's poison. And so it was in this case."

MacMorran, listening intently, scarcely responded to what Marston said to him. Also, he was unable to distinguish Palmer's reply. He felt that he must establish contact with Anthony Bathurst as soon as possible. He began to push his way, therefore, through the crowd making its departure, to the raised platform near the 'mike.'

Chapter XXXII
REACTIONS. (POST-SABBATH)

ANTHONY met him as he began to ascend the platform. MacMorran suffered himself to be drawn on one side. "Satisfied, sir?" inquired the Inspector.

Anthony grinned at him. "What about yourself, Andrew? Were you?"

"I think you're right—but, of course, it's more or less a shot in the dark. Crayle fitted in splendidly . . . and young Findlay. At the same time, I've news for you. Listen to this." Anthony listened with becoming attention. "So Coventry disagreed, did he? One man's meat—eh?" He chuckled. "Do you think Palmer noticed that you were lying handy, Andrew?"

"I'm pretty certain that he didn't. He hasn't seen a lot of me in the past and to-day I've managed to keep well in the background."

"Did he glance at you when he was talking to Coventry?"

"Not that I noticed."

"In your direction?"

"Don't think so."

"Well, it doesn't matter much. Now with regard to the other arrangements. All O.K."

MacMorran nodded. "Everything. Every step taken by them will be well covered. My lady, the loving wife, hasn't known it—but there's been a man on her tail all the afternoon. I gave him the most explicit instructions not to lose sight of her."

"Not the man you employed before, I hope, Andrew?" Anthony grinned at him again.

"Once bitten twice shy, Mr. Bathurst. Or in other words the burnt child fears the fire."

"Enigmatic. However, seems all right to me. It's up to you now, Andrew."

"If the move is made—as you seem confident it will be."

"My dear chap! The birds have heard the sound of the gun. But not in the wheat and stubble this time. Having heard said gun, said birds will rise. When they rise we, you and I, Andrew, shall see them. See them and recognize them. Then, Andrew, you can do your stuff."

"How long do you give me, Mr. Bathurst?"

"You saw his face. Better than I did. I was on the platform. How long do you?"

"To-night," answered MacMorran after a hard think.

"I agree, Andrew. To-night's the night. I shall be at my flat. Give me a ring directly you want me . . . and I'll introduce you to the snarling man."

A smile of contentment spread over MacMorran's features. "What about Marston?" he asked curiously.

"He'll be there," replied Mr. Bathurst, "I've seen to that."

"Do you think he'll enjoy it? He seemed a bit off song in the room where Carlton Sands was murdered."

"At any rate it will be a new experience for him. His life in Sussex is colourless. Don't you remember how he insisted on that point?"

This time it was MacMorran's turn to chuckle. "You're right, Mr. Bathurst. Well—here's to the next time."

"Thank you, Andrew, but it will *not* be the time for dancing."

The telephone bell rang in Anthony's flat at almost exactly half-past eight. MacMorran's voice at the other end was quiet but ominous. "They're off. Left the house together but separated after going about a hundred yards. Took different taxis. To Liverpool Street. You can guess what that means. Two of my men went after them. But listen to this. The lady's travelling as a young man."

"She's used to that, Andrew. Won't occasion her any worry. Seen Bergner no doubt. Liverpool Street means Harwich. Harwich probably means Brussels."

"That's right, sir. The boat leaves about twenty to eleven. The train arrives with some few minutes to spare. Now listen to me, Mr. Bathurst. The Commissioner's coming with us. Will you pick us up in your car?"

"In ten minutes, Andrew. At the corner of Fanshawe Street. All right? . . . Good. And shove a revolver in your pocket. Then we shall have two with us."

Anthony took his charges aboard at the corner of Fanshawe Street at 8.42. Once clear of London, he felt confident he could knock holes in the distance all right. As they tore down through the county of Essex he was irresistibly reminded of the night he went after Ramsay, the Mapleton murderer. Sir Austin Kemble was unusually quiet and even MacMorran and Anthony seemed disinclined for anything more than desultory conversation. As they approached their destination, Sir Austin brightened up. Anthony encouraged him. "What time does the boat leave?" asked the Commissioner.

"About ten-forty, sir. And we should be there in less than five minutes." He looked at his watch. "We shall do it comfortably, sir."

The car ran alongside the quay. "As far as numbers are concerned," declared MacMorran, "we've got plenty in hand. Hoad and Riches are on the train and there are three of us here which makes it five to two in our favour."

"Plus," added Anthony, "the element of surprise."

They parked the car and made their way to the platform. "She's signalled," said Sir Austin, "not long now."

The noise of the train could be heard in the near distance. "Here she comes," he continued. The boat train, slowing down, ran alongside the platform. Anthony touched his companions on the arms and shepherded them into the shadow. The train stopped and doors were thrown open. Figures emerged and flitted along the platform towards the landing-stage where the boat lay waiting. Porters mingled with them and took baggage from their hands.

"There are my two chaps," said MacMorran quietly. "Look—Hoad and Riches, about two-thirds down the length of the train. *And* Marston as well."

"Where they are," replied Mr. Bathurst, "the birds will be also. Hoping to be in Brussels in the morning. False optimism. Yes—there they are—look—just in front of your two fellows."

"Get ready, MacMorran. They'll be abreast of us within half a minute."

Anthony's hand went to the revolver in his pocket. He and the Commissioner ranged themselves on each side of the Inspector. The seconds that passed seemed more like minutes. The crucial moment came. MacMorran stepped forward and stood in the path of the two people.

"One moment, please," said MacMorran. "Would you mind stepping this way—I'd like a word with you."

The stouter figure of the two people thus addressed, stopped short in astonishment. "What do you mean?" he demanded truculently. Then he seemed to see MacMorran's features properly, for the first time, and to realize who it was that barred his way. "What's the meaning of this?" he said fiercely.

"You know," returned MacMorran tersely.

The man's hand went like a flash to his side pocket. But the Inspector was too quick for him. A quick movement by MacMorran and cold steel bit into his wrists. "You are arrested, Peter Crayle, for the murders of Aubrey Coventry and Carlton Sands, and I warn you that anything you may say will be used as evidence against you. Hoad—see to Mrs. Crayle—will you?"

Anthony saw a chill look of fear cross the face of Valerie Moffatt as Hoad stepped forward and took her by the arm. The man who had been handcuffed raised his hands in a vicious attempt at resistance. But MacMorran, taking no chances, jerked him into swift surrender.

"Get the car, Riches," he cried to the other plain-clothes man ... "there are two people here who want safe housing for the night."

Anthony watched the five figures depart. He turned to the Commissioner. "I think, Sir Austin, that for you and me and Marston here ... a little light refreshment is indicated ... what do you say, sir?"

The Commissioner was acquiescence itself. There was one point about Bathurst—he knew how to do things properly. As for Marston—he was still trembling with excitement. As he had been promised . . . he had obeyed Mr. Bathurst's instructions and had been in at the death.

CHAPTER XXXIII
MR. BATHURST SUMS UP

CHIEF-Inspector MacMorran took the chair which Anthony offered him. "You may shed your anxiety, Mr. Bathurst."

"Concerning what and which, Andrew?"

"Getting a verdict."

"Oh, and why do you say that, Andrew?"

MacMorran's reply was curt. "He's confessed. Made a clean breast of things."

"On the whole, I'm not terribly surprised. They've been man and wife some time, I take it, Inspector?"

"Some weeks. Married down in the country somewhere. The old man's in high feather."

Anthony smiled. "I know. I had grub with him at Murillo's on Tuesday evening. Help yourself, Andrew. You deserve a celebration." Anthony pointed to the decanter.

MacMorran was not slow to take the opportunity. "Fill in the gaps for me, will you, Mr. Bathurst?"

Anthony stretched his lithe length in the arm-chair and drew luxuriously at a cigarette. MacMorran went on. "There are still a good many as far as I am concerned, and Sir Austin tells me you did it for him on Tuesday—so what about it for me, Mr. Bathurst?"

Anthony shook his head. "Not one of my happiest efforts, Andrew, by a long chalk. So much of the story seemed inconsequent and this fact, I think, was mainly responsible for my being so long in grasping the right threads. What shall I take first, Andrew . . . the story of the crime or my various deductions as they came to me?"

"Just as you like, Mr. Bathurst."

"I'll take the crime first then, Andrew. The trouble began, I think, with Hubert Palmer. What exactly is Palmer's occupation?"

"A sort of B.B.C. producer . . . that's what I should call him . . . thinks out new series for Radio presentation."

"Exactly. And one of his series, you would find, I suggest, if you took the trouble to investigate, was probably on 'Great Painters' or something of that kind. I expect it was turned down . . . but Crayle, no doubt, knew of it . . . and picked out some chunks of expert knowledge re Holbein and Rembrandt."

MacMorran nodded.

"And got the idea that Coventry's pictures might be genuine . . . is that the idea?"

"You've got it, Andrew. He was a frequent visitor to the house in Danvers Gate, had taken the opportunity to examine the pictures, and had carefully noted certain signs (which Marston has since described to us) that helped to foster the idea. Consultation with Carlton Sands probably clinched the matter and Crayle, in desperate financial straits (he plays the horses and the market) and extremely desirous of marriage, determined on a bold coup. He used the name of Silas Montgomery because he knew that name would bait Coventry and, by employing Austin, fixed up the fatal early morning interview. Immediately following, notice, the 'Seven Arts' Ball."

MacMorran frowned. "Why did he use the fellow Austin for that?"

Anthony smiled. "Think, Andrew. That is where I was so slow. Absurdly so . . . because it brings us close to the kernel of the entire matter."

"I can't get it."

"*He didn't want Coventry to recognize his voice.* Note, too, how he contrived to spell a word incorrectly. The word 'precisely.' That fact would help to hide his identity when questions came to be asked."

MacMorran's face cleared. "Of course. I see it now."

"His idea was to arrive disguised in the blue overalls, tie Coventry up, blindfold him, and get away with the pictures. Replace them with his 'duds' (marvellous copies, remember) and behold—when Coventry recovered—what had happened to him beyond the assault—and what had he been robbed of? Coventry was unaware, recollect, of the value of his pictures, and I doubt very much whether he would have noticed the substitution for a long time. His condition would have been one of sheer mystification. But Crayle's plans went amiss."

"How?"

"I'll tell you that later. He strangled Coventry with one of the ropes he had brought with him. He was younger and stronger and doubtless took Coventry at many disadvantages."

"But his alibi? We checked up on it."

"I'll deal with that later too, Andrew. For the present, I'll stick to the crime proper. Well, he got away with the two pictures and through the offices of Carlton Sands contacted Bronson Van Hoyt. The man who would pay a big price and ask no questions. From then, however, our friend began to make mistakes. When he disposed of his suit of blue overalls he left behind the clues that took us to Southwick. You will recall those two slips of paper, Andrew?"

MacMorran nodded. "Ay. How on earth did he come to do that?"

"It's all conjecture, of course, but I think Coventry had given him the address of Gaunt, Marston and Co. in the first place some time before the murder. Probably in answer to a seemingly innocent question with regard to copies of pictures generally, and he destroyed the paper at the same time as he packed his parcel of clothes for disposal. Two of the tell-tale pieces fell into the cap he had worn . . . and he failed to notice the occurrence. That was his vital false step. His second one was to murder Carlton Sands after doing his best to murder me."

MacMorran screwed up his face. "How did he know we were on to Sands?"

"Through young Coventry. Don't you remember how we asked questions . . . pregnant questions about the pictures in the Coventry house? I *meant* Coventry to talk. That was why I let him see so much. I hoped it would force action on the part of the murderer. It did. Very effectively! He knew that we were getting very warm indeed. So much so, that he decided to remove both Sands and me. He very nearly brought off the double."

"There's still a lot I don't get yet. Tell me how you got hold of the threads."

Anthony lit another cigarette. "Go back to the evening of the 'Seven Arts' Ball. And the appearance of the 'snarler.' Ever thought much about that, Andrew?"

"You bet I have."

"Get this into your nut then. Crayle desired to *establish the man's identity*. The 'snarler' would be the man the police wanted when they started hunting for Coventry's murderer! He decided to show himself to Aubrey Coventry both *before* the ball, when Coventry alone should see him, and *during* the ball, when Coventry, *plus others*, should see him. Obviously the people the snarling man couldn't be, if his identity came to be questioned and seriously scrutinized, would be those who were with or near Coventry while the dance was going on. He was hanging round Coventry's house when the latter walked into the park and he followed him there so that Coventry should notice him for the first time. When, by a sheer stroke of coincidence, Coventry asked him for a light, he 'snarled' in reply. It was all part of his original plan, except that by sheer force of circumstance he became the 'snarler' some hours before he had intended to."

"I don't understand," ventured the Inspector.

"Don't hurry me, Andrew. You will very shortly. I'll go on. What was Crayle's costume at the ball?"

"He appeared as a discus thrower, whatever that may be."

"Exactly, Andrew, which meant a very light costume indeed in the Greek style. Quite a simple matter to slip dungarees over it and a wig! A few touches here and there and the 'snarling mechanic' was there again . . . for Coventry and (mark you!) several others, to see this time. Remember the statements of the two door-keepers Wood and McCorkell when we interviewed them? Nobody of that type went in and the back of the premises presented a complete barrier to entrance!"

"I see. Yes. Anyhow—go on."

"In time Crayle returned with the two Coventrys to their house in Danvers Gate and very probably wished them good-night. From there he went to his flat. Picked up his lady love, changed back into the 'snarler,' and gave her the costume of the discus thrower! Which she donned and wore at the night club in Rothwell Street.

To establish Mr. Crayle's alibi! Such a costume made recognition an absolute certainty. Incidentally, Andrew, it was then that I formed my first half-suspicion. D'ye know what it was?"

"I certainly do not. Tell me."

"That an hour and a half's spell on gin and lime didn't sound like the man who was supposed to be the hero of it. Anyhow that's neither here nor there. I'll proceed. With his copies from Gaunt, Marston & Co., and his ropes and anaesthetic for tying and dosing Coventry, he picks up Sewell's taxi and arrives at Coventry's house. His 'pinkish' complexion was caused by touches of make-up. Coventry himself, you must note, is sitting up, all keyed up and dithery. Waiting for the Napoleon of Wall Street, Mr. Silas Montgomery. I'll endeavour to sketch for you what I imagine must have happened. But first of all I'll ask you a question. What was it that Crayle must not do in contact with Coventry?"

"I'm on to that," said MacMorran laconically. "He mustn't speak."

"Andrew, you're not as daft as you look. You've hit it. But it was the two note-books that gave it away to me. When Coventry let him in and saw the blue overalls for the third time I suggest he said in astonishment, 'Are you Silas Montgomery?' What was the sequel? I think it may be accepted that Crayle feigned dumbness and asked for pencil and paper for the purpose of communication and to explain the conditions of the telephone messages. That was why the *wrong* note-book was in front of each chair! Don't you see, Andrew? Coventry wrote on his and pushed it to Crayle, who did likewise and gave his to Coventry. It came to me suddenly that the presence of these two books in the inappropriate positions on the table—because we *knew* where Coventry had sat—meant one thing and one thing only! That Silas Montgomery or his represent-ative had either been deaf and dumb or feigned those conditions. In other words there we had again similar conditions to those of 'the snarling man.'"

MacMorran nodded approval. "Good work—that."

"The pleasure's mine, Andrew."

"Why did Crayle kill him?"

"Because in some way, probably as he was about to dope Coven-try, after he had tied him up, Coventry recognized him and accused him by name. That was where Crayle's plan went astray, as I said just now."

"Why didn't he resort to mere burglary . . . and leave murder alone . . . in his original plans I mean?"

Anthony Bathurst shook his head. "He was no burglar, Andrew. No tools or anything of that kind. Would have been helpless and hopeless at a forced entry. The only way he could get in was by having the front door opened to him. All invitation and ceremony. He knew that well enough."

"What was your point with regard to the cap? You asked for it towards the end of the case. I've racked my br-rains, rather, over that cap."

Anthony smiled. "I had it subjected to a series of experiments by an analytical chemist, to try to find out the trade of the man who had habitually worn it. It was quite clean, if you remember, and gave no external clues that were recognizable or would help us. My scientific friend reported that it was a painter's cap. I've made some inquiries and I'm told that the B.B.C. headquarters at Broadcasting House were painted about a week before Coventry was murdered . . . you can imagine how Crayle came by it . . . he wanted one for his special purpose, saw one lying about, and 'won' it."

The Inspector grinned. "More marks for you. But rather a long shot, I must say."

"I can take criticism, Andrew—indeed I deserve it. But long shots, when they do turn up, pay better than hot pots."

The Inspector nodded. "So they tell me. I don't hold with such goings on myself and my old woman's dead set against wastin' money. How did you work that Reactions game?"

"Mainly through Findlay Neilson, your distinguished relation. Sent him a special letter, outlining the whole campaign. Crayle thought that the entire idea emanated from Neilson himself and had nothing about it that was different from the ordinary programme. He didn't connect Neilson with Scotland Yard. To him it was all normal. But when he refused the bait offered him as Holbein, he *knew* that we were hot on his track. He did just what I wanted him to do. Tried to clear immediately. And don't forget this, Andrew, as an interesting facet of psychology. If he had answered 'Holbein' he would have won the game for his side. That was arranged beforehand by myself and my three more distinguished colleagues who so kindly lent me their invaluable assistance. But Crayle *deliberately refused an honour* which would have been as unction to his scheming soul . . . he loves the limelight . . . because he was afraid to divulge his knowledge of the master."

"Yes. I follow all that. It was smart work on your part."

"No bouquets, Andrew. Stick to the script. Oh, there's one other thing. Perhaps the cleverest touch our pair of criminals put up. Miss Moffatt's well-advertised refusal of the marriage lines until the mystery of her uncle's death was solved. Crayle's depression was well done."

"A deep depression," sighed MacMorran with a chuckle.

"Excellent, Andrew. You're emerging from your coma."

"Who was the young man who called at Marston's with the order for the duplicates . . . horn-rimmed glasses and toothbrush moustache? The—"

Anthony interrupted him. "The one you arrested a few evenings ago, Andrew. Didn't I tell you she was used to male costume?"

"An accessory all the way—eh? Well, we live and learn." Mac-Morran rose to go. "I promised the old woman I wouldn't be late this evening. I like to think I'm a man of my word. I wouldn't have her imagine I'd formed other-r affections." He turned suddenly. "That reminds me, Mr. Bathurst, what had Rayner to do with Vere Valentine—Mrs. Sere? Just another example of the eternal triangle?"

Anthony smiled and shook his head. "Don't think so. Wait a minute. This is a revelation I've promised myself . . . although I have a shrewd idea." He went to the telephone and dialled. MacMorran heard spoken words. Mr. Bathurst's smile broadened. More words were spoken. MacMorran heard them with feelings of surprise. The conversation developed. Eventually he heard Anthony say: "Have no fears, Miss Valentine. I'll lock it away for ever—in the dungeon of my heart."

Mr. Bathurst replaced the receiver. "As I thought, Andrew. A skeleton in the Valentine cupboard. She is Rayner's niece. Rayner's sister was a nice girl but somebody 'done her wrong.' It's been kept quiet . . . she's now a respectable married woman with no one the wiser. Which, on the whole, I suppose, is just as well for all parties concerned or unconcerned."

MacMorran nodded. "I agree. After all, there's no need for dirty washing to be hung out in public. . . ."

Mr. Bathurst remonstrated. His grey eyes twinkled. "Aren't you forgetting something, Andrew?"

"How do you mean?"

"Well, haven't I, during the last few days, heard a vague reference in that connection to the Siegfried Line?"

Chief-Inspector Andrew MacMorran swallowed hard.

THE END

9 781914 150678